China Coup

The publisher and the University of California Press Foundation gratefully acknowledge the generous support of the Sue Tsao Endowment Fund in Chinese Studies.

China Coup

THE GREAT LEAP TO FREEDOM

Roger Garside

UNIVERSITY OF CALIFORNIA PRESS

University of California Press
Oakland, California

© 2021 by Roger Garside

Library of Congress Cataloging-in-Publication Data

Names: Garside, Roger, author.
Title: China Coup : The Great Leap to Freedom / Roger Garside.
Description: Oakland, California : University of California Press, [2021] |
    Includes bibliographical references and index.
Identifiers: LCCN 2020035735 (print) | LCCN 2020035736 (ebook) |
    ISBN 9780520380974 (cloth) | ISBN 9780520380981 (ebook)
Subjects: LCSH: Coups d'état—China—Forecasting. | China—Politics
    and government—2002-
Classification: LCC DS779.46 .G365 2021 (print) | LCC DS779.46 (ebook) |
    DDC 951.06/2—dc23
LC record available at https://lccn.loc.gov/2020035735
LC ebook record available at https://lccn.loc.gov/2020035736

Manufactured in the United States of America

29 28 27 26 25 24 23 22 21
10 9 8 7 6 5 4 3 2 1

To all those whose love and friendship have nourished me.

Contents

Preface

Before the next National Congress of the Communist Party of China, due in November 2022, President Xi Jinping will be removed from office by a coup d'état mounted by rivals in the top leadership who will end the tyranny of the one-party dictatorship and launch a transition to democracy and the rule of law.

The main body of this book, Part 2, explains *why* it *will* happen. Parts 1 and 3 tell *how* it may happen; they are semi-fictional—the people named are real, while the storyline is fiction.

"Revolution has always seemed 'impossible' until it occurred, after which everyone sagely agreed that it was 'inevitable,'" wrote one expert on the Soviet Union before its collapse.[1]

Two decades after its collapse, Leon Aron, director of Russian studies at the American Enterprise Institute, commented: "In the years leading up to 1991, virtually no Western expert, scholar, official, or politician foresaw the impending collapse of the Soviet Union, and with it one-party dictatorship, the state-owned economy, and the Kremlin's control over its domestic and Eastern European empires. Neither, with one exception, did Soviet dissidents nor, judging by their memoirs, did the future revolutionaries themselves."[2]

The future I predict depends on men and women in China, the United States, and its liberal, democratic allies displaying courage and wisdom. These qualities have been in short supply in recent years, except in places like Hong Kong and Taiwan, but there is good reason to believe they are not extinct.

We cannot know the future of China with certainty any more than we can know the future of other countries. Since the manuscript of this book has been completed, there have been major developments in China's policy towards international financial markets and institutions that have changed the context for the story that I tell in Part 1. They will have far-reaching consequences for China domestically and internationally, but they have reinforced my view of the underlying realities which that story is designed to illustrate.

While we cannot know the future of China with certainty, we can use our knowledge and our judgment to identify its most likely trajectory in broad terms. My career at the front line of political and economic change has embraced diplomacy, development banking, university teaching, and the development of capital markets in countries making the transition from a command economy to a market economy. (A full account is in the afterword.) The interaction between economics, finance, and politics I have witnessed has led me to the view of China's future that I offer in this book.

1 *The Coup*

1   *The Coup*

Li Keqiang, China's premier and second-ranking member of its Communist Party, stares in horror at the Reuters Chinese-language feed on his computer screen. He is reading a press release by the US Securities and Exchange Commission (SEC) announcing the imminent suspension of trading on all US exchanges of the securities issued by five of the Chinese companies with the highest capital valuations in the American markets. The reason given is that the SEC lacks confidence in the veracity of the financial information those companies supply to investors. The suspension will last from 9:30 a.m. Eastern Standard Time on Monday, 28 March, to 11:59 p.m. EST on Friday, 8 April.

Since the first China-registered company was admitted to listing on the New York Stock Exchange in 1992, nearly two hundred more have been listed on major US exchanges, raising tens of billions of dollars each year. For investors, a US listing carries with it the assumption that US rules and regulatory oversight apply, but when it comes to Chinese companies, that simply is not true. Beijing routinely blocks the efforts of the US Public Company Accounting Oversight Board (PCAOB) to gain access to the accounts of these companies held in China and the right to inspect their assets, so that it can verify the information they supply. Chinese law requires that financial records remain in China, and Beijing restricts access to accounting information, citing national security and state secrecy.

The US Congress has long been indignant that Chinese companies should be permitted to access the US capital markets, and apparently mislead American investors, while obstructing the legitimate demands of the SEC. The indignation is all the greater because US competitors of these companies have been subjected to discrimination or outright bans in China.

When US President Barack Obama urged President Xi Jinping to change Chinese law to allow disclosure, he refused and used a joint press conference with the US president to make clear how strongly he resented the pressure. On this issue, he has overridden the advice of Li and others, because he believes that China is now strong enough to defy attempts by the United States to influence Chinese law making.

Li has no illusions about Chinese financial and reporting standards. The scandals are legendary. He remembers the case of Sino Forest, which overstated the value of its forests in Yunnan by US$900 million, and Luckin Coffee, whose share price lost $5.5 billion when it was revealed that 40 percent of its sales had been fabricated in one quarter.[1] Over the years, US regulators have acted against Chinese companies for problems of financial information, and dozens have been delisted, but never companies of such size as those now suspended for noncompliance, whose total capitalization is well over one trillion US dollars. They have been out of compliance for three years, so their time is up.

Li is all too aware that three weeks ago an international consortium of news media, consisting of the *New York Times*, the *Asahi*

Shimbun in Tokyo, *The Guardian* in London, and the *Süddeutsche Zeitung* in Munich, featured front-page reports based on leaked documents that show that the accounts of two of the five, ChinaPay and JieChu, contained "material inaccuracies." These companies are both leaders in China's financial services. They are highly innovative and have achieved phenomenal growth for a decade by financing China's private sector corporate borrowers, which are ill served by the state-owned banks, and depositors, who are denied a proper rate of return by those banks. They harness fintech brilliantly, but have engaged in shadow banking, taking risks they have concealed from the financial regulators, except for those whose complicity they have bought with large bribes. Naturally, the companies have denied the accusations just published, denouncing the documents as forgeries. The SEC has responded by saying that if they will grant the PCAOB full access to their books, the truth or falsehood of the allegations can be established.

Legislation was passed in 2020 designed to ensure that all companies on American stock exchanges, whether registered in the United States or abroad, that fail to comply with US disclosure requirements for three consecutive years are liable to be delisted from US stock exchanges.[2] Since the revelations about ChinaPay, JieChu and the other three Chinese companies, the SEC and the White House have come under renewed pressure from congressional leaders to enforce this law, starting with these cases.

As Sino-American relations have deteriorated, pressure has mounted for the United States to adopt other measures to harden its stance towards China in the financial field. Leading members of Congress such as Senator Marco Rubio of Florida have for some years been pointing out that pension plans of everyday Americans are heavily invested in companies that serve the Chinese Communist

Party and, they argue, are furthering the regime's efforts to under-mine the United States. In 2019, former Chinese Finance Minister Lou Jiwei warned of a "financial war" between China and the United States using "long-arm jurisdiction," and his prediction was validated a few months later, when President Trump ordered the main pension fund of the US government to stop investing in Chinese equities.[3] In June 2020, the President went further when he ordered his Working Group on Financial Markets to make "recom-mendations for additional actions the SEC or any other Federal agency or department should take as a means to protect investors in Chinese companies, or companies from other countries that do not comply with United States securities laws and investor protections." This raised the specter of far wider sanctions, includ-ing a ban on *all* American pension funds investing in Chinese corporations.[4]

The deeper background is that American enthusiasm for trade and investment in China has waned, and hopes that economic reform would lead to political change in China have collapsed. According to current assessments, economic reform has stalled because China's leaders fear it will undermine their grip on power. American enthusiasm has turned to hostility due to a growing rec-ognition that China is:

- forcing US companies to hand over intellectual property to joint-venture partners,
- engaging in state-directed cyber theft of American intellec-tual property on a scale unprecedented in history,
- imprisoning over a million Uighurs for "thought reform" in Xinjiang,
- abolishing freedom and the rule of law in Hong Kong,

- building and militarizing islands in the South China Sea in order to turn this key international trade route into "a Chinese lake," in defiance of international law.[5]

The initial coverup of the outbreak of coronavirus in Wuhan has convinced Americans that the Communist leaders of China cannot be trusted.

All this has caused a profound sea change in American opinion towards China. This is evident not just in the executive branch of government but across the Republican-Democrat divide in Congress, in the media, in large corporations,[6] and in universities. Increasingly public opinion leaders take the view that the Chinese Communist regime—as distinct from the Chinese people—has been using weapons of economic warfare and regional military power in pursuit of political supremacy on the world stage.

In this highly charged climate, the SEC has decided to suspend, initially for the standard period of ten business days, ChinaPay and JieChu and the other three big companies that have failed to comply with its demands for access. It further puts on notice *all* Chinese companies whose securities are being traded on US exchanges: *provide assurances within ten business days that you too will grant the SEC immediate access to your accounts held in China, or you too will face suspension.*

Shaken, Li summons Wang Yang by phone to discuss the ominous announcement. Wang ranks fourth in the Party hierarchy. He is Li's closest political ally. Before Xi made clear his opposition to radical economic reform and political liberalization, Wang had worked daringly for both, as Party chief in China's richest and most populous province, Guangdong. Soon after Xi Jinping had assumed office, Li and Wang became convinced that Xi's policies were causing the

Party to overreach at home, and China to overreach abroad. They shared their misgivings with each other but concealed them from others, prudently thinking one thing and saying another. As time passed their misgivings turned to alarm, and eventually they understood that some other members of the Politburo shared that alarm. But Xi had centralized decision making in his own hands and was deaf to all voices of caution.

Waiting for Wang, Li ponders the wider context of the confrontation with the SEC in its wider context. He knows well that over the past decade, the China strategy of successive US presidents has rotated 180 degrees, from benign engagement to hostility. Obama's mostly symbolic "Pivot to Asia" in 2010 was succeeded by the very real trade war launched by Trump. After a clumsy start, the United States assembled a team with a sophisticated understanding of geoeconomic warfare. In response to "Made in China 2025," a blueprint to upgrade the manufacturing capabilities of Chinese industries, the Americans began systematically blocking China's acquisition of technologies needed to catch up and overtake them in the fields of artificial intelligence and quantum computing. More fundamentally, their strategy is based on recognition of where the true fighting strength of the US and other liberal economies lies, above all in the markets for capital and currencies, and where their defenses are weak, as in the field of cyber warfare, the supply of rare earth minerals, and the manufacture of active ingredients for generic medicines.

The SEC suspension of Chinese companies on US exchanges is an initiative by an autonomous agency, but what neither the SEC nor China's premier knows is that the documents published in the international press have been "acquired" by US intelligence agencies and fed to the press through an independent-seeming third party. Taking its lead from the White House and a Congress united on this issue, the US government is escalating the Sino-American economic war from trade and investment in goods and technology to action against China in the field of capital markets.

For years now, Li and Wang have recognized that China is on a collision course with what is still, by a wide margin, the world's most powerful nation. Trump's catalog of mistakes in dealing with allies and rivals alike has diminished America's standing around the world, again and again playing into the hands of its detractors, but Li and Wang are well aware of the factors that have produced the sea change in American attitudes towards China and caused even Europeans to question their readiness to subordinate political values to supposed economic advantage in dealing with China. Besides, Li and Wang understand very well that economically, militarily, and politically the United States still far outweighs China. A radical rethink of strategy has long been essential. But Xi is in thrall to a vision of himself as the strong man who would resist the calls for political reform at home and confront the United States and its allies abroad. At home, he has put his faith in the Social Credit System, which will soon be ready for nationwide application, to strengthen "the dictatorship of the people," oblivious to its impotence to defend the Chinese financial system from its fatal weaknesses. In Sino-American relations, Xi, in Li's view, is autistic: he is unable to grasp that across the political spectrum US attitudes have undergone a sea change, and China must adjust its strategy in response.

When Wang joins Li, the two men sit side by side on a sofa, with notepads on the low table in front of them, on which they can silently communicate their more controversial thoughts. They present a contrast with the man who dominates their thoughts, Xi Jinping. Xi is a "princeling," the son of a leader of the first generation of revolutionaries; his career was jump-started by his family connections. Li and Wang had to rely on their own talents: Li's father was a mid-level official and Wang's a manual laborer. Xi stands almost six feet tall. His jowls are heavy, and he is overweight; a photograph of Xi walking beside President Obama juxtaposed with a Disney image of Winnie the Pooh walking with his friend Tigger went viral in China, until banned by censors.[7] During a three-nation tour of Europe in 2019, he walked with a slight limp and seemed to be suffering from a back problem. Li is 5 feet 9 inches in height, slim and agile. The eyes behind his rimless spectacles are always alert, and his mobile face breaks easily into a smile. Wang is about the same height as Li, with a relaxed, urbane manner. He avoids the stilted language of many of his peers and has the self-confidence to joke with foreign journalists; his eyes are shrewd and his black hair elegantly grey at the temples.

Li and Wang were both born in 1955 and Xi in 1953, so all three were young adults in the heady, hope-fueled years of the early 1980s, when, to the young at least, China's future, political as well as economic, seemed open. Li was a brilliant student, an outstanding member of the renowned "class of 1982." This class had passed one of the most competitive exams in the history of China and would produce some of the nation's most talented people in a wide array of fields. For the first time since 1949, students were free to read and absorb ideas and knowledge from around the world. Li seized the opportunities to study the laws and institutions of liberal democracy,[8] and his PhD in economics covered privatization and capital markets, highly controversial subjects at the time.[9] Xi's academic record was undistinguished, his undergraduate studies were in the politically neutral field of chemical engineering, and he has been credibly accused of having plagiarized his PhD thesis.[10]

Li leads the discussion with Wang: "If Comrade Jinping wants to defuse this confrontation, he can use his authority as president to waive the law that prohibits our companies from granting this access. As general secretary he can instruct the Party cells in the companies to ensure they comply with the SEC's demand. Responsibility for compliance or failure to do so lies fairly and squarely with him. But he won't, will he?"

"No," Wang agrees, "he will see this as a contest of wills, and it will reinforce his conviction that he is the strong man defending our regime against all its enemies, at home and abroad. Of course, in the short term the suspension is going to disrupt American markets and hit international investors. But in the longer term it will strike a far harder blow on our companies. Until the SEC is satisfied, US exchanges won't trade their existing securities, or admit new ones, and our companies need access to the US capital markets to finance their international operations. If they they move to Hong Kong, the long arm of American finance and law will reach them there too." What Wang and Li know, but Wang does not say, is that the rich and powerful of China benefit hugely from these operations. By listing their companies overseas and in Hong Kong, China's business elites, and by extension their political associates, have effectively put billions of dollars of assets beyond the country's capital controls. Apart from their legitimate business expenses, they can use some of the dollars they raise to reward their political friends for past favors or buy future ones; they can finance their children's education overseas; they can create a store of wealth safe from domestic political risks and beyond the reach of anticorruption investigators and their enemies within China's borders.

"Yes," says Li, "and this is just the latest step in the long-term American offensive against us. If this confrontation is not resolved, the Americans will escalate. You and I have studied their options. We have discussed this at length. We know that if they block us from their markets in capital and currencies, and from their banking system, it will be devastating for us."

"When trading opens on Monday," says Wang, "there will be heavy selling on our stock markets. The kind of intervention we organized in 2015 will not stabilize the market for long because the trigger for the crisis now is not domestic but international; and it is not only a matter of market sentiment but of legal sanctions."[11]

"You and I know," responds Li, "that this drama on the market is not going to play out in isolation. On Monday, a collapse of stock market prices will trigger a chain reaction that will turn a bad situation into a full-scale crisis. You and I have anticipated such a crisis for years, without knowing what would trigger it. Now we do know. The rice is almost cooked."

That homely phrase, spoken in a low voice, crashes like thunder in Wang's ear.

"Indeed," responds Wang. It is all he needs to say. The seemingly innocuous phrase "the rice is cooked" is a code agreed between them for implementing an audacious contingency plan they have worked out over the past few years. These men recognized that China's economic slowdown was taking place in an environment poisoned by an array of deep-seated problems, political, social, and moral, which would interact at some point to cause a crisis. They have long resolved to be ready to seize that moment to move against Xi Jinping himself. Nothing less offers an escape from the dead end in which his policies have trapped China. His China Dream is a waking nightmare.

Their objective is not a simple change of leaders. They have come to the conclusion that many of China's problems have arisen precisely because the economic reforms introduced after 1979 were not accompanied by political reforms. The tension between social and economic change on the one hand and an unchanging political system on the other has made the status quo unsustainable. The nationwide application of the Social Credit System is reinforcing their control but not resolving any problems. At home and abroad, problems have been accumulating for years. The two men have concluded that none of them can be resolved without a radical change of political structure. In the Soviet Union, in the early 1990s, Boris Yeltsin had come to the same conclusion. He lacked the skills, character, and physical stamina needed to govern Russia well in the extremely difficult circumstances that followed his revolution, but hindsight has not discredited his judgment that economic and political reform must go hand in hand.

Pragmatism is one of the strongest characteristics of the Chinese people, and Li and Wang's approach to political change is above all pragmatic. They have not undergone some Damascene conversion to the ideals of liberal democracy. They have simply recognized that the model of economic reform without political reform has outlived its usefulness. This is no new insight. Back in 2011–12, Li, then the first vice premier, had played a decisive role in the biggest-ever collaborative project between the Chinese government and the World Bank, which had produced *China 2030*, a wide-ranging, far-reaching report that indicated, in suitably diplomatic language, that the communist regime would have to embrace pluralism and relax its suffocating grip on society if China was to avoid the "middle-income trap" that had ensnared Latin America and North Africa.[12] Indeed, they are convinced that the model of economic without political reform has not only outlived its usefulness: it has become counterproductive. Dangerously so. If they do not act decisively now, their own power and wealth will be in peril. Their personal interests and those of the nation make radical change imperative and urgent.

Now that the crisis that they have long anticipated is breaking, these two men are steeled with excitement but very nervous: they are about to challenge the second most powerful man in the world. The penalty for failure will be death, or life imprisonment. On their skill, judgment, and courage will depend the fate of a nation of 1.4 billion people, and the outcome of their challenge will have repercussions around the world.

Of course, the efficiency of China's security apparatus has made conspiracy very risky. The failure of the plot by Bo Xilai, Party chief of Chongqing, and Zhou Yongkang, the security chief, to seize power in 2012 stood as a reminder of that. But Li and Wang believe they are smarter than them.

Unlike Leonid Brezhnev when he was plotting to overthrow Nikita Khrushchev in 1964, the two men had decided at the outset to move quickly to recruit only a small number of absolutely essential people.

Li and Wang Yang had first approached Wang Qishan, vice president of the Republic. With his lean, ascetic look, his balding head and rimless spectacles, Wang might be mistaken for an academic. Indeed, his father was a leading professor of engineering, and he himself was appointed for a time to research the history of China in the nineteenth and twentieth centuries in the prestigious Academy of Social Sciences. But Wang is anything but an ivory-tower academic. He entered the world of princelings when he married the daughter of a first-generation revolutionary, and he made a brilliant career developing China's postsocialist financial system. He has gained tremendous respect for his capacity to handle the most difficult tasks.[13] Deeply steeped in China's history, he sees the communist period as part of China's longer struggle for modernization. He has had close ties to Xi Jinping since they met as "sent-down youths" toiling in the countryside in the Cultural Revolution. In 2012, Xi entrusted him with running the anticorruption campaign, a job that made him many enemies but gave him unrivaled knowledge of the dark secrets of the most powerful people in the land. In 2017, he stepped down from the Politburo, probably because an unwritten rule then in force barred anyone aged 68 or older from appointment to it, and was appointed vice president of the Republic. He was given the rare privilege of attending meetings of its Standing Committee as a nonvoting member.[14] While he is close to Xi, he is very much his own man; in Communist Party politics, personal loyalty counts for little.

When Li Keqiang and Wang Yang approach him, they do not spell out their arguments at length; they think they know his mind. So Li sets out their thinking tersely and then sums it up: "Qishan, you know, we know, and many others around us know that China is traveling in a direction that holds great dangers for the nation, for the Party, and for us personally. We know the problems and the solutions, but we are prisoners of the political system. We are rulers of the largest nation in the world and the second largest economy, but we are slaves, slaves to the Great God Party. We will remain immobilized in impotence unless we smash the idol, dethrone its High Priest, and break out of this prison. Now is the time to act."

"I have been waiting for you, waiting to see if you would dare to act. I will work with you," replies the vice president.

The three men agree that, in the contingency planning for a coup, Wang Qishan would concentrate on constitutional and institutional aspects, while Wang Yang would lead on economic issues, with the two of them reporting back to Li.

This triumvirate of plotters knew they could only succeed if they had the military on their side. The two military members of the Politburo were Air Force General Xu Qiliang and General Zhang Youxia of the land forces. The triumvirate were convinced that these men took a hard-headed view of the strategic balance. China was taking great strides to modernize its armed forces, and narrowing the gap with the Americans, but was still well behind in every aspect of warfare. If political miscalculation led to military conflict with the United States, it was the armed forces that would immediately suffer on a massive scale. Like the triumvirate, they believed that Xi was leading China to overreach internationally and was overly influenced by retired generals who trumpeted chauvinist nonsense from the safety of their think tanks.

With backing from the Wangs, Li arranged secret meetings for the three of them with the two generals separately.

They met first with Xu. It did not prove too difficult for them to persuade him to join them in developing a contingency plan in case Xi Jinping led China into a military confrontation with the United States (a confrontation most likely to occur over disputed islands in the South China Sea). They knew that it would be much harder to persuade him of the disadvantages of a simple palace coup in which the leaders of the Party changed but the political system stayed the same. Li had set out the arguments in a handwritten note that he handed to Xu.

It began by describing how the Americans are moving beyond the trade war to more broad-ranging economic hostilities, and warning that Xi did not take proper account of American superiority in this field and had been slow to recognize the strategy the Americans had developed for geoeconomic warfare.

The note continued:

You know very well the disparity between their military and ours, but their superiority in economic power is much greater, and carries no risk of nuclear war. Comrade Jinping was very slow to recognize that the strategies we have been pursuing against the USA, especially the acquisition of intellectual property through forced transfers and intelligence-gathering, which served us well for years, have now become counterproductive. These strategies, together with his strengthening of the state sector, restricting the private sector, and total rejection of political reform, have led to a sea change in American attitudes towards us. He has made an enemy of the world's most powerful nation. They are using their economic power not just to secure better terms for trade and investment, but to press us to relaunch our transition to a market economy, and that is quite clever, because as you know many of us believe that is in China's best interests. It is economic reform, free markets—to the extent that we have them—that have given us economic growth. We need more of them, not less. The recession and unemployment caused by the coronavirus have made this more urgent than ever.

The Americans began this push with trade, but now they have begun to exploit their superior strength in the markets for currencies and capital. Their Justice Department is conducting legal proceedings against some of our biggest banks in relation to the breaking of UN sanctions on North Korea.[15] This could lead to the exclusion of those banks from the US financial system, and that would terminate their international operations. That would be a sentence of death.

Eventually, the Americans could go even further: they could freeze our holdings of Treasury bonds and ban us from future purchases—shut us out of the world's reserve currency. They have many other buyers, but we have no alternative. The Euro and yen are simply not realistic alternatives for our foreign exchange reserves.

Hundreds of billions of dollars of US pension funds, mutual funds, foundations, endowments, and retirement plans are invested in the stocks and bonds of Chinese companies listed in the United States, Hong Kong, and the mainland. They have already stopped the main pension fund of the US government from investing in Chinese equities. They could order *all* US companies and individuals to divest from all our state-controlled companies such as those in the banking, petroleum, and petrochemicals sectors.[16] Then they could move on to target private sector companies. They have many attractive alternatives for their investments. We could not find other investors to replace them on anything like the same scale. This would be a devastating blow to our economy.

This is war without firing a shot, and a war we cannot win. It is also a war we should not be fighting. Our highest objectives are to make China secure and prosperous. To renew our economic growth, we need to relaunch the transition to the market economy. If that is also an American objective, so much the better. But further economic reform cannot be achieved with our one-party political system. It requires political reform, a transition to democracy. Without it, we cannot overcome the vested interests that are blocking economic and every other kind of reform at every level. We should be opening up the "commanding heights" of the economy, banking, utilities and transport, to allow our dynamic, profitable private companies to compete with corrupt, sclerotic state-owned companies, but vested interests are blocking that. We should be rebalancing our economy by relying more on household consumption, but that would require a substantial transfer of wealth and income from provincial and municipal governments and state-owned entities to households. Vested interests are blocking that too, and only in a democratic system can we mobilize the force of public opinion to overcome them.

In fact, we need political reform to resolve a whole range of other problems we cannot solve with a one-party system. Look at Hong Kong, Xinjiang, Tibet, and Taiwan. The strategies pursued by Xi have alienated the people in all those regions. He did not invent these strategies, but he has reinforced them, he has persisted in them long after they have become counterproductive, and he refuses to consider any reform that would allow us to address the root causes of these problems. With our present system, no negotiation, no compromise can be contemplated on the issues that are alienating the Hongkongers, the Uyghurs, the Tibetan Buddhists, and the Taiwanese. That is why the United States is imposing sanctions on our officials who implement our strategies, has removed the trade and investment privileges accorded to Hong Kong, and is threatening to restrict our access to its capital markets.[17]

The target of America's hostility is not China, but our one-party system. If we change our political system, we shall benefit China economically and socially, and we shall open the door to peace with America. So, we need not just a change of personnel, but a change of system.

When General Xu finished reading, he sat in silence for a minute, absorbing the shock. Could he believe what Li had written? Was he hallucinating? No, he knew Li to be a rational man, and Li was sitting there in front of him.

Li gave him time to recover, retrieved the note, and broke the silence by saying:

"Of course, all that goes totally against the line the Party has been preaching to the public for years, but who believes the Party line nowadays? Who reads the *People's Daily,* except Party officials who need to parrot the current formulations? They don't believe all that stuff either, do they?

"With decades of practice, we Chinese have become the world's greatest company of actors, pretending to believe what we don't. Just think back to the *tsunami* of popular outrage that burst out when Dr. Li Wenliang was silenced for warning of the outbreak of the coronavirus in Wuhan. People cast all pretence aside.

"Of course, there are millions of us in the Party and our friends who have done very well by the current system, but it is on its last legs now. After over forty years of spectacular economic and social change, the tension between a changed society and a paralyzed political system will bring down the political structure in chaos if we do not take the initiative in reforming it, radically. Only if we lead the change will we stand a chance of surviving it. To put it crudely, our personal self-interest is at stake as much the national interest."

Somewhat hesitantly, General Xu accepted the force of the arguments deployed by his civilian colleagues, and Li burned the note in front of him. The meeting with General Zhang followed a similar pattern, to the same conclusion.

Two other members of the Politburo were essential to success: Guo Shengkun, the head of China's domestic security apparatus, who had to be persuaded not to frustrate the conspiracy, and Zhao Leji, who had taken over from Wang Qishan as head of the anticorruption commission in 2012. He had thereby acquired similar leverage over other Politburo members through knowledge of their shady activities; he could compile dossiers of their assets controlled through companies in tax havens where disclosure of beneficial ownership was not required, of bribes they had paid in advancing their own careers or received for advancing those of others, and of the business dealings of their families.

When the conspirators approached them, Zhao and Guo faced a stark choice: betray them or join them? If they betrayed them, there would be a struggle for power that the plotters would probably win, since they included two members of the Standing Committee of the Politburo, the two most senior generals, and the well-connected vice president. They joined the plot.

The conspirators' calculations of the national interest were interwoven, of course, with their own political interests: in the event of a crisis the best hope of preserving their own power and wealth would lie in leading the top-down revolution, or "refolution," to use the term coined to describe the combination of reform and revolution that transformed Hungary and Poland in 1989.[18]

In the contingency planning, the generals took responsibility for the military and security details (the People's Armed Police was under direct military command), and provided the premises, transport, and communications for plotters to keep in touch and meet in secret. Each of them worked with a tight circle of handpicked members of their own staff. They referred to themselves simply as "the Friends."

Now, on the day of the SEC's announcement, Li Keqiang and Wang Yang contact the other Friends and arrange to meet them at

1 a.m. on Sunday, three hours hence, at a secret location guarded by the military. When they meet, Li Keqiang summarizes the likely impact of the SEC announcement on China's financial markets, and the immediate follow-on effects in the property and foreign exchange markets. For the benefit of those Friends who are not as familiar with the economic developments as he and Wang Yang are, he begins with a blunt description of the background and recent developments:

> "After the global financial crisis of 2008, we adopted the strategy of massively increasing the supply of credit to the economy. Much of it was used for nonproductive purposes, like property speculation and building infrastructure we do not need, such as roads to nowhere and airports without air traffic. It kept people employed, but it brought diminishing returns: in 2008 every additional unit of credit increased output by one unit; by 2020 it was taking four units of credit to produce one extra unit of output. Even before the coronavirus struck, our whole system was infected with debt. The measures we have had to take to deal with the recession and unemployment since then have added to that.
>
> "The only road to a strong recovery is to allow our dynamic, profitable private sector to expand and reduce the loss-making state-owned sector, but Comrade Jinping has always resisted that because it will undermine our Party's monopoly of political power, and he is adamantly opposed to political reform.
>
> "Of course, political reform would carry huge risks for the nation, and for us personally, but the risks of continuing with our present system are greater. What do we see now? Problems are mounting in a property market already weakened by the coronavirus. It is much too dependent on debt. It is riddled with corruption

and the falsification of collateral pledged against loans. In Beijing and Shanghai we have some of the most overvalued housing in the world, and they are our most politically sensitive cities. Construction companies are laying people off in large numbers.

"Falling prices on stock and property markets are interacting to reinforce downward movement on both. Companies and households in difficulty are selling shares to meet mortgage payments and property loan repayments. That's pushing prices down further. Demand for our exports has not recovered from the coronavirus. Unemployment soared when the disease broke out, and it is rising again now. Our social welfare system is still seriously underfunded.

"All these problems are coming together in the most vulnerable part of our financial system—shadow banking and the interbank market—as investors lose their appetite for high-risk, high-return products. City and regional banks are especially exposed, and there are some two hundred of them. The national regulators have tried for years to get a grip on them, but they are colluding with regional bosses who depend on them to make their local economies look good.

"There is going to be turmoil in our financial markets, and the financial crisis will quickly expand into a wider economic crisis. Faced with a crisis at home, I expect Comrade Jinping to ramp up external tension as a distraction for the public, and to rally leading comrades behind him. If he misjudges that, we shall face a double crisis, international as well as domestic. This is just the kind of situation for which we have prepared our contingency plan. If we fail to act in time, our country will face disaster, our Party will be annihilated, and we shall not enjoy a peaceful old age. Comrade Jinping has already personalized the confrontation with the SEC, and he will surely lead from the front from here on. We must remove him now. If we do not act now, he will use the coming National Congress of the Party to reappoint him and force us into retirement. The opportunity to launch a transition to democracy with a swift, surgical strike will have been lost, but the causes of instability will not have been eliminated. If we do act now, we believe our comrades in the Politburo will accept our lead. Do you agree?"

It was more of an assertion than a question. The Friends all expressed their agreement. The die was now cast and there was no turning back.

On Li's instructions, the two Wangs and General Xu arrange to meet each day, however briefly, to judge when the moment to act has come, then contact the others.

On the Monday, the main index of large-cap stocks falls almost to its daily limit of 10 percent. Small-cap stocks and high-tech names also fare badly. Chinese bond yields spike to 5 percent. China's government spokesman denounces the SEC's action and reassures investors that the fundamentals of China's physical economy remain strong. But on Tuesday the market falls again, this time by 8.25 percent. That day, China's leading finance officials, regulators, and central bankers hold emergency meetings to decide their response to the market turmoil. There is no official statement, but in the late afternoon rumors fly around that the state is planning to intervene in the market as it did in 2015: it will organize a buying program of $500 billion, by state-owned financial institutions, the "National Team." This settles the market. On Wednesday, the official announcement of the buying program brings a cautious rally.

On Thursday, the buying by the National Team holds the market flat, and Xi tells the Politburo Standing Committee that afternoon that they have the situation under control. Supported by a majority of the committee, he brushes aside expressions of doubt by Premier Li and Vice Premier Wang Yang, insisting that he should issue a public demand to his US counterpart that he intervene to get the SEC to cancel the suspension of Chinese companies from trading.

At noon EST on Friday, the White House announces the rejection of Xi's demand and affirms the executive's respect for the independence of the SEC. By then it is 1 a.m. throughout China, and market traders are taking their rest after a roller-coaster week.

The dominant players in China's financial markets have the whole weekend to reflect on the fact that the SEC is standing firm, and their government is refusing to negotiate on the SEC's demands.

When the Friends gather to review the situation, they are more convinced than ever that Xi has fatally miscalculated the balance of forces and is leading China into a dead-end street.

When the market opens on Monday, sellers, taking a negative view of the weekend's stand-off, test the resolve of the National Team to hold prices at their current levels. Over the course of the day, doubts grow as to the strength of the National Team's willingness to commit their resources to the full; not only do many of its key players resent the fact that they were investigated for insider trading in the wake of the 2015 market crash, but they are much more pessimistic about the wider context now. The index ends the day 3 percent down.

In Washington, members of Congress, smelling blood, raise the incendiary issue of Chinese banks facilitating the breaking of

United Nations sanctions against North Korea by Chinese companies, operations on which the US Justice Department and indeed the UN have long held documentary evidence.

On Tuesday, there are runs on some of China's city and regional banks in Shandong, Liaoning, and Guizhou Provinces. The quality of information about them is too poor to enable the People's Bank of China (PBoC), the central bank, to intervene in time to save the weakest. Under tight censorship, news media do not mention the bank runs, but the news spreads on WeChat.

Li Keqiang begins to think about the speeches he will make to the nation and the Central Committee of the Party when he launches the coup d'état. Since he will be leading a political revolution, nothing less, there will be no point in pandering to opponents of change by paying lip service to their views or using the wooden language Party leaders usually employ at great length. He must set the tone for the new era by being direct and brief. Since this will be a top-down revolution, not a bottom-up manifestation of people power, he will not have the immediate backing of crowds on the streets or public opinion expressed in mass media. But he can overawe the reactionaries by conjuring up the possibility that, if need be, he will mobilize crowds, freeing deep currents of long-suppressed resentment, as Yeltsin did in the Soviet Union. Everyone present will know that the regime's budget for internal security exceeds that for the military because it believes that the Chinese people present a greater threat to it than the armies of foreign powers. They know that they pay tribute to the attractive power of democracy by the ruthless way they suppress discussion of it and punish those who ever dare to advocate it. In addition to these intangibles, they will see that Li has the backing of the leaders of China's armed forces, and that is raw power.

Li will be bold in promising to empower people who have been treated as political infants all their lives. He will deploy the explosive power of acknowledging truths that have been buried for decades, truths about the tragedies inflicted on China by Mao and the Party itself. He will acknowledge the power of advocating values and ideas suppressed for decades. He will show that he is unafraid of the reactionaries in the Party leadership, by broadcasting to the nation before meeting with the Central Committee.

On Wednesday, contagion spreads to even the big, well-funded national banks; their stock prices are hammered, and depositors start to make panic withdrawals from them too, forcing the central bank to intervene to keep them adequately funded. The index falls almost its full limit.

On Thursday, large and very angry crowds gather at the locked doors of the failed city and regional banks, demanding compensation. When the police arrive in force, they refuse to disperse. Clashes break out, causing injuries to police as well as protesters. Fired up by the example of these depositors, unemployed workers who have waited for weeks and months for their benefits gather at the gates of those former employers who are still in business on a reduced scale; others gather outside the mayor's office. Reports spread by WeChat video streams, which appear on foreign websites, until the streaming service is suspended. Netizens show their usual linguistic ingenuity to defy the censors' attempts to stop them from spreading the stories.

Although China's stock markets are not heavily dependent on foreign investors, nor are Chinese banks tightly interwoven with foreign counterparts, alarm about China's economic prospects and even its political stability has gathered momentum in international markets, especially in Hong Kong. In the currency market, the renminbi falls to its lower daily limit. The PBoC continues to intervene to stabilize the banking system. Despite the continuing efforts of the National Team, the stock market again falls almost to its lower limit, so that by the end of the day, it is down by a cumulative 35.3 percent since the start of the crisis.

News reaches the Party leaders of civil disturbances spreading around the country. Confidential reports from police chiefs warn that their officers, many of whom have lost much of their life savings as the stock market and property asset bubbles have burst or whose relatives have seen their businesses fail, are reluctant to risk injury in clashes with protesters. A growing number of social media censors are allowing negative news posts to remain undeleted for too long. Exchange control officials are accepting large bribes to allow capital to flee the country and are joining the flow. Like the police officers and censors, most of these officials have been doing these jobs for pragmatic reasons: they are self-interested, not motivated by political loyalty. Indeed, their work exposes them more than most people to the dark side of the regime and the corrupt behavior of its high officials, making them cynical. Their first priority is self-preservation. Now that their own finances are being hit hard, organizational discipline is weakening, and political trouble is looming.

At this moment there is an extraordinary development. On Tianfu Square in the heart of Chengdu, capital of Sichuan Province, a large crowd has gathered around a powerful and eloquent orator who is denouncing the lies and official corruption which, he claims, have created the financial house of cards that is now collapsing, destroying the savings of the people. He blames the one-party dictatorship for the problems, which he says have reduced China to a moral swamp. He calls for a spiritual revolution and a new China under a new constitution, based on democracy and the rule of law, and the separation of the state and religion.

The speaker's name is Wang Yi. Back in 2018, when he was senior pastor of the Early Rain Covenant Church, an illegal, unregistered Protestant church in Chengdu, he was arrested and later sentenced to nine years in prison for "subversion of state power." He is supposed to be still serving that term, but word spreads through the crowd that while in prison he converted the prison governor to Christianity, and the governor arranged his escape. A constitutional lawyer before he became a pastor, Wang had gained a national and international reputation for defending the rights of poor and powerless defendants. Under his leadership, the Early Rain Church became famous for commemorating the victims of the Sichuan earthquake and the massacre on Tiananmen Square on 4 June 1989, and Wang's writings on religion and law were widely followed on the internet. Knowing his reputation and popularity, and facing the destruction of their own savings, the police on Tianfu Square hold back, awaiting orders from above. News of Wang's escape and appearance on the square spreads like wildfire through social media to Christians across China, who begin to gather in their own cities, holding homemade crosses, symbols of their faith that for years had been burned and banned, and echoing Wang's demands.

On Friday morning, the full Politburo meets in emergency session. Xi opens the proceedings by pointing out that the US president has come under mounting pressure at home and abroad to intervene with the SEC to avoid causing wider instability on international markets; China should stand its ground. When news arrives that the stock market rout is continuing, taking the index down by its 10 percent limit, and bringing the cumulative fall since 28 March to 42 percent, the Politburo orders the immediate closure of the market "until normal conditions are restored," an action without precedent since 1949. Faced with reports that capital flight is accelerating, it orders suspension of repatriation of profits by foreign-invested companies for the next eight weeks. With senior police officers reporting that their rank-and-file subordinates may refuse orders to confront the swelling crowds of angry protesters, the Politburo orders the deployment onto the streets of the People's Armed Police (PAP). The PAP is the iron fist and ultimate guardian of the regime against the people and even, if necessary, against the army. Since 2018 it has been jointly commanded by the Central Committee and the Central Military Commission, of which Generals Xu and Zhang are the senior vice chairmen under Xi.

On Saturday 2 April, news media give saturation coverage of Xi Jinping, dressed in military uniform, visiting the Joint Operations Command Center of the armed forces. They stress his role as commander-in-chief. He then makes a TV broadcast to the nation, dressed in military uniform. He denounces the Freedom of Navigation Operations (FONOPs) that the US Navy (and the navies of its principal allies) have been conducting in disputed waters around islands in the South China Sea since 2015 and demands an end to these "provocations." He declares an Air Defense Identification Zone (ADIZ) around the Paracel Islands, to "identify, monitor, control and react to aircraft entering the zone with potential air threats." He orders a task force including an aircraft carrier, fifteen surface combatants, and ten attack submarines to set sail south for the zone from Hainan Island. People's Liberation Army (PLA) Air Force fighter/attack aircraft to be deployed to bases along China's southeast coastline. Xi claims that FONOPs are disrupting the legitimate activities of Chinese fishing fleets. What he does not mention is that the fishing vessels are under command of the Chinese Navy, and he has just ordered dozens of them to swarm around US Navy vessels conducting their operations, forcing them to leave "Chinese" waters to avoid a collision. When the Friends meet later that day, the generals express extreme alarm at the orders Xi has given; the risk of an accidental collision and an armed response by the Americans is unacceptably high. They agree that if a collision occurs they should implement the contingency plan.

A few hours later, the US SEC announces that the five Chinese companies suspended from trading ten business days earlier have not given the assurances demanded on access to their accounts in China, and the suspension has therefore been extended for another ten days. The SEC further announces that since the other Chinese companies whose shares are traded in the United States have also failed to comply with its instructions on access, they will all now be suspended from trading. There is a surge of speculation that when the new foreign exchange trading week begins in Sydney on Monday the PBoC will announce a major devaluation of the renminbi.

Heavy patrolling by the People's Armed Police maintains order on the streets of China's major cities over the weekend, but there are fears that when banks open for business on Monday, there will be renewed disturbances. In the event, crowds gather, but there are only sporadic outbreaks of violence.

This uneasy calm is broken on Monday at 2 p.m., when international news media report that a PLA Navy ship has rammed a US Navy destroyer engaged in a FONOP in waters around the Paracel Islands. The American destroyer *USS Jeremiah Denton*, which had maneuvered to avoid hitting three fishing vessels that had put themselves in its path, was struck by the prow of a much heavier Chinese destroyer, the *Nanchang*, which had been following it and had held to its course. It was a glancing blow and the damage was above the waterline, but it resulted in the death of five US sailors and the wounding of six others. The US government issues an ultimatum demanding that within 48 hours China accept responsibility for the incident and agree to immediate talks on measures to avoid future confrontations in the South China Sea. In parallel with the very public ultimatum, the US president uses the red hotline to warn Xi that if China rejects the ultimatum, the United States will immediately inflict devastating damage to unspecified Chinese military installations. In his response to the president, Xi stalls for time. He then schedules a full Politburo meeting for 7:30 p.m.

The Friends quickly make contact and, using the prearranged code, agree to implement the contingency plan when the Politburo gathers in Zhongnanhai, the compound where the leaders live and work in central Beijing. As usual, the Politburo will meet in the Huairen Hall, a two-story Chinese-style hall, where the Dowager Empress Cixi once worked. Ironically, given the drama that is about to unfold there, its name translates in English as the Hall of Cherished Compassion.

Xi opens the meeting with a short statement reaffirming the positions he has taken on the financial and now military confrontations with the United States, and he then calls on Li Keqiang to update the meeting on the military situation. Supremely confident as always, he has no foreboding of what is to come. To his utter astonishment, the hitherto uncontroversial, technocratic premier launches into an all-out attack on the president's handling of both confrontations, placing the blame for the double crisis the nation and the Party now face squarely on Xi. This is the first overt move in the contingency plan agreed by the Friends. As Xi is about to launch into a furious riposte, Li insists that the other Friends be heard first and sternly brushes aside Xi's sputtering objections. The Friends speak in turn. Air Force General Xu declares that Xi's blundering has put China in peril of an American military onslaught. General Zhang briefly supports General Xu from the point of view of the land forces. Wang Yang warns that the financial markets and the economy stand on the brink of disaster, putting the immediate crisis in the context of years of mistaken priorities and bad management by Xi who, having centralized power in his own hands, must accept the blame. They are followed by Guo Shengkun, the security chief, and Zhao Leji, who claims to have compiled a dossier of corruption on a massive scale by Xi's close relatives who have continued in business, contrary to assurances given by him when he was appointed to lead the Party. As a nonmember of the Politburo, attending as usual by special invitation, Wang Qishan is saved the pain of speaking against his friend and ally of over fifty years.

From being the head of the pack, Xi has been turned upon and attacked by his apparently obedient followers. Again he tries to intervene, but he has lost his bluster. Again Li silences him, saying that every member of the Politburo must first be heard. The remaining members are invited to speak in order of seniority. Particular attention is paid to the highly respected Vice Premier Liu He, Xi's closest economic adviser. He damns Xi with faint praise, others equivocate, and none offers a robust defense. It is evident that Xi has alienated the majority of the Politburo. With the poise of a skilled prosecutor summing up irrefutable evidence against a defendant in a capital case, Li addresses Xi like a one-man execution squad:

"You have centralized greater authority in your hands than any leader since Chairman Mao, and what have you done with it? Have you used it to lead us into a new era of economic reform? No, you have capitulated to the power of vested interests. Have you adapted our political system to match the social transformation our nation has achieved? No, you have led us backwards, suppressing civil society, overplaying the hand of the Party, and opening the way to staying supreme leader for the rest of your life. Have you enhanced China's international standing? No, you have made enemies of the world's strongest nation and its allies, all of whom had previously been well disposed towards us. And that has led us into the double peril we face tonight. Is there is any reason why you should not resign all your posts?"

"This is outrageous!" Xi expostulates, "history will condemn you. Resign? What a farce! I see guns trained on me by men I trusted to defend China and our Party. I not only resign from my posts, but from the Party, which has now been captured by renegades. History will condemn you for the vile traitors that you are!"

Ignoring the counterattack by the now broken chief, Li thanks him and assures him that he, his wife, and his daughter will enjoy the protection of the state in his "retirement," and that a comfortable villa awaits them in a coastal province to which they will be escorted, with every courtesy, by a detachment of PAP, who are then summoned to the meeting room and informed of Xi's dismissal. In his luxurious prison, Xi will have time to reflect upon his mistakes, while China makes a transition to democracy and the rule of law. When that transition has been achieved, Xi will be offered his freedom on condition that he publicly pledges the same allegiance to the new order and the same obedience to its laws as will be required of every citizen of China.

The meeting resumes under the chairmanship of Li, who proposes three steps for immediate action:

- He will speak on the hotline to the US president to defuse the military and financial confrontations.
- He will make a public broadcast at noon the next day, Tuesday.
- The Central Committee of the Party will meet immediately after the broadcast.

Wang Yang proposes that Li be nominated for election by the Central Committee as general secretary of the Party; Li proposes that he recommend to the National People's Congress (NPC) that Wang Qishan be elected president of the Republic, and that Wang Qishan should then nominate Wang Yang for premier.

The meeting agrees to all these points and further agrees that, in speaking to the US president, Li will

- say that, following Xi's resignation, the Politburo has agreed to the leadership changes (Wang Yang and Wang Qishan will be at his side to confirm these);
- acknowledge China's responsibility for the fatal collision in the SCS and propose a bilateral meeting in Singapore to discuss measures to avoid any repetition;
- give an assurance that the government will act immediately to permit Chinese companies to comply with SEC information requirements;

- ask that the US government keep secret the leadership changes until they are announced in China in "the coming hours."

Li makes the call, which defuses the Sino-American crisis. The meeting then resumes to discuss the Friends' plans in depth.

Li sets out the strategy the Friends have agreed to. He hammers home the point that the model of economic reform without political reform has become counterproductive in every sphere of national life. A mere change of personnel and policies will be futile. The system must be changed. Unless the nation can be convinced that this is about to happen, the small crowds now on the streets will rapidly swell, the erosion of authority within the security apparatus will become a collapse, and confidence in China's financial institutions will totally evaporate, with disastrous consequences. The Politburo must unite behind a far-reaching program of political and economic reform, and carry the Central Committee with them. Initiatives must be taken to gain the trust of people in China's peripheral regions who have been deeply alienated: the people of Tibet, Xinjiang, Inner Mongolia, Taiwan, and Hong Kong. In his broadcast to the nation, Li must say enough to persuade the people that they are going to be politically empowered, but not so much that the Central Committee feels it is being forced to sign up to a detailed blueprint. The challenge will test Li's political skills to the utmost.

In the discussion that follows, voices of caution are raised, warning that because China lacks any experience of popular democracy a leap to universal suffrage will bring chaos, and arguing that a program of gradual reform would be more prudent. Li, backed by Wang Yang, rebuts this, saying that the history of reform in China shows that small steps to democracy would, in the future as in the past, be stopped in their tracks by vested interests, while larger steps that empower only part of the population would arouse unstoppable demands to extend the vote to the whole population. They are living in twenty-first-century China, not nineteenth-century Britain. He accepts that radical reform carries big risks but insists that nothing less will be effective and sustainable. The situation demands boldness, not timidity.

Eventually, the Friends win the argument. Li is authorized to speak again to the American President to say that the Politburo has agreed that major constitutional and policy changes are needed, and to outline the timetable for his broadcast and the Central Committee meeting.

Mass media are authorized to alert the nation to an address to be carried by television and radio at noon, Tuesday.

As soon as the Politburo meeting ends, the security and military chiefs order implementation of the contingency plan. PAP detachments locate all members of the Central Committee, inform them of the plans for "a major public announcement" to be followed by a Plenary session of the Committee, and explain the arrangements for their movements: they will be escorted immediately by military transport to the site of the meeting, to await its opening. It will be held, as usual, in the Jingxi Hotel, a drab Soviet-style building run by the military in a closely guarded compound in northwest Beijing; there they will stay until it ends. On arrival at the Jingxi, they are informed of the leadership changes. In the meantime, they are allowed no contact with anyone. Their phones and computers are taken into "safekeeping." Their personal staff and family members are informed of their movements and asked to remain at home, where they will be "under police protection." No detail has been left unattended.

Around the country, PAP detachments are deployed to TV and radio stations, news media offices, and financial institutions, where they are to await further orders. All PAP and police leave is canceled.

As he is driven from Zhongnanhai to the Jingxi Hotel, Li Keqiang remembers that two days before, when he had come to the family breakfast table, he had found that his wife, a professor of English, had laid beside his place the two books on British history that Li and his classmates had excitedly translated into Chinese in the early 1980s: a history of the British constitution and Lord Denning's *The Due Process of Law*. The principles he had absorbed then had been buried for years but now came alive in his mind again. Into his mind flashed images of China's last great political crisis, in 1989, which led to the sacking of General Secretary Zhao Ziyang on suspicion of favoring political reform. Zhao had been held in house arrest for the remainder of his life. Li knew that Zhao, with plenty of time to think, had indeed concluded that parliamentary democracy was the best form of government in the world.[19] Now Li was about to launch China into a democratic revolution. Would he succeed where Zhao had failed? And if he failed?

2 *Why a Coup?*

2 *Totalitarian China: Outwardly Strong, Inwardly Weak*

Robert Conquest, the great Anglo-American historian of the Soviet Union, defined a totalitarian state as one that recognizes no limits to its authority in any sphere of public or private life and that extends that authority to whatever length feasible.[1] The regime imposed by the Communist Party of China fits that description. In the Great Leap Forward, Mao Zedong attempted to extend the authority of the Party to the furthest limits conceivable, and in doing so created the greatest man-made disaster in the history of the world. His successors recognized that it was not feasible to extend the Party's authority as far as Mao had attempted. Otherwise it would lose its grip on power. But as the constitution of the People's Republic makes clear in principle, it reserves the right to impose its authority in any sphere of public or private life, and the Party frequently reminds society of this in practice.

It is the absence of any restrictions on the Party that constitutes the principal difference between a totalitarian and an authoritarian regime.[2] Only if we recognize this reality can we understand China today and stand a chance of accurately predicting its future.

The version of totalitarianism practiced by Xi's China is far more subtle and sophisticated than those of either Hitler's Germany or Stalin's Soviet Union. It does not rely on mass terror. It has no need to do so because it can now harness technologies of power and reach that not even George Orwell, let alone Hitler or Stalin, could dream of.

After the death of Mao, the Party adopted a strategy of economic reform without political reform. It has allowed a great increase in de facto economic and social freedom so that the industrious and enterprising Chinese people can generate economic growth, but it has not abandoned its authority in any sphere of life.

Article 1 of the Constitution adopted in 1982 puts it plainly: "The People's Republic of China is a socialist state under the people's democratic dictatorship," and the preamble makes clear the intention that this should continue: "Under the leadership of the Communist Party of China . . ., the Chinese people of all nationalities will continue to adhere to the people's democratic dictatorship and follow the socialist road." Thus, the National People's Congress is subordinate to the Party, as is every other organ of state power, including the government, the armed forces, the judiciary, the police, and so on. This is not a formality—the Party remains determined to act as the final arbiter of right and wrong, truth and falsehood, justice and injustice, and of what may or may not be known and remembered, as it has since it came to power in 1949. It is above the law: indeed the law is whatever the Party says it is, prospectively and retrospectively. For instance, there is no legal definition in China of a "state secret," but if a journalist publishes a fact that the Party considers to be seriously damaging to its interests, it will deem that fact to be a state secret, give instructions to the court appointed to "try" the accused, and have the journalist sent to jail; it will even dictate the length of sentence. So, the PRC is ruled, as its constitution declares, by a dictatorship, one best described as absolutist.

The Communist Party of China (CPC) has the essential characteristics of a Marxist-Leninist party on the model established by Lenin in the Soviet Union and maintained by all his successors until Mikhail Gorbachev. Its organizational structure and its formal methods of control over its own members are essentially unchanged from when it seized control of the mainland in 1949. Nowadays, it prefers to adopt a posture described by Professor Perry Link as that of "a giant anaconda coiled in an overhead chandelier. Normally the great snake doesn't move. It doesn't have to. It feels no need to be clear about its prohibitions. Its constant silent message is 'You yourself decide,' after which, more often than not, everyone in its shadow makes his or her large and small adjustments—all quite 'naturally.'"[3]

The Party prefers to exercise its power backstage, behind any number of different curtains marked "Government," "Military," "State-owned Bank," or "Judiciary," but these are instruments of the will of the Party, which still calls the shots when it chooses. The state has no legitimate, distinct existence of its own: it exists, in its various manifestations, to do the bidding of the Party. And, just as the KGB was the Siamese twin of the Communist Party of the Soviet Union, so the Public Security Bureau is the Siamese twin of the CPC, enforcing its will where persuasion is judged insufficient, using violence as a matter of routine. The role of the police pioneered by Lenin and Stalin remains essentially unchanged, although its methods have been adapted to the mixed economy and the digital age.

Despite spending more on internal security than on defense against its external enemies,[4] and despite great economic growth, the regime does not feel secure, and with good reason.

The reasons are not hard to identify. As subsequent chapters will show, the absence of political reform means that economic growth has come at great moral, environmental, social, intellectual, and cultural cost. This strategy has resulted in great social inequality and social injustice. Now the economy itself faces mounting problems, at home and abroad, so that an economic drama is being played out in an environment that is toxic.

The deep-seated, long-term problems faced by China are the product of the totalitarian regime imposed by the Party, and the very nature of the regime makes it impossible to deal with *any* of the problems at the radical level required to remedy them. To change one part of the system would require changes in the other parts, and this would destroy the Party's monopoly on political power.

For three decades from 1978, the Party pursued, with fits and starts, a strategy of transition toward a market economy. In 2008 it halted that transition because it recognized that further reform would undermine its totalitarian grip on political power. Since then it has not resumed it.

Because the Party maintains a regime that is totalitarian in character, it denies any space or legitimacy to efforts by others to fill with positive values the moral vacuum created by its loss of faith in its own communist creed (chapter 4). In practice, materialism, greed, and hedonism have largely replaced it.

A regime that was authoritarian might well tolerate a diversity of religious faiths, as happens in Singapore for example, but the CPC, being totalitarian in character and atheist by doctrine, cannot do so. In one region of China, Xinjiang, the Party believes that it is feasible to impose atheism on the people and, as we shall see in chapter 5, is using the most highly developed form of police state in its attempt to do so. This is the most naked manifestation of its totalitarian character. Elsewhere, its attempts to control religions through regulation have largely failed, and yet it cannot officially confer legitimacy on the unregulated worship and teaching that most of the hundreds of millions of religiously active people prefer (chapter 5). The result is the most far-reaching demonstration to date that this totalitarian regime is failing to impose its orthodoxy (atheism), but cannot and will not openly come to terms with reality (widespread religious faith and practice).

In a country as large and populous as China, effective protection of the environment cries out for national-scale organizations that mobilize the public to support the implementation of policies and expose abuse or failure on the part of local officials. But the totalitarian regime is paranoid about the development of national-scale organizations that could morph into a political opposition (chapter 6).

As will be discussed in chapter 8, Xi has cast aside the caution displayed by his predecessors in the conduct of foreign affairs and adopted a much more assertive strategy. Insensitive, heavy-handed behavior has become more frequent. The most glaring and dangerous example of this has been in dealing with the United States. For far too long for its own good, the regime failed to recognize that its actions were alienating the world's most powerful nation. This blindness has to be attributed in part to a totalitarian system which, to put it mildly, does not engender respect for those whose values and outlook are markedly, or—in this case—fundamentally different. As America has awoken to the totalitarian nature of the Chinese communists, a nature the latter had been careful to mask for a long time, its strategy of benign engagement has turned to nascent hostility. No people on earth is less forgiving than the Americans when they believe that their trust and friendship have been betrayed. Their trust will not be restored without systemic change in China.

The "autistic" insensitivity that has alienated America has had the same effect on the inhabitants of the regions on China's periphery: Tibet, Xinjiang, Hong Kong, and Taiwan. It is not a traditional defect in China's national character. Far from it. It has been engendered by a political system that does not allow for true compromise or sincere negotiation.

The most dramatic illustration of the Party's totalitarian character is the Social Credit System (SCS) which it is now developing through pilot operations in preparation for national application. From the many pilot operations, it is clear that, when applied nationwide, the system will calculate a credit score for every citizen and business in China, including foreign individuals and businesses. It will reward behavior that the Party deems to be "trust-keeping" and punish what it deems "trust-breaking." The concept of trust on which it is based is ill-defined, leaving great scope for arbitrary interpretation, and the punishments are wide-ranging, disproportionate, and equally arbitrary. Trust-breaking behavior may merely breach social and moral norms that are not codified as legal rules yet are imposed by the government at will. It is likely to substitute a rule of so-called trust for the notion of "governing the country in accordance with the law" enshrined in China's constitution.[5]

Information on the system is being shared across over thirty government agencies and CPC organizations. When fully operational, it will incorporate mass surveillance using facial recognition, predictive policing, and big data analysis technology. The number of surveillance cameras in China was expected to reach 626 million by the end of 2020.[6]

China's legal system is already filled with examples of language so vague that it (deliberately) leaves room for arbitrary application.

Among the most notorious are what legal experts refer to as "pocket crimes" such as "picking quarrels and provoking trouble" and "gathering a crowd to disturb order in a public place," offenses so broadly defined and ambiguously worded that prosecutors can apply them to almost any activity they deem undesirable, even if it may not otherwise meet the standards of criminality. The SCS grants the party-state new authority to impose a complex web of sanctions to punish people for expressions of opinion or actions of which the Party does not approve. Sanctions in the SCS extend far beyond unfavorable treatment in a purely business sense. They involve expansive and enormous disadvantages in myriad areas, from employment, professional qualifications, and social mobility to various socioeconomic activities, such as organizing environmental protests or attending unregulated churches. Behavior ranging from "spreading rumors" on the internet to "rejecting university admission" is deemed "trust-breaking."

As of June 2019, twenty-seven million air tickets and six million high-speed rail tickets had been denied to people who were deemed "untrustworthy."[7] The system had been used to ban children from certain schools, prevent low scorers from renting hotel rooms, and blacklist individuals from procuring employment. Examples of behavior for which people have been punished, in addition to dishonest and fraudulent financial behavior, include playing loud music or eating on public transport, jaywalking, making reservations at restaurants but not showing up, failing to correctly sort personal waste, and fraudulently using other people's public transportation ID cards.[8]

Individuals and companies can check their status on a national website, but there are no meaningful checks on the accuracy of the information fed into the system, and it is quite unclear how those subject to sanctions can appeal against wrongful punishment. There is no debate in public media about the issues raised by the system. Indeed, in China, unlike in liberal democracies, there is no public debate on the political and moral issues raised by computerized data gathering.

To a society universally acknowledged to be suffering from a lack of trust and truth, this system has a superficial appeal. However, the underlying purpose is not to instill trust and truth but to reinforce control by a totalitarian regime, whose abuse of power and disregard for truth over decades have created this pair of deficits.

The development program is running a little behind plan, and as the target date of end-2020 for nationwide rollout approached, no claims for achieving that were made, but given the massive resources being devoted to it and the rapid progress made in China in other applications of relevant technologies, the delay may not be very long. Once applied in China, the regime can look forward to applying it abroad.

If one focuses only on its powers and capacity, China's party-state looks invincible, but as the fate of Nazi Germany and the Soviet Union proved, totalitarian states are neither invincible nor omnipotent. As we shall consider in some depth in the chapters that follow, China's totalitarian regime is outwardly strong but inwardly weak.

The body politic of China is like a man suffering from an advanced stage of uremia. His kidneys can no longer eliminate urea, which is now accumulating in his bloodstream to a level that is life-threatening. The patient can only be saved by a kidney transplant. So, in China, prolongation of the one-party regime is intensifying the nation's problems. The only remedy is a democracy transplant.

3   *The Looming Economic Crisis*

Xi Jinping has proclaimed a vision of a China of greater wealth and power, without explaining how this will be achieved. The reality is that the economy has slowed, and no recovery can be expected in the foreseeable future. Some major regions have been in recession for years. A high level of corporate debt, much of it incurred by loss-making state-owned enterprises (SOEs), constitutes a threat not only to China, but also to the global economy. Major parts of the financial system are vulnerable. Deep structural reforms are required, but the Party will not make them due to fears that reforms would destroy its grip on power.

Since 1979, a limited transition to free markets has allowed the growth of a dynamic, efficient, and profitable private sector, which produces between two-thirds and three-quarters of China's gross domestic product (GDP), is the driving force of exports, and creates 90 percent of new jobs. SOEs are bloated, inefficient, sclerotic, and a drain on the economy. A large share of the profits from the private sector are forcibly directed to SOEs, through state-owned banks. The level of activity of SOEs has been kept artificially high by massive injections of credit and protection from international and domestic competition, but their return on investment has been declining for years and is now low. The ratio of state banks' nonperforming loans is high and rising. Investment has been massively misallocated, and "zombie" SOEs have been kept on life support. SOE corporate debt has reached a dangerous level, and price bubbles have developed in both the property and stock markets.

But to maintain its grip on the political system, the Party has kept the "commanding heights of the economy" in state ownership. Private companies are denied entry to sectors reserved for SOEs and suffer discrimination in both public procurement and land use. They have been deprived of their due share of investment funds by the banking system and the capital markets, both of which are rigged against them. According to the International Monetary Fund (IMF), the state sector produces only 22 percent of GDP but accounts for 55 percent of total corporate debt.

In the fable of Sinbad the Sailor, the Old Man of the Sea tricked Sinbad into letting him ride on his back, twisted his legs around Sinbad's neck and would not let go. He rode him day and night without respite, plucking fruit for himself from the trees as they passed. Like the Old Man of the Sea, the state sector is riding on the back of the private sector and refuses to let go. Worse, the Old Man is sucking blood from the neck of Sinbad.

Nonstate companies like Huawei, Alibaba, and Tencent (the developer of WeChat) have demonstrated great prowess at copying, adopting, and developing technologies and business models invented elsewhere. Protected against foreign competition in their domestic market, they have grown at phenomenal speed to great size. High-tech start-ups are flourishing, and by 2017 China had nurtured 164 "unicorns"—private companies with a valuation of at least $1 billion—passing the US total of 132. China leads the world in the application of fintech and is good at the development of customer-facing technology. But no Chinese company has yet disrupted an industry in the international marketplace in the way Amazon, Facebook, and Uber have. Nor has China given birth to the kind of world-beating companies like Toyota and Sony that emerged in Japan in the 1970s. Discrimination against the private sector and deficiencies in the legal system are serious handicaps. Xi Jinping's strategy of reinforcing the dictatorship of the Communist Party of China (CPC), which discourages original thought, and the continued prevalence of corruption in academic and research institutions both militate against an enabling environment for fundamental research and innovation. The forced transfer of intellectual property by foreign companies to their Chinese partners in joint ventures and state-directed cyber theft of foreign industrial secrets are not adequate substitutes.

Ninety-five percent of Chinese farms are under 2 hectares (cf. India, with 85%). This is highly inefficient, but in the absence of a satisfactory social welfare system, family-managed subsistence farming is the only safety net in case of large-scale urban unemployment. Moreover, for doctrinal political reasons, the state remains the ultimate owner of all agricultural land, which prevents the consolidation of landholdings into privately owned farms on an efficient scale.

Since the global financial crisis of 2008, China has avoided recession by flooding the economy with credit. The IMF reckons that between 2008 and 2018, the ratio of gross debt to GDP rose from 135 percent to 300 percent. Credit has grown at twice the rate of GDP, until the total quantity of bank deposits, i.e. money, in China is more than double that of the United States, even though the US economy is 60 percent larger than China's. Much of the credit has been used for unproductive purposes, such as servicing nonperforming loans, building infrastructure with no economic use, and speculation in the property and stock markets. Because China is not a market economy, it has been able to defy the economic equivalent of the law of gravity for a long time, but as the American economist Herbert Stein remarked: "If something cannot go on forever, it will stop."[1]

The IMF has warned that the high level of corporate debt constitutes a threat not only to China, but also to the global economy, which must be tackled through far-reaching reforms. Because many liabilities have been created off the balance sheet, the exact level of this corporate debt is unknown, but *no nation with a debt mountain as high as China's has ever reduced it without either recession or prolonged inflation.* The recessions have either been sharp and short-lived, or more gradual and long-lasting (such as Japan's "Lost 20 Years" from 1991 to 2010).

When eventually the Party makes a serious and sustained attempt at "managed deleveraging," its smooth management is likely to prove beyond the wit of man in such a large, opaque, diverse, and complex economy. Instead, it will result in unemployment on a large scale, falls in property and stock prices, and grave instability in the financial system, which will cause the collapse of second- or third-tier banks and bring a high risk of wider financial contagion.

To handle the expansion of credit, the financial system has grown at a phenomenal rate.[2] Not surprisingly, the system for regulation and supervision has not kept up, so that much of it resembles a gigantic Ponzi scheme; it is the Achilles' heel of China's economy. Major parts of it are vulnerable. A huge shadow-banking industry has grown up, opaque and for a long time largely unregulated. The true level of nonperforming loans is of great concern. Second- and third-tier financial institutions are at risk. In 2018 the regime began to take remedial action, but tighter regulation without systemic reform will simply contribute to the same outcome as debt reduction.

The Party has elevated the struggle against debt and financial risk to be one of three "key battles" to be fought.[3] In October 2017, the chairman of China's central bank chose a moment of the highest political sensitivity—when the Party was holding its Nineteenth National People's Congress—to warn that China risked a Minsky moment,[4] when systemic financial instability can manifest itself after a long period of growth and excessive growth of debt, causing a collapse of asset prices.

The National Institute of Finance and Development, a Chinese government–affiliated think tank, has warned: "China is currently extremely likely to experience a financial panic." Kenneth Rogoff, professor of public policy at Harvard University, has identified China as "the leading candidate for being at the center of the next big financial crisis."[5]

Capital flight has become a major concern, suggesting a loss of confidence in the Party's management of the economy. Tightening of controls has succeeded in restraining it, but loss of confidence coupled with entrepreneurs' resentment of being treated as second-class citizens is a major political risk to the regime.

Uncertainty about the true state of the economy and disbelief in official statistics are greatly magnified by the Party's suppression of objective reporting and analysis.

On 15 March 2007, Wen Jiabao, China's premier at that time, described the Chinese economy as "unstable, unbalanced, uncoordinated, and unsustainable."[6] That was before China began its massive expansion of debt. Six years later, in November 2013, Xi Jinping declared that China's development remained "unbalanced, uncoordinated and unsustainable," and since then the dependence on credit to fuel growth has continued, compounding the problems (only in 2018 did initial signs appear of an attempt to curb credit growth).[7] In November 2013, the Central Committee adopted a program of economic reform with sixty-six specific decision points, very largely based on *China 2030*, the joint report by the Chinese government and the World Bank mentioned in chapter 1, which articulated a broad consensus in senior levels of the Party and the state. If fully implemented, it would have increased the role of markets in determining the allocation of resources in the economy. Since the spring of 2017, a study by the Asia Society Policy Institute and the Rhodium Group has tracked progress and backsliding in policy assessment areas. Only two, innovation and the environment, have consistently shown progress. Official policy has if anything tended to favor SOEs in relation to the private sector.[8]

Radical restructuring is needed to put the economy on a sounder footing. There is no lack of intellectual understanding of what needs to be done, and an overwhelming majority of China's economists vigorously criticize current economic arrangements and demand liberal alternatives.[9] The 2013 reform program is testimony to the strength of their views.

Zhang Weiying, one of the most prominent liberal economists in the country and a professor at prestigious Peking University, spoke for many in his profession in a lecture in October 2018.[10] He lashed out at those who attribute China's economic growth to an exceptional "China model," which includes a powerful one-party state, a colossal state sector, and "wise" industrial policy, saying it is not only factually wrong, but also detrimental to the country's future. He alleged that this misconception inevitably led to antagonism between China and the West.

Zhang said that the trade war not only reflected conflict between China and the United States, but between China and the larger Western world. It also went beyond trade to reflect the clash over value systems, he said.

A strong believer in the free market, Zhang said China's rapid growth in past decades stemmed not from the "China model" but a "universal model" which relied on marketization, entrepreneurship, and three centuries of accumulating technology in the West, like the success stories of other developed economies.

"Blindly emphasising the 'China model' would lead us onto a path of strengthening state-owned enterprises, expansion of state power and overly relying on industrial policy, which would lead to a reversal of reform progress, wasting previous reform efforts, and the eventual stagnation of economic growth," he said.

Chinese economists know that while a centralized state can marshal resources for selected projects, *no state ruled by an 'authoritarian' regime—let alone a totalitarian one—has yet moved from the ranks of middle-income nations to those of high income, except some oil-rich economies, of which China is not one.* Many know, but few dare to say, that the obstacles to reform are political, as follows:

· Further privatization would undermine the one-party dictatorship.
· Party officials, managers, and workers in SOEs have a vested interest in the status quo.[11]
· Powerful families suck money out of SOEs.
· The real estate industry also has a vested interest in the status quo.
· Layoffs and shutdowns could cause mass unrest.

Since late 2018, faced with the prospect of years of slower growth and strong pressure for reform from the United States, Xi Jinping, Liu He (his principal economic adviser), and other leading figures have begun to speak of internal market reforms in terms not heard since 2013, but the deadlock between the need for those reforms and Xi's determination to defend the political status quo remains unresolved. In the words of Zhang Ming, a political scientist at Renmin University in Beijing, "Many economic problems that we face are actually political problems in disguise, such as the nature of the economy, the nature of the ownership system in the country and groups of vested interests."[12] The frustration of economic liberals grows, there is mounting dissatisfaction and distrust in the private sector, and the unspoken deal with the people, "We let you make money, and you let us rule" is undermined, year by year. The victims of Xi's anticorruption campaign take pleasure in his discomfort. Ambitious members of the top leadership are on the alert for an opportunity to remove him.

As of this writing, the full effects on the economy of the coronavirus pandemic have yet to emerge, but it is sure that the problems outlined above have intensified. Chapter 7 will look at these effects in a little more detail.

In the conditions described above, a financial crisis would lead to an economic and then a political crisis, as illustrated in chapter 1.

4   *No Trust, No Truth*

In December 2012, just a month after being appointed general secretary of the Communist Party of China (CPC), Xi Jinping warned the Party's supreme body, the Politburo: "Corruption has become so widespread that it will ultimately destroy the party and the nation." He was not the first Chinese leader to acknowledge that China was facing a moral crisis. In 2011, after several horrifying food and drug safety scandals, Prime Minister Wen Jiabao said: "These scandals are strong enough to show that the moral decay and loss of trust have reached an extremely serious point."[1] Wen added: "A country that fails to embody the high moral standards of its citizens can never become a truly powerful country or a respected nation."

State media regularly mention a "threefold crisis of faith," with the three being confidence, trust, and faith.[2] In a large official survey on "social diseases" in China conducted in 2014, "loss of trust" was ranked the top such condition. Eighty-eight percent of respondents believed that China has been beset with a "social disease of moral decay and the loss of trust."[3] According to a ten-thousand-character Party document on the moral state of the nation issued in 2019, "money worship, hedonism, and extreme individualism are still prominent."[4]

That China's leaders should be forced to acknowledge the state of "moral decay and loss of trust" when their Party has governed the nation without sharing power and without interruption for over seven decades is a terrible indictment of its rule.

This society, which once was ruled by morals rather than laws, knows that it has lost its moral compass. Moral questioning began to afflict China well before the communists came to power. From the middle of the nineteenth century, the impact of European and American power, culture, social mores, ideas, and Christian faith sowed doubt on the settled certainties of Chinese ethics, religion, and cultural self-confidence. Wave upon wave of fresh ideas and new thoughts crowded in. But in their seventy years of rule, the communists have done much greater damage.

Soon after coming to power, they used the dynamics of social hostility and exploited real or imagined grievances to impose land reform and to take private businesses into public ownership. In villages and companies throughout the land, people were dragooned into acts of violence to destroy the old order and establish the new. This violence was their baptism into the new political order, and their participation made them complicit in its creation. In destroying the old order, the Party members destroyed the educated gentry, who had been vitally important in the transmission of public ethics from one generation to the next.

The CPC tried to create a totalitarian regime that would control not only the actions but the thoughts of every individual. Mao Zedong used the term *brainwashing*, and the aim was not just compliance but conviction. Vast programs of "re-education" were organized. Indoctrination became a permanent feature of everyday life. Precommunist China had perhaps the richest tradition of ethics in the world. The Stalinist party substituted its alien ideology for traditional morals.

The Anti-Rightist Campaign of 1957–59 targeted educated people in general and persecuted five hundred thousand, sending them into internal exile or prison camp, or condemning them to death. It silenced China's finest minds. The conscience of the nation was heard no more in Mao's lifetime.

One year later, in 1958, Mao insisted on launching the Great Leap Forward. In political and economic terms, this was an attempt to impose communism in one bound and replace poverty with abundance for all. In terms of China's security, Mao hoped it would produce enough grain for sale to the Soviet Union to finance the purchase of know-how and matériel for building nuclear weapons, a goal that appealed to his thirst for power and glory. He was going to seize the leadership of world revolution.

Instead of prosperity, it brought starvation, death, and disease. Instead of security and prestige, it brought hostility from even China's communist allies, and humiliation on the world stage.

The Great Leap inflicted incalculable damage on family life. Private houses were destroyed, communal canteens replaced eating at home, and in the most "advanced" communes, husbands and wives were compelled to live in separate dormitories, their children were forced into ill-organized boarding kindergartens, and the old were segregated in retirement homes. In the words of one historian, "coercion, terror and systematic violence were the foundation of the Great Leap Forward."[5] To protect their own careers, enforce their authority, fulfill their targets, and protect their personal rice bowls at a time of famine, Party cadres turned the countryside of China into killing fields. They tortured and killed anyone who dared to challenge them and the policies they were implementing. They forced husbands to torture their wives and to kill their children if they were disobedient.[6] In some areas where supplies of food were exhausted, people turned to cannibalism.[7] The pain and suffering of the people were disregarded as their wishes and feelings were subordinated to Party policies that caused forty-six million premature deaths through starvation and disease.[8]

To this day, the Party continues to suppress this history, and acknowledges only "three years of natural disasters" or "three years of difficulty."

Without totalitarian dictatorship, the Great Leap would never have been launched because opposition to the extreme collectivization of social and economic life would have come from parties representing farmers, and agronomists would have told the Party leaders that Mao's unscientific ideas on increasing crop yields were absurd and would bring disaster. The leaders suppressed the truth about its dire effects, and Mao could with impunity make remarks such as "When there is not enough to eat, people starve to death. It is better to let half the people die so that the other half can eat their fill."[9] Because of the totalitarian system, Mao was able to deny reality and persist in his policies, to protect his own position, long after the depth of the disaster became evident, even to him.

The attempt to collectivize the entire nation was abandoned, but the regime continued to rely upon a totalitarian system of control over every aspect of society and every medium of expression. An essential feature of the control system was the insistence that the common people spy and report on each other, creating an atmosphere of anxiety and distrust.[10]

When he launched the Cultural Revolution in 1966, Mao replaced Party doctrine with his Thought and made himself a demi-god. When this, his last attempt at revolution, degenerated into internecine strife, and the brightest of his "revolutionary successors" embraced free-thinking individualism rather than collective ideals, he and the Party he still led were seen to be deeply discredited, both morally and ideologically. The Chinese people had become consummate performers in an unending game of political pretense, going through the motions of demonstrating loyalty to the latest shift in party line, without believing a word of it. Housewives and factory workers waved their freshly inscribed banners or shouted in chorus the newly minted slogan with easily discernible detachment. Schoolchildren were better at it: a visitor to the same primary school at an interval of a few months could observe the same beautifully drilled eight-year-olds dance on the stage shouting "Strike down Deng Xiaoping!" on the orders of Mao and the Gang of Four, on the first occasion, and six months later, "Strike down the Gang of Four!" with an equal show of conviction. At their age, neither slogan meant much to them, but from an early age they were being taught that in Chinese politics there is no such thing as objective truth: "truth" is whatever the Party dictates at a given moment in time.

The disasters China's one-party dictatorship has either created or aggravated during the seven decades of CPC rule have taught those it rules to pretend to forget the truth. The vital importance of doing so has been impressed by parents upon their children in generation after generation, and censorship has reinforced apparent amnesia with genuine ignorance.

By the time of Mao's death, a moral and intellectual vacuum existed in the public sphere, and the Party made no attempt to develop a new set of moral or political ideals. His successor Deng Xiaoping, and Deng's allies, realized that the Party must abandon its insistence on empty displays of conviction by the people. They must settle for compliance and control if they were to survive in power. Self-preservation became the CPC's guiding principle. The rulers bought the tolerance of their subjects principally by increasing their economic freedom. They struck an unspoken deal with them: "We let you make money, you let us rule." At no time since the end of the Cultural Revolution in 1976 has the regime offered the people anything beyond stability, economic growth, and, more recently, assertive nationalism. As Marxists, the Party has always given materialism highest priority, but this has been accentuated in the Reform Era. Economic reforms without political reform, freedom of expression or freedom of religion have encouraged materialism, greed, and hedonism, creating a breeding ground for cynicism. Four decades of spectacular economic growth, radical social change, and cultural change brought by opening to the world have exacerbated moral confusion and uncertainty.

Totalitarianism exalts the Party and demeans the individual and civil society. Every aspect of human activity is subordinate to the Party's goal of control. There is no ideal—truth, justice, equity, harmony, virtue, beauty, or freedom—to which appeal can be made in official, public discourse. The problems of social and gender inequality, both of which loom large in China, cannot be properly examined, let alone tackled. Complaints from Chinese abound on the internet that truth has been relativized and lying normalized. A nationwide survey found that nearly 60 percent of respondents agreed that "people's values differ and therefore there should be no good or bad, right or wrong regarding moral issues."[11]

As anthropologists like Arthur Kleinman and Yunxiang Yan have described, this situation has given rise to widespread and extreme manifestations of the phenomenon of the "divided self," identified long ago by Sigmund Freud.[12] Or, as novelist Ma Jian puts it: "Everyone in China must have two personalities, one for public display, one hidden within."[13] Much of the time, Chinese, like the subjects of other communist parties in the past, practice public conformity without inner conviction.[14]

The CPC no longer believes in socialism, let alone communism, and it destroyed what remained of its own moral authority by the military massacre of June 1989. In April and May of that year, the biggest popular movement for democracy and the rule of law that the world has ever seen swept the country. On a single day, 18 May, six million people joined demonstrations in 132 cities across the country. The Party leaders realized that their rule was within days of extinction unless they were to launch an effective counterattack. Their immediate response was to use the so-called People's army to crush the people by force, in and around the nerve center of the movement, Tiananmen Square. Three years later they reinforced their unspoken deal with their subjects ("We let you make money, you let us rule") by more far-reaching economic reforms and a greater opening to the world, still without any dilution of the Party's political monopoly.

To rebuild the loyalty of those who would continue to rule in the Party's name, they created conditions in which officials at all levels could loot state property. They countered the biggest democracy movement in history by making the greatest opportunity for predation the world has ever seen. Corruption in China is not the unfortunate by-product of rapid economic growth, or a failure to foresee the consequences of system design, but the result of strategic choices by the CPC. Decentralization of administrative power without clear definition of legal ownership has encouraged the looting of state property by power holders at every level. This has kept officials loyal to the regime and hostile to systemic change.[15]

The most spectacular example to date has been that of Zhou Yongkang, who was the third most powerful politician in China. He was a member of the Politburo Standing Committee, China's highest decision-making body, and oversaw China's security apparatus and law enforcement institutions, with power stretching into courts, prosecution agencies, police forces, paramilitary forces, and intelligence organs. He was the Chinese equivalent of Lavrentiy Beria, chief of the Soviet security and secret police apparatus under Stalin. In 2015 Zhou was convicted of bribery, abuse of power, and the intentional disclosure of state secrets.

It is not only their rulers whom the common people distrust: their distrust runs horizontally as well as vertically. They shake their heads, and whisper to visitors: "In China there is no trust and no truth."

The second major strand of the political strategy of the regime has been to build a socioeconomic system that allows the rich and middle class to exploit the poor in the cities and countryside, for example by banning free trade unions, and through regressive fiscal and social security policies. The direct tax burden on individuals is very light. Personal income taxes account for only 5 percent of government revenue, only 2 percent of the population pay them, and there are no taxes on the value of property or on capital gains from financial assets. The hundreds of millions of peasants who have migrated to the cities are denied the full range of social security benefits and public services available to registered city dwellers. It is not surprising, therefore, that the level of income inequality is high and rising, exacerbating social tensions.

China's moral crisis has featured in many scholarly studies by academics in China and abroad.[16] He Huaihong, professor of philosophy at Peking University, has written a thoughtful and wide-ranging study of what he calls China's "moral miasma," *Social Ethics in a Changing China—Moral Decay or Ethical Awakening?*, published by the world's most influential social science research center, the Brookings Institution.[17] He believes that corruption is not just a problem of governmental officials; it is a "failure of society" and signifies the collapse of ethical codes in the nation. In his introduction to He Huaihong's book, Cheng Li of Brookings commented: "The country's ethical and moral problems are all too clear from the long list of widely occurring phenomena, such as commercial fraud, tax fraud, financial deception, shoddy and dangerous engineering projects, fake products, tainted milk, poisonous bread, toxic pills, and decline in professional ethics among teachers, doctors, lawyers, Buddhist monks, and especially government officials."[18] In *China's Crony Capitalism*,[19] Minxin Pei, professor of government at Claremont McKenna College, California, has explained the dynamics and the full extent of corruption in China with power and precision. Hu Jiwei, a former editor of the *People's Daily*, once told Professor Roderick MacFarquhar of Harvard University that corruption is worse now than it was under the Nationalists who ruled China before. Corruption was one of the main reasons why they lost China.

Corruption pollutes schools and universities, where plagiarism is rife and academic advancement is for sale; law enforcement agencies; and the highest reaches of the military, where promotion can be bought and procurement perverted. It is a key to retaining power. The CPC has turned the state sector of the economy into a walled garden within which its officials can plunder with impunity. Just over half of the nation's assets have been kept in it, including the commanding heights of banking, insurance, transportation, power generation and distribution, steel production, urban real estate, and telecommunications. Because the rulers have refused all demands for political reform, they can to this day protect the walled garden with the full panoply of instruments of repression of an unreformed Leninist state. Relations between companies in the private sector of the economy, where ownership is better defined, is less affected.

Corruption hinders the Party and state from achieving essential goals like curbing pollution of the environment, as chapter 6, "An Environmental Catastrophe," will show. The decentralization of administrative authority without political reform, which encourages systemic corruption, has wreaked havoc on China's natural environment. The state has promulgated a thousand regulations to protect the environment, but corrupt officials often fail to implement them, because they are in cahoots with polluting industrialists. Corruption pervades the environmental protection system, from monitoring to enforcement. Environmental oversight is as lax as financial controls in the state sector. The state agencies tasked with implementing regulations are even weaker than those that are supposed to investigate corruption. According to a former head of a local environmental protection bureau, an entire industry involving local governments, assessment agencies, and project developers has grown up around the falsification of environmental impact assessments.

Chinese critics have pointed out that the absence of political reform means that the evil cannot be fought through a free press, an independent judiciary, or political remedy. More than two years after the anticorruption campaign was launched by Xi Jinping, Professor Jiang Hong of Shanghai University of Finance and Economics said, in a speech that was later deleted from the public record: "To permanently cure corruption, we need political reform to put power into the cage of a system and to fundamentally clear the soil that creates corruption."[20] He proposed that every legal citizen be allowed to participate in elections and to compete to be elected.[21] The campaign has not spared high-ranking officials, but only 0.5 percent of officials have been seriously sanctioned. Xi is widely accused of targeting his enemies; he has used the Party apparatus instead of the courts and has addressed the symptoms, not the underlying causes. Thus his campaign has brought a short-term reduction in the symptoms of corruption, but a thorough, long-term reduction would require systemic change of a kind that he has explicitly rejected.

As this book has already made clear, the Chinese people have long been deeply sceptical of their rulers' motives, and the conduct of this campaign must have deepened their scepticism, inflicting further damage on the moral health of society.

Concern for the state of social ethics is often expressed via social media. In 2011, an instance of public callousness became notorious in this way. A toddler lay dying in the middle of the street, hemorrhaging after being run over by a van. Eighteen pedestrians turned a blind eye to her as they passed by. This scene was recorded by a nearby closed circuit camera and was posted on the internet. It was viewed by millions of Chinese, who were deeply unsettled by it. Many voiced the view that three decades of economic growth at any price had left nothing but moral confusion in its wake. Six months later, Han Han, the young author of China's most widely followed personal blog, which registered well over three hundred million hits, was still citing the incident as a sign of "Chinese society's cold selfishness."[22] At another time, Han Han wrote: "[the Party] taught us cruelty and [power] struggle in the first few decades—and greed and selfishness in the ensuing few decades. Our culture and tradi-tional morality have been shattered. The same goes for trust among us. Gone too is any semblance of faith and consensus."[23]

Over the past decade, the Chinese media have reported count-less terrible stories from daily life: in fear of legal liability or black-mail, bystanders offer no help when a little girl is hit by a car or an elderly person falls in the street. When a twenty-year-old female contestant on a television dating show was asked by an unem-ployed suitor if she would ride a bicycle with him on a date, she replied, "I would rather cry in a BMW." Her answer became a national sensation, online and in print, under the headline "I would rather cry in a BMW than smile on a bicycle."

A social commentator in a Party-controlled national daily paper asked whether the young woman had spoken only for her-self, and wrote, in answer to his own question: "No. Her opinion resonates with youth; they have grown up in a society that is quickly accumulating material wealth. They are snobbish. They worship money, cars and houses because the highly developing economy has made them do so."[24]

Leading playwrights and theater directors who have grown up in the Reform Era have often targeted the culture of materialism and lack of authenticity that they believe now permeates Chinese society. The most-performed contemporary play, *Rhinoceros in Love*, which has been performed more than two thousand times and seen by more than a million people over eighteen years, is an out-standing example of this. It has achieved a cult following among the generation now in their twenties and thirties. Its male protagonist, Ma Lu, a zookeeper, sees parallels between his charge, an aging black rhino from which the zoo has no intention of breeding, and his own lonely existence. Ma Lu falls obsessively in love with Ming Ming, who coldly rejects him; she in turn is obsessed by a man who treats her with abusive contempt. Ma Lu engages a "love coach," who gives him nonsensical lessons on how to woo Ming Ming, to no avail. The play is bizarre and absurdist, but, according to Meng Jinghui, China's leading theatrical director who first staged it (and whose wife wrote it), young audiences see it as embodying an ideal of romantic commitment that eludes them in a society steeped in consumerism, commercialization, money, and sex.[25]

Jia Zhangke, internationally acclaimed filmmaker, has written: "We're a very money-driven society. We want to focus on the economy rather than the people driven by that economy. So I look the whole way from individuals who neglect their emotions to the society that neglects individuals."[26]

The moral ethos of today's China has been brilliantly captured by the writer Yan Lianke in satirical novels (for one of which he was awarded the Franz Kafka Prize in 2014), but he has also made powerful nonfictional observations on Chinese politics and ethics. He has said: "Truth is buried, conscience is castrated and our language is raped by money and power."[27] He claims that by controlling every aspect of people's lives, communism has infantilized generations of Chinese: "People's sense of themselves as individuals has atrophied, so much so that they have lost common-sense ideas of how to behave ethically without strict parameters."[28] Even more fundamentally, he believes that "To live in China in 2018 is to inhabit a reality that makes you question the very nature of reality."[29]

The depth of distrust that pervades relations between rulers and ruled is reflected in the fact that the internal security budget exceeds the national defense budget, suggesting that the Party fears domestic threats to its control more than external ones,[30] as foreshadowed by China's greatest writer of the twentieth century, Lu Xun, who wrote, before the communists came to power: "Once upon a time, there was a country whose rulers completely succeeded in crushing the people; and yet they still believed that the people were their most dangerous enemy."[31] When Milovan Djilas was a leader of the Yugoslav Communist Party, he had a similar experience with Stalin and his Politburo, who made him feel "that these men had no confidence at all in the legitimacy of their rule. . . . They acted like a group of conspirators scheming to suppress, squash, circumvent or hoodwink the inhabitants of some conquered land, not their own."[32]

The absence of the rule of law and the prevalence of corruption have contributed to the climate of distrust horizontally as well as vertically. It is indicative of the moral climate that, with the complicity of the Party, Chinese organizations have used computer hacking to carry out the biggest theft of intellectual property of all time, stealing industrial and commercial secrets from America and Europe in the Great Cyber Heist.[33]

When this pattern of behavior is viewed alongside these assaults on truth, both historical and contemporary, it is no surprise that the moral crisis of China today is so often summed up in the phrase: "No trust, no truth."

To Gorbachev's Prime Minister Nikolai Ryzhkov, the "moral state of the society" in 1985 was the "most terrifying" feature of Soviet society, and many Chinese will recognize China today in his description of the Soviet Union of that time: "[We] stole from ourselves, took and gave bribes, lied in the reports, in newspapers, from high podiums, wallowed in our lies, hung medals on one another. And all of this—from top to bottom and from bottom to top."[34]

The political centrality of the moral condition of a nation has been underlined by Leon Aron, a Moscow-born scholar of Russian affairs, who asked a few years ago: "How, between 1985 and 1989, in the absence of sharply worsening economic, political, demographic, and other structural conditions, did the [Soviet] state and its economic system suddenly begin to be seen as shameful, illegitimate, and intolerable by enough men and women to become doomed?" And he answered his own question thus: "Merciless moral scrutiny of the country's past and present, within a few short years, hollowed out the mighty Soviet state, deprived it of legitimacy, and turned it into a burned-out shell that crumbled in August 1991."[35]

As we have seen, the crisis of morals in China long predates Xi Jinping's assumption of supreme power, but his critics can legitimately ask: how effective has his response been to the crisis he himself has acknowledged? His response has been based on the premise that Gorbachev and his fellow reformers made a fatal mistake in allowing Soviet citizens to engage in the "merciless moral scrutiny of the country's past and present" to which Aron refers. Instead, Xi has reinforced censorship and suppressed both public scrutiny of the moral state of the nation and any open search for remedies. As noted above, he has relied on an anticorruption campaign that attacks the symptoms, not the systemic causes; has sidelined the legal system; and has acted as cover for his attacks on his political rivals. Anecdotal evidence suggests this has gained him some short-term political popularity and reduced some of the more brazen manifestations of official corruption, but its short-term character and ultimate futility offer his rivals weapons with which to attack him.

5   *Who Rules: God or the Party?*

On 30 December 2019, a court imposed a sentence of nine years' imprisonment and three years' deprivation of political rights on Wang Yi, senior pastor of the Early Rain Covenant Church in Chengdu, capital of Sichuan Province, for "inciting subversion of state power and illegal business operations."

Why would the Communist Party of China impose such a heavy sentence on a pastor whose church never numbered more than seven hundred in its congregation, in a city of nine million people and a nation of 1.4 billion? The sentence was only two year shorter than that imposed in 2009 on Liu Xiaobo, the Nobel Peace Laureate who headed a campaign with no less an objective than to move China from a one-party dictatorship to an elective democracy.

If we view this action in the broad context of the Party's relations with religion, we can see that it was not a manifestation of doctrinal hostility or paranoia but a carefully considered and meticulously planned move in a long-term, nationwide strategy to counter what it sees as an existential threat to its monopoly of power.

With China's supreme political authority bankrupt morally and ideologically, and society as a whole in a moral crisis, hundreds of millions of people have turned to religion in search of values and the meaning of life. This poses a huge dilemma for a Party that keeps atheism as a core tenet of its formal ideology.

The most far-reaching attempts to eliminate religion from China were made under Chairman Mao during the Cultural Revolution, which succeeded only in suppressing its outward manifestations. After Mao's death, the Party explicitly recognized that it could not eradicate religion entirely.[1] In the decades that followed until Xi Jinping became Party leader, the treatment accorded to those practicing religion varied greatly from one region of China to another, and from one religion to another, but everywhere it was true that instead of seeking to eliminate religion the Party sought to control it, or to contain it where it could not control it. Relations between the Party and religious entities varied from extremely conflictual to cooperative. In the late 1990s and the subsequent decade, Party leaders spoke of separating politics and religion, and they declared that religions could make a contribution to the "harmonious society" they were then proclaiming to be a national goal. In 2002, General Secretary Jiang Zemin was asked, "If you could issue one decree that you were sure would be obeyed in China, what would it be"? He replied: "I would make Christianity the official religion of China."[2] That was the moment when a Party leader came closest to emulating the Roman Emperor Theodosius, who issued an edict making Christianity, which had been persecuted sporadically, the official religion of the empire.

Religious groups and places of worship were supposed to be registered by the "patriotic religious associations" formed by Buddhists, Daoists, Muslims, Catholics, and Protestants. They were subject to restrictions and controls under the State Administration for Religious Affairs, which, in the case of Christian churches, was tasked with exercising control over the training and appointment of priests and the content of sermons. That system of control remains essentially in place but, as we shall see later, since 2011 an explicit strategy of eradication has been adopted toward those Christian churches that refuse to be controlled. In practice, if not in name, a strategy of eradication has also been adopted toward Islam in Xinjiang.

In China at least 350 million religious believers and tens of millions of others engage in various spiritual meditation practices and folk-religious rituals.[3] This phenomenal growth of religion in post-Mao China has occurred in parallel with rising living standards. It is of great importance in all its manifestations not only for China but globally and historically. Yet for China domestically, it is the growth of Christianity, from about 4 million in 1949 to somewhere between 75 and 120 million today, that is of the greatest social and political significance, and will therefore be the focus of this chapter.

The growth of Christianity, and especially Protestant Christianity, is of especial significance for three reasons: the people attracted to Christianity, its vision of an alternative society, and the rapidity of its growth. Its growth has mainly occurred not in remote border regions but in the cultural heartland among the ethnic Chinese or Han majority, who make up 92 percent of China's population, and among younger, better educated, upwardly mobile people who hold positions of influence in society, such as lawyers, doctors, educators, scientists, and business leaders. In short, these are the very people who are supposed to be leading the modernization of China. As Ian Johnson, a leading authority on religion in contemporary China has written: "This makes Christianity the first foreign religion to gain a central place in China since Buddhism's arrival two millennia ago."[4]

The second reason why Christianity is of special significance is that it offers a vision of society, indeed of life itself, that is a radical alternative to that of the CPC; it holds firmly to the belief that God and not the Party is the supreme authority. In contrast to a Party that no longer believes its own ideology and whose members mostly join it out of self-interest, Christianity in China is a faith strongly held by its adherents, whose careers are more likely to be hampered than helped by their joining a church. In a society in *spiritual* confusion, Christianity offers an answer to the question, what is the meaning of life? In a country that has lost its *moral* compass, Christianity offers values centered on love and service to others. Chinese Christians have been very active in social welfare work, disaster relief, and using law to defend the poor and powerless. In a one-party dictatorship, unregistered Christian churches offer autonomous communities, with increasingly democratic leadership structures. In a society where distrust is the norm, their close-knit, often cell-based organizations are communities of trust and shared values. The Party does much to isolate China from the world, through censorship and the Great Firewall and denouncing universal values; field research shows that many Chinese Christians are attracted by the universal character of the worldwide church, and they associate Christianity with progressive ideas and the modernity of America and free societies in East Asia, such as South Korea. In contrast to a totalitarianism that exalts the Party and demeans the individual, Christianity teaches that God loves every individual and wants to set him or her free. In defiance of a totalitarian regime that claims a right to be the ultimate arbiter of truth and falsehood, good and evil, Christianity affirms that there is a higher power to which that right belongs. It teaches that every individual is responsible for seeking truth and virtue, with the guidance of the Holy Spirit, the Bible, and the Church. Many claim that they have thereby found liberation from man-made mental shackles.

And thirdly, Christianity has been growing faster than any other religion in China. Part of the attraction of Christianity for many Chinese is that, unlike Buddhism or Daoism, it is associated with prosperous, democratic countries in Europe and America, and has played a dynamic role in social and economic development in many countries. *The Protestant Ethic and the Spirit of Capitalism* by the German sociologist Max Weber, which draws a link between the ethics of ascetic Protestantism and the emergence of the spirit of modern capitalism, has been much studied on university campuses.

When Wang Yi converted to Christianity in 2005, he joined the Calvinist sector of Protestantism, which presents the greatest challenge to the Party due to its theology and the people who are attracted to it. A selective interpretation of Calvinism has attractions for young intellectuals in a society suffering from "a threefold crisis" of trust, confidence, and faith, and ruled by a totalitarian regime. Calvinism offers them a vision of a radically changed Chinese society,[5] and an inspiration for a twinning of spiritual and political change. Calvinists stress that God is the transcendent source of all values, and that law derives from the authority of God. Freedom of conscience is a cardinal tenet for Calvinists like Wang. They assert that, with divine guidance, consciences may rise above abusive laws and resist the authority of tyrants. For them, freedom of religion is the most fundamental freedom, from which all others flow. For Calvinists, China's democratization and Christianization are linked. At a time when the CPC is aggressively attempting to Sinicize Christianity, Calvinists proclaim the goal of Christianizing China.

Calvinism is only one strand of Chinese Protestantism, which is largely evangelical and pentecostal. But they have an importance out of all proportion to their numbers, because their combination of faith; constitutional, legal, and political principles; vision for radical social change; and high intellectual standards makes them a vanguard of revolutionary potential.

Wang Yi has articulated the beliefs and standpoints of Chinese Protestants with outstanding clarity and courage. Before his conversion to Christianity, he had gained a high profile in several fields. He began his professional career as a lecturer in constitutional law and a human rights lawyer, defending the poor and vulnerable, a field in which about one-quarter of the lawyers were Christians. He had gained a national reputation as a lawyer and social activist, as well as a widely followed blogger on cinema and the author of two books analyzing Hollywood and European films.

In 2004, he was included in the list of "50 Most Influential Public Intellectuals of China" by the respected *Southern People Weekly*. In 2006, he was chosen to be one of three Chinese human rights attorneys to discuss religious freedom in China with President George W. Bush in the White House. In that same year, the Party detained or drove most human rights lawyers like him out of the legal profession.

After his conversion to Christianity, Wang put his religious beliefs into practice by his leadership of the Early Rain Reformed Church, which he founded as an unregistered church in Chengdu in 2008. In 2011, he was ordained and became its senior pastor. Under him, Early Rain established its own religious school, college, and seminary. These were all illegal, but Wang was unapologetic, arguing that the Party-state has no right to separate religion from education. When challenged as to why an expert in constitutional law should initiate an illegal act, and why indeed he should found and lead an unregistered church which contravenes the law by its very existence, Wang insisted that the party-state had for decades "trampled on its own constitution and laws," and in any case, as Calvin taught, Christians are not bound by laws that contravene the will of God. Early Rain developed the West China Presbytery with other unregistered churches in Chengdu. It held annual acts of commemoration of the victims of the 1989 Tiananmen Massacre and the Sichuan Earthquake, in defiance of the policies of the Party. Early Rain campaigned against forced abortion and supported the families of political dissidents jailed by the Party. It publicly acknowledged the vital role that Protestant missionaries played in bringing modern knowledge, ideas, and values into China through translation, publication, education, and medicine in the nineteenth and early twentieth centuries, all of which history is suppressed by the Party. A non-Christian visitor to Early Rain commented to Wang that the church lived in truth, "as if you weren't living under the Communist Party."[6] It was the freest group he had seen in all China; no other group spread its faith or discussed Chinese society so freely. The churches that people like Wang found and lead are manifestations, on a small scale, of their vision of a changed China.

In October 1517, Martin Luther nailed a document to the door of the Wittenberg Castle church. Concerned with true repentance and sorrow for sin, Luther's 95 Theses became the foundation of the Reformation. In August 2015 Wang led the elders of his church in posting their own 95 Theses online.[7] They set out the views of the Early Rain Covenant Church on relations between church and state, rejecting the Sinicization of Christianity, and attacking the state-registered churches. They did not spark a Chinese equivalent to the Reformation, but within six months they had attracted 38,000 hits.[8]

While most churches are careful not to engage in overtly political activities, it is clear from interviews and other evidence that many Christians share the longing of people like Wang Yi for China to change. When they recite The Lord's Prayer they invest the words, "Thy kingdom come!" (*"Yuan nide guo jianglin!"*) with a meaning that is secular as well as spiritual.[9]

Here is how the pastor of what was in 2018 Beijing's most dynamic unregistered church described his vison of Christianity's role in shaping China's future: "China's society is awaiting a huge transformation, like a pregnant woman who is just about to give birth; however, she needs the strength to do so. Many people are looking to the church to provide this strength to help the Chinese society give birth to a new day. I believe the next thirty years in China will be similar to the period of the 1920s to the 1940s. At that time a thousand years of feudal rule collapsed, and a new republic was established. This was also the most dynamic period in history for the church in China. The church was active in every area of society—education, culture, politics and economics. The significant transition in the next 30 years will be from the Party's authoritarian rule to the emergence of a modern nation. There is no force that will be able to stop this development, for whoever gets in the way will be destroyed. I believe that the elites of today have the potential to play an important role in this social change. I am particularly looking forward to how Christians can play a role similar to that of believers one hundred years ago who, during a time of epic change, made a great contribution to the Chinese people and nation."[10]

Party leaders are well aware of the reasons why many of their subjects are attracted to Christianity. They also know the role played by Christians, especially in Poland and East Germany, in the downfall of communism in Eastern and Central Europe, a phenomenon that has been required study in the Central Party School.[11] China's Christians today account for only 5–10 percent of the population, far less than in Europe in the 1970s and 1980s, but the recent history of a country on China's very doorstep, South Korea, stands as a warning to China's leaders: the number of Christians in South Korea grew from only 3 percent of the population in 1969 to about 20 percent in 1979, and by 2005 had reached 29 percent, a growth in absolute numbers of 1,400 percent in under forty years.[12] They must be aware too that in the 1970s Korean Christians played a role in undermining the military dictatorship far greater than their percentage of the population.[13] All of which explains why CPC leaders try hard to constrain the growth of Christianity, while pursuing a less hostile policy toward (non-Tibetan) Buddhism and Daoism.

Those Chinese Christians who place a high priority on political safety join the officially registered and regulated Protestant or Catholic churches. Some of these attract a membership of several thousands; for instance, the Chongyi Church in Hangzhou can accommodate a congregation of 5,500. But in general the fastest growing, most dynamic Christian churches are self-governing Protestant churches that neither register with the authorities, nor accept control and regulation. They reject what they see as the dead hand of control by the party-state, and regard as absurd the pretension of an atheist party to dictate who shall be ordained priests and what they shall preach. They account for about two-thirds of China's estimated sixty million Protestants and half of its estimated twelve million Catholics.

While the 95 Theses of the Early Rain Covenant Church denounced the registered churches in uncompromising terms, in general it is true to say that the mutual mistrust or even hostility that marked relations between the registered and unregistered churches has diminished over time, helped by the way in which some registered churches have resisted attempts by the party-state to distort fundamentals of Christian doctrine.[14] Many on both sides of the divide have come to believe that there is more that unites than divides them in terms of common values and beliefs, surrounded by a society in a moral crisis and repressed by the party-state.

With some high-profile exceptions, these churches have developed a pattern of organization and activity that takes account of the political context in which they must operate. Most congregations have respected the three "red lines" set for churches by the party-state: do not organize across provincial boundaries, keep a low public profile, and keep your contacts with foreign churches close to zero.[15] They are acutely aware that in no field does the Party tolerate the formation of large organizations that might become a force against it.[16]

Many churches organize themselves in cells, where the faithful meet once or twice a week in small groups, often numbering three to five and seldom over a dozen individuals, for prayer, study of the Bible and theology, or discussion of church affairs. Cells join together for Sunday worship as a single larger group, but the cell builds mutual trust, shared values, and solidarity. Above the cells comes a structure of central leadership, which, in the best examples, is democratically elected and engages in consultation with the membership on crucial decisions.[17] In their decision making, they rely not only on rational analysis but also on prayer for divine guidance to a degree rare in many more established churches. With their combination of cellular organization and strong central leadership, the unregistered churches resemble an underground political party or a guerrilla movement. Not only does it enable them to avoid unwanted attention, it gives them resilience in time of oppression.

So too does their flexibility: when the police drive them out of one apartment, they soon reappear in another. They travel light, not weighed down by elaborate church furniture. A neon-lit cross is more likely than a large, solid crucifix; an electronic keyboard and guitars, rather than an organ with many pipes; and a light table will serve for the altar. Doctrinally too, these Protestants travel light, with a strong, uncomplicated faith, reminiscent of the early churches of Christendom.

It is not only at the tactical level that the unregistered churches resemble nonviolent guerrillas; viewed as a whole, the struggle between them and the party-state resembles one between a guerrilla movement and an army of occupation. There is asymmetry between the slender resources of the churches and the massive forces of the party-state. Unregistered churches are a movement, whereas the party-state is a tightly structured organization. They are motivated by a faith; those whose task it is to monitor and control them are doing a job for a salary. They are flexible and mobile; the party-state is cumbersome and slow-moving. They usually form quietly, with minimal publicity. They try new tactics, retaining what succeeds, abandoning what does not, probing, advancing, or withdrawing.

In the 1980s, the center of gravity of Chinese Christianity was in the countryside. In the 1990s it shifted to the cities, which saw great growth of unregistered house churches.

Late in the first decade of the twenty-first century, politically astute leaders of urban churches like Wang Yi and "Ezra" Jin Mingri, senior pastor at the Zion Church, one of the largest in Beijing, adopted a strategy of open communication with officials of the Religious Affairs Bureau and the security services. These officials bear a heavy responsibility for ensuring that religious activities do not cause "social instability," which the Party dreads above everything. Yet they lack the resources and manpower to discharge their responsibility effectively. They are numerically overwhelmed, and many, especially the security officials, understand little of Christianity. Their morale and willpower suffer from their low political priority and low status in the bureaucratic pecking order.[18] Pastor Jin set out to reassure them that the church he was founding would observe the regime's "red lines" and would not cause instability. He gave the authorities the details they needed about himself, his congregation, and his church's activities, without allowing them to interfere in their essential religious autonomy. Encouraged by his example, more and more unregistered churches have done the same, and gone on, over time, to explain the essentials of their faith to officials, who responded reasonably. Tens of thousands of unregistered churches in China have developed this modus vivendi with their local authorities and, until recently, thereby gained space in which to operate.[19]

. . .

For the first thirty years of the Reform Era, the Party prioritized social stability in its policy on religion and not inflaming international criticism on human rights grounds. On paper, unregistered churches were illegal, but in practice they were mostly tolerated provided they observed the "red lines." Indeed, in the early years of the new millennium, the Party took the view that religion could contribute to the "harmonious society" it was promoting, provided religious organizations observed certain guidelines. Religious publications were available for purchase online, and often the restrictive regulations were not rigorously enforced. Even unregistered churches had their own websites (on which they published articles and sermons), educated children in the faith, ran seminaries, and organized networks across provincial lines. Under these conditions, Protestant churches grew so vigorously that in 2006 the head of the State Administration for Religious Affairs told a closed-door meeting at Peking University that Protestants in China numbered 110 million, forty million more than the membership of the Communist Party of China at that time.[20]

Clearly, this growth posed a massive dilemma for the Party. While Party leaders recognized that churches could contribute to society through social work and the moral example of Christians, they were confronted by the phenomenal growth of faith that, according to their ideology, was supposed to die out. As they moved around the country or read police reports, they encountered ever more churches and Christians, each one testifying to belief in a power whose authority transcended theirs. Inside the churches, and inside their homes, Christians revered crosses and images of Jesus Christ, not the national flag or the portrait of a Party leader. Through their faith, Christians belonged to a universal church numbering some two billion believers and propagating universal values at odds with those of the Party. These Christians were praying daily that God's kingdom would come to earth, and that was not part of any five-year plan of the party-state. Whatever their true number, Protestants constituted a great body of people, by far the largest body outside the CPC, whose allegiance was to an authority and a creed other than those of the Party. What were the Party leaders to do about it?

Faced with this situation, in 2008 the CPC undertook a major review of their policy toward unregistered churches. A year-long research project began involving government departments, universities, private organizations, and scholars from unregistered churches, culminating in a conference to consider its findings, which were presented in a 675-page collection of dissertations. A consensus emerged that the existence of house churches should be recognized. It was argued that the existing situation, in which unregistered churches flouted the letter of the law, actually undermined the authority of the party-state, and the best way forward would be to legalize them.[21]

The Party had to consider the far-reaching political implications of this radical concession not only for the place of religion in China but in other fields also. A concession would show that the Party was willing to accept reduced authority in the face of popular pressure. To grant freedom of religious belief would encourage pressure for freedoms of expression, of assembly, and of association. At the same time, the Party was considering whether to pursue the transition to a market economy, which had yielded huge economic benefits, or abandon it lest its continuation contribute to undermining its monopoly on political power. The Party stood at a fork in the political road: a choice between an authoritarian and a totalitarian polity. In the wider world, liberal democracy was still reeling from the global financial crisis; this encouraged hardliners in the leadership.

The Party both rejected the proposals for religious freedom and abandoned the transition to the market economy. In September 2011, a secret government document reportedly set out a three-phase plan for completely eradicating unregistered churches over a period of ten years.[22] Although this particular report has not been corroborated, subsequent events have made clear that government bodies throughout China were implementing a strategy and guidelines along these lines for the better part of the 2010s. This strategy was in line with the overall political strategy that Xi Jinping began to pursue when he became Party leader the following year: the tightening of censorship,[23] the persecution of human rights lawyers, the suppression of civil society in general, the denunciation of universal values, and the reimposition of CPC control over every field of the nation's life.

Revised religious affairs regulations came into force in 2018 that place much tighter restrictions on and oversight of religious activity. The tightening includes the financing of religious groups and the construction of religious buildings, as well as restrictions on religious schooling, the times and locations of religious celebrations, and contact with Christian organizations abroad. Other regulations followed that severely restrict online communication by religious groups, a principal means of contacting the faithful and spreading the gospel to others. A key objective of the strategy is to prevent the transmission of religious faith to children.[24] The new regulations require all religions to be *Sinicized*, a vague term that can interpreted to mean whatever the Party decides.

It became evident that the Party had ordered a major escalation of persecution to coincide with the date the new regulations came into force. This was dramatically reflected in statistics compiled by the United States–based ChinaAid, the nongovernmental organization best organized to collect and monitor reports on the persecution of Christians in China.[25] (ChinaAid points out that its coverage cannot be comprehensive and cautions that while it has confidence in the accuracy of the trends shown, its absolute numbers are incomplete.) In 2018, more than one million people were persecuted, compared to 4,322 in 2011. Of those persecuted, more than ten thousand were church leaders. In that year, more than fifty thousand people were abused, compared to seventy-six in 2011. The number of those who were detained for some hours or

TABLE 1. Comparison of persecution by year in six categories

Year	2011	2017	2018
No. of persecution cases	93	1,265	>10,000
No. of people persecuted	4,322	>223,200 (church leaders, >1,900)	>1,000,000 (church leaders, >10,000)
No. of people detained	1,289	>3,700 (church leaders, >650)	>5,000 (church leaders, >1,000)
No. of people sentenced	4	>347	>500
No. of abuse cases	24	>300	>2,000
No. of people abused	76	>2,000	>50,000

days rose from just under 1,289 in 2011 to over five thousand in 2018. In 2018, more than five hundred people were sentenced to prison terms, 125 times more than 2011, when four were sentenced. Table 1 provides these statistics in tabular form.

Given the size of China, the number of Christians and their adherence to a global faith, it would be folly for the Party to engage in an all-out assault simultaneously across the nation, as Stalin did, dynamiting hundreds of churches and executing hundreds of thousands of priests, monks, and nuns all in a short space of time. That would maximize internal resistance and international condemnation. Instead, the Party has adopted a strategy of progressive strangulation and suffocation. Its intention is that in a few years all unregistered places of worship will be closed, preventing corporate worship; while all unlicensed priests and lay leaders of congregations will be prevented from serving their congregations through intimidation, imprisonment, or application of sanctions under the Social Credit System. Unregistered churches will be bankrupted through punitive fines; their seminaries will be closed, cutting off the supply of newly trained priests or lay leaders. The transmission of religious knowledge will be prevented through the banning of publications, broadcasting, and online communication. The religious education of children will be increasingly suppressed.

That is the strategy, and the annual Persecution Reports published by ChinaAid record meticulously how vigorously it is being implemented. Across the country, local authorities are conducting repeated raids and harassment to pressure churches to disband, imposing administrative penalties so heavy they bankrupt them, confiscating their assets, cutting off their electricity and water supplies, and compelling landlords to evict them. The online presence of influential churches and missionary organizations has been removed or blocked. Members of congregations are being subjected to unlawful detentions and disappearances, physical assault, death threats, and surveillance. They have been denied access to lawyers. Lawyers who take up their cases are themselves being arrested. Thousands of crosses and bibles are being burned in public and major churches demolished; Christmas celebrations are being banned or obstructed.[26] The Party is increasingly targeting state-sanctioned churches and their leaders. Innumerable examples demonstrate that the campaign against Christianity has unleashed a recrudescence of the lawless assaults and reckless mindset of the Cultural Revolution, with the difference that this time it is officials of the party-state and their agents, not gangs of youths, who are the assailants.

In July 2018, more than thirty of Beijing's hundreds of unregistered Protestant churches took the rare step of releasing a joint statement complaining of "unceasing interference" and the "assault and obstruction" of regular activities of believers since the new regulations came into effect. Despite this, most unregistered churches have maintained their nonconfrontational strategy.

The struggle between the Party and the churches is illustrated by the following stories.

Shouwang Church, Beijing

Shouwang Church in Beijing was founded in 1993 and grew to become the largest of about three thousand unregistered churches in the city, with some one thousand members. Its name means "lookout" in Mandarin. The choice evokes a passage in the Old Testament of the Bible, in which God commands the people of Israel, who are being oppressed by the pagan kingdom of Babylon, to post a lookout on a watchtower "and let him announce what he sees." What he sees is the approach of a group of horsemen, who announce the destruction of Babylon. The link between Babylon and China's atheist party-state is not hard to discern.

Its congregation was representative of unregistered urban churches in the Reform Era in that it attracted many well-educated people, entrepreneurs, academics, students, journalists, doctors, lawyers, and other professionals to be baptized. It elected as its senior pastor Jin Tianming, who had become a Christian while studying chemical engineering at China's leading science university.

Like Early Rain Covenant Church in Chengdu, the church formed part of the "New Calvinism" movement within Chinese Protestantism. Professor Sun Yi of Renmin University, a leading Chinese scholar of Calvin and the Reformed tradition, was elected to be one of its elders.

At first, Shouwang followed the usual policy of small meetings in apartments. By 2003, it had developed into a network of fifteen unregistered groups or "house churches" who met in this way. Even so, its growth attracted the attention of the authorities, who would send the police to seize the worship books and break up the gatherings, always on the pretext of complaints from the neighbors.

The church was a pioneer in combining a network of cells with a well-organized central leadership whose decision making was based on extensive consultation and democratic voting.

Recognizing that they could not escape the attention of the authorities, the leaders of Shouwang decided the best strategy would be to "go public." They would rent space in an office block that would be empty on Sundays, so there would be no neighbors to whom complaints could be attributed. They would take the initiative in communicating with the government.

Indeed, they went beyond simple communication. They tried to register their church with the state. The Religious Affairs Regulations of 2005 contained provisions that supposedly granted unregistered churches the right to regularize their position by registering directly with the state without joining the officially sanctioned associations, yet provided no procedure for doing so. Shouwang applied and was rejected three times. It had failed to register but had exposed these provisions of the regulations as a sham.

Shouwang Church rented office space but was always prevented from buying a property upon which to make its permanent home, almost certainly because of Party pressure. In 2009, when its landlord terminated its lease on rented premises, the church tried to buy an entire floor of a building in the university neighborhood with US$6 million it had raised in donations, but the sale was canceled, again probably under pressure from authorities. So Shouwang rented a big conference room from an up-market restaurant. Several months later, that contract also was canceled under official pressure, leaving the worshippers without premises, so they began holding services outdoors, on a square near Peking

University in the Haidian District. These gatherings initially attracted as many as one thousand worshippers, but they were then much reduced by police action. According to foreign press reports, Beijing police at times used as many as four thousand five hundred officers to provide surveillance of the square, and of the homes of about five hundred church members, to deter them from congregating. Members of the congregation were repeatedly arrested and forced to sign a disavowal of their spiritual guide before being released. Senior Pastor Jin Tianming and other leaders of the church were placed under house arrest. As a result, church members reverted to worshipping discreetly in smaller groups in homes or elsewhere. There is no report of Shouwang doing anything at any stage that upset "social stability," yet their peaceful efforts to worship discreetly were continually disrupted or blocked by the party-state.

In 2010, Shouwang helped to gather two hundred delegates from around the country in preparation for attending a landmark international evangelical conference in South Africa, the Third Lausanne Congress.[27] This was the first time such a delegation from China had assembled to attend an international gathering. It was a wonderful opportunity to make contact with the universal church. Alarmed by the church's capacity to coordinate and their desire to present themselves as the legitimate representatives of Chinese Protestantism (only unregistered churches had been invited), the authorities banned the delegates from leaving the country. When, at the last moment, they were prevented from leaving, it was a big disappointment, but two years' preparation had brought a large number of rural and urban churches closer together.

Then the "jasmine revolutions" started, and fearing the Arab world's revolutionary spirit would spread, the CPC strengthened its resolve to ensure that Shouwang should stay dispersed, and succeeded in doing so.

A minority of the original congregation continued to worship together, but in small groups. Pastor Jin Tianming preferred to remain under house arrest rather than submit to the will of the Party. In April 2018, he stepped down as senior pastor of Shouwang to focus on his calling to be involved in missions. When in December of that year the authorities detained Early Rain's senior pastor and over one hundred members in Chengdu, Jin Tianming issued a statement of solidarity.

On one side of the historical balance sheet of the struggle between the authorities and the church are four positive points: (a) Shouwang had the satisfaction of exposing a key provision of the religious regulations for the sham it was; (b) many members of its congregation demonstrated the strength of their faith by repeatedly gathering in public to worship, knowing that some of them would be detained for hours or days; (c) their elders gained valuable experience in leadership under pressure that they brought to wherever they worship now; and (d) images of church members worshipping as snow falls around them have survived on the internet as vivid reminders of their struggle. But the Party has been able to disperse Beijing's largest church and severely disrupt its corporate life of religious education, training, and worship. Above all, the authorities have prevented it from celebrating Holy Communion as a united body.

Removing Crosses: The Zhejiang Campaign

One of the most striking examples of the much more aggressive policy pursued since Xi Jinping came to power has occurred in Zhejiang

Province, where the authorities conducted a three-year campaign, beginning in March 2013, just six months after Xi assumed the leadership of the Party. It bore the hallmarks of a pilot project designed to test an approach that, if deemed successful, could be rolled out nationally. Documents obtained by the *New York Times* showed that it was carefully planned; it was conceived and conducted on a large scale, and the strategy was high profile and full-frontal. The choice of Zhejiang was hardly fortuitous: it is home to one of China's largest, boldest, and most vibrant Christian populations, and Xi knows it well, since he was first secretary of the Party there from 2002 to 2007. The campaign was launched in Wenzhou, a city with over a million Christians (about 11% of its 2010 population, and a massive increase over the 1949 total of seventy thousand), in two thousand churches.[28] The church is so strongly established here that private sector companies adopt biblical names. Registered churches enjoy good relations with unregistered ones, affording some of the latter regulatory cover and preacher exchanges. Until the Zhejiang campaign was launched, the Christian churches, unregistered as well as registered, had for many years developed good relations with the local authorities. The city, often called the "Jerusalem of the East" or "China's Jerusalem," is renowned not only for its Christian community, but for its spirit of enterprise at home and abroad, being a great source of entrepreneurs who have established themselves in trade around the world. It is inconceivable in the Chinese political system that a highly aggressive, widespread campaign against this well-known and well-connected Christian community would have been launched without careful consideration and approval at the very highest level in Beijing.

Beginning in March 2013, the Zhejiang authorities focused their campaign mainly on the outward manifestations of Christianity:

church buildings, and especially the essential symbol of the faith, the cross. By mid-2016, crosses had been removed from the rooftops or façades of at least one thousand five hundred churches, and over two hundred churches had been demolished.[29]

From Wenzhou and other cities, the campaign soon spread across the province, even to rural villages. Most of the structures targeted were unregistered Protestant churches, but several dozen Catholic sites of worship and even some officially sanctioned churches had their crosses removed, or were also demolished. In some places, church members resisted, facing hundreds of riot police officers. They would encircle their church to protect its crosses, holding hands to create a "human wall"; or they conducted a sit-in while chanting hymns. In some instances riot police and demolition crews dispersed the gatherings by force, but particularly in smaller villages or with lower-profile churches, believers have succeeded in fending off destruction.

In one ugly confrontation, about fifty church members were injured. Sanjiang Church in Wenzhou was the largest to be demolished. It could accommodate two thousand worshippers. The complex of which it formed part occupies more than one hundred thousand square feet of land. Completed in 2013, it cost its members more than 20 million yuan ($2.92 million). It is an unregistered church, but before the provincial Party leaders had launched the campaign to remove crosses, the local authorities had actually praised its construction as a model project, a contradiction that shows how far the campaign departed from established local practice and demonstrates the inconsistencies that can arise in a society where there is no rule of law.[30]

Sometimes Zhejiang Christians put up new crosses right after the old ones were torn down. Others took to manufacturing large numbers of smaller crosses to be placed on cars, on homes, or by the side of the road, in an effort to foil the government campaign's core aim of rendering the region's Christian presence less visible.

Although unregistered churches were predictably the most numerous targets, pastors from state-regulated churches were also persecuted, to the surprise of most observers. A few of them had broken with a lifetime of subservience to the Party to protest against the cross removals. Their disobedience was met with detention and imprisonment, punishments that had previously been reserved for their unregistered counterparts. In the highest profile case, the senior pastor of China's largest church, Chongyi, a registered church in the provincial capital, was detained incommunicado for three months for protesting against the cross removals, then released. He was arrested again, but the People's Procuratorate finally dropped all charges against him. The pastor of another registered church in the province who also protested against the campaign was jailed for fourteen years on a charge of "corruption and inciting people to disturb social order." ("It's easy for them to fabricate a crime and accuse you," said the pastor of a large unregistered church in Wenzhou.)[31] For the first time, unregistered church leaders crossed the divide to stand beside their former adversaries, to protest against these judgments. Prominent Protestant and Catholic leaders across China, including senior figures in the government's religious affairs bureaucracy, spoke out against it in sermons and on social media.[32]

As with Shouwang and other churches, the party-state has oppressed a Christian community that has never been reported to have disrupted social stability. The Party center may have judged that while it achieved some success in the short term in removing symbols of Christianity, it provoked determined resistance, including from influential members of the official "patriotic" religious associations, brought closer together Protestants and Catholics as well as members of registered and unregistered churches, aroused greater long-term hostility toward the CPC, and gave rise to widespread negative publicity abroad. Pictures of bruised and beaten Christians flooded social media and the websites of overseas Christian advocacy groups.[33]

In 2018, campaigns of cross removal similar to the one piloted in Zhejiang were rolled out in Henan, Jilin, Hebei, and Jiangxi Provinces and the Xinjiang "Autonomous" Region. Like Xi Jinping's anticorruption campaign, the cross removals dealt with the symptoms, not the underlying causes.

Henan Province

Henan province has one of the highest proportions of Christians in any province of China; its estimated several million followers of Christ constitute one of the largest bodies of Christians in East Asia. Most are Protestant and most attend unregistered churches. They have been targeted for oppression from time to time in the past, but in 2018 the provincial Party launched a campaign of harassment and persecution of Christians of all denominations in Henan of a ferocity unseen since the Cultural Revolution.

By the end of September that year, more than two-thirds of the ten thousand churches in the province had been shut down, including many officially registered, and over seven thousand crosses demolished.[34] Under government instructions it became commonplace for crosses and bibles to be burned, and the Apostles' Creed and the Ten Commandments to be torn from a church.[35] Inspectors explained that Xi Jinping objected to the First Commandment, "Thou shalt have no others gods before me." Unemployed people were hired to barge into churches to smash and destroy windows and doors, and snatch away stools and books used for church worship.[36] One church that was allowed to stay open was required to hang Xi Jinping's and Mao Zedong's pictures on the left and right side of its cross. A notice banning prayer and religious discussions in schools called schools "a battlefield" for constructing socialism.

As with the campaign of cross removal in Zhejiang, it is clear that this campaign has been conducted with the full authority of the Party center in Beijing.

Zion Church, Beijing

While Shouwang and the Zhejiang churches were suffering persecution, others were allowed for a while to grow without major conflict with the state. An example of those is Zion Church, whose history was sketched out for me in 2017 by the assistant pastor.

> Our senior pastor, Dr. Ezra Jin, was an undergraduate at Peking University at the time of the 1989 democracy movement, witnessed its suppression, and lost faith in the Communist Party. He tells us, "Like all my peers, I felt an immense sense of hopelessness." A few years later, he was converted to Christianity. He began his ministry with ten years as a pastor in a registered church in Beijing. In about 2003, he went for postgraduate study in theology in Virginia, USA. After four years, friends in Beijing appealed to him to return home and join their efforts to develop the ministry outside the state-controlled structure.
>
> He agreed, and in 2007 founded Zion Church in a small space with room only for a congregation of twenty, most of whom were old men or penniless students, but some of them urged him to rent

a bigger space. They found a larger space, in the building we now occupy, but the rent was many times what they were paying before, and they would be sharing the floor with a nightclub! You know what kind of people run nightclubs in Beijing, and what goes on in them. Ezra and most of the congregation felt, "It's too big, too expensive, too risky," but other friends urged him on, saying, "Beijing Christians have a big need for more churches. In three months your congregation will grow to fill this space." He prayed to God, and heard God telling him to go ahead. He went ahead, and in six weeks they raised enough money to pay ten months' rent. One hundred fifty-seven people attended their first service in the enlarged premises, and I was one of them. We followed the lead set by Shouwang of being open to the government.

There were setbacks. In 2010, in addition to leading Zion, Ezra was running a big seminary in six thousand square meters of rented space in a separate building. The government wanted to scare him, so they forced the landlord to break the seminary's rental contract.

There were new challenges. In 2013, our landlord came to us and said, 'I want you to take over the whole of this third floor. The owners of the nightclub haven't been paying their rent, and you always pay on time. Take it over!' But it was eight thousand square meters, it was going to cost us ten times more rent, and we would need $450,000 to convert and furnish it. We called a meeting of the congregation. Almost everyone felt it was too risky, but a new member said, "You have been praying for new premises for two years. Now you have this opportunity, and what's your response? 'Lord we have no money.' Where is your faith?" We took it.

Now we worship in an auditorium many businesses would be proud to have, with a bookshop and a cafe just outside. We have three services every Sunday, with a total congregation of seven hundred, of whom about half are university graduates. About two hundred children and teenagers are being taught the gospel. We have eight branch churches in Beijing, and plan to have one in every district of the city. We have held thirty to forty meetings for churches from all over China, and others are following our lead in being open to the government. When we moved our seminary to this building, the government made no objection, and three hundred people have graduated from it.

Ezra Jin is self-confident, articulate, and resilient. He is a gifted leader who has displayed extraordinary skill in navigating through the dangerous waters of religion in China, for which there are no charts and where sudden squalls can, without warning, hit from any direction. He is a bold risk taker but does not seek political confrontation. He believes most officials have accepted that the church is too strong to be destroyed and can play a constructive role in society. He does not want financial aid from abroad and, as his assistant pastor said to me, "Many business leaders are ready to make big donations to churches, so they do not need foreign money. The church in China should relate to the world church on a basis of equality. It can look abroad for advanced theological training, or to learn standards of management, while foreign churches can learn from the experience of Chinese Christians of practicing their faith under very difficult circumstances."

The careful, nonconfrontational approach adopted by Zion, and the skilled, diplomatic leadership of its senior pastor won precious time for his church. But these factors did not save it after the new religious regulations came into effect in 2018.

In April of that year, the city authorities asked the church to install twenty-four closed-circuit television cameras in the building for "security." Pastor Jin told Reuters: "They wanted to put cameras in the sanctuary where we worship. The church decided this was not appropriate. Our services are a sacred time."

When the request was refused, police and state security agents started harassing churchgoers: calling them, visiting them, contacting their workplaces and asking them to sign declarations, promise not to attend the church, and renounce their faith. The police even threatened them with losing their apartments, school placements, or jobs if they did not stop attending.[37] In August 2018, the church and its landlord were set to renew a five-year lease that was about to expire, when the landlord backed out under pressure from the authorities. One Sunday in September, some sixty government workers arrived, accompanied by buses, police cars, and fire trucks. They seized bibles, confiscated the contents of their Christian bookstore, and sealed the premises.[38] Since that time, Zion Church has not been able to celebrate Holy Communion as body whole and entire.

There are churches who have defiantly crossed the "red lines" of the regime. Regional governments have taken severe actions against some that have grown exceptionally strong and prominent. These actions include forcible closure, the confiscation (or looting) of church assets, destruction of churches and other property, short-term detention of members of the congregation, putting their leaders under house arrest, or jailing them, sometimes for many years. These actions are clothed in legal justifications such as the infringement of planning regulations, which is often technically justified, because local authorities often deny churches planning permission as a way of blocking their growth. More aggressively, the party-state can further allege that a church poses a threat to "social stability," which is seldom if ever justified by the facts.

Some churches have been prepared to move boldly without the cover of law when they judged that the party-state was masking its true intent with the trappings of legality. Facing a party-state apparatus with vastly greater resources of manpower, money, and organization, they have refused to be cowed. When the riot police, paid thugs, and bulldozers have moved in, they have not shrunk from being beaten or jailed for long years on trumped-up charges.

A striking example of this very assertive approach is the network of Protestant churches in the city of Linfen, which lies on the banks of the Fen River in Shanxi Province, in China's interior.

The Linfen Network, Shanxi Province

Before 1978, Linfen city was famous for its spring water and greenery, but the great growth of China's economy has changed that. Shanxi has one-third of China's coal deposits, and Linfen has become a coal mining center. As a result, it was listed in 2006 as one of the ten most polluted cities in the world. With industrialization, prosperity, and pollution has come a growth in Christianity. Of the four million people in the city and its surrounding area, fifty thousand belong to a network of unregistered churches, the second largest in China. Around 2005, their church leaders applied to the local Religious Affairs and Land Bureaus for permission to occupy land and construct a complex of buildings. The spiritual center of this complex was to be a church large enough to hold over a thousand worshippers. Since this Patriotic community was not part of the state-controlled Three-Self Protestant Movement, this was a bold but peaceful challenge to the resolve of the party-state to implement its regulations. They received no reply, which is a typical tactic of the party-state in its attempt to thwart the growth of religion. Eventually, they went ahead without permission and built the whole complex including the megachurch with their own resources, of course. They named their church the Golden Lampstand, after the seven-branched candlestick of pure gold, a symbol of light and joy, carried by the people of Israel on their long journey through the Sinai desert in search of their Promised Land.

On 13 September 2009, as the church was nearing completion, about four hundred police, officials, and hired thugs descended on the site. They attacked church members who were sleeping there, ransacked the buildings, and looted property inside. Two bulldozers decimated the foundations of the new church building, reducing it to a heap of brick and metal. The attackers also damaged the Good News Cloth Shoes Factory in Linfen, one of the primary sources of income for the whole Linfen church network. When the dust settled, seventeen buildings at the factory complex had been reduced to rubble. Access to the factory site was closed off, and power, water, and all communications to the county capital Fushan were severed. More than thirty church members had to be hospitalized in critical condition. As news of the attack spread and day broke, hundreds of fellow members of the Linfen network rushed to the church site to aid the wounded. The authorities also moved to prevent worship elsewhere in the Linfen network, stationing police at other sites. Despite threats, a prayer rally was held the next day. More than one thousand prayed together in the rain.

When, days later, state military police stood twenty-four-hour guard around the Linfen church buildings, barring believers from worshipping there, the Linfen leaders resolved to file a complaint with the central government. A week later, alarmed by the reaction from the fifty thousand church members, the Fushan County government entered into covert negotiations with Linfen's Pastor

Yang Li and two of her staff. They offered the church 1.4 million yuan in compensation, provided they would keep silent about the attack; but they would not lift the church ban. The church leaders refused the offer and rebuilt the megachurch from their own resources, at a cost of 17 million yuan ($2.48 million).

The local government accused Pastor Yang of "illegally holding religious activities" and "illegally sharing the gospel" with youth. She, her husband, and eight others were all tried two months later with little attorney-client access or attorney access to the documents to be used by the prosecution. They were all convicted of criminal offenses. Pastor Yang was sentenced to seven years in jail; the others were given lesser sentences.[39]

There had been no report at any stage of Golden Lampstand Church disrupting "social stability," yet the authorities had attacked it and violently disrupted its efforts to conduct their worship and other activities in peace.

The spirit of the Linfen Christian network was not broken. In one sign of its strength, it continued to organize annual training courses. In early 2016 it held a six-day training program for more than four hundred preachers and deacons from every parish in the metropolitan area.

On 9 January 2018, a month before China's new regulations on religious affairs were due to come into force, paramilitary People's Armed Police forces used excavators and dynamite to demolish the rebuilt church. "I think this might be a new pattern against any independent house church with an existing building or intention to build one," said Bob Fu, founder of ChinaAid.[40] As we have seen, the months that followed showed how prescient he was.

· · ·

The success of the Party in the first decade of the twenty-first century in suppressing the Falun Gong, the spiritual practice that combines meditation and qigong exercises with a moral philosophy centered on the tenets of truthfulness, compassion, and forbearance, is also an encouragement to the Party. After emerging in 1992, the Falun Gong movement attracted tens of millions of practitioners; official estimates placed the number at seventy million in 1999, about as many as Chinese Christians today. Viewing it as a major threat due to its size, independence, and spiritual teachings, the CPC persecuted it with the utmost severity and achieved virtually total suppression. No nation took effective action to punish this outrageous violation of human rights.

Now, its campaign against Islam in Xinjiang also seems aimed at its eradication.[41] Of a population of twenty-one million, at least one million have been imprisoned in "re-education" camps. A detailed and carefully researched study published by Human Rights Watch in 2018 concluded: "The government's religious restrictions are so stringent that it has effectively outlawed Islam." The application of high-technology security apparatuses has turned Xinjiang into the most sophisticated and pervasive police state the world has ever seen. It may enable the Party to overcome deeply held religious faith. The rest of the Islamic world has been supine in the face of the Chinese communists' persecution of their coreligionists in Xinjiang.

At the beginning of chapter 2, I quoted the warning of Robert Conquest: a totalitarian state is one that recognizes no limits to its authority in any sphere of public or private life and that extends that authority to whatever length feasible.[42] The CPC's actions in Xinjiang are a demonstration to the world of how it acts when it enjoys unfettered power. The eradication of unregistered Christian churches is only phase 1 of its strategy; if it achieves that, it will move on to phase 2, the eradication of those that are registered. But will it succeed in phase 1?

Xi Jinping may for now feel pleased with the results of the assault on Christianity. The large churches destroyed in the last eighteen months have not been rebuilt, the crosses that were removed have not reappeared, and the congregations dispersed have not regrouped. He can note with satisfaction that liberal democratic governments, other than the US government, have failed to express outrage, let alone impose sanctions.

But a longer historical view casts doubt on Xi's chances of ultimate victory. Mao's Cultural Revolution suppressed every outward manifestation of Christianity, but many Christians kept the faith alive in their hearts and resumed their worship after Mao's death. After four decades of phenomenal growth, the resilience of Christian faith now is likely to be greater than during the Cultural Revolution. It is now thoroughly indigenous in its leadership and financing; Christians no longer have to ask themselves: am I following a faith that is part of an imperialist legacy? The attacks on registered churches in recent years have awakened their leaders and congregations to the reality that there is no refuge to be found in accepting the control of the Party: all Christians now face a common enemy. The contrast I drew early in this chapter between Christians and the Party shows the strong grounds Christians have for a robust faith in their religion and its place in Chinese society. The war on Christianity is asymmetrical: force one side, faith on the other. Lacking ideological conviction, the Party has to employ bulldozers and dynamite, politically controlled prisons, camps, and courts. The Christians are armed with what they carry within them.

Let us return to the question with which this chapter began: why would the Party leaders impose a sentence of nine years in prison on the pastor of a small church in Chengdu? Do they really believe that he is capable of subverting state power? Yes. The congregation of the Early Rain Covenant Church numbered only seven hundred, and there were only 303 original signatories to the *Charter 08* manifesto to which Liu Xiaobo put his name in 2008, but the Party leaders fear Christianity as they fear democracy. The severity of the nine-year sentence on Wang Yi is the measure of their fear of Christianity, as the eleven-year sentence on Liu was the measure of their fear of democracy. These sentences are recognition of the power of the faith and ideals these men represent. That is what they calculate, not the size of Wang's congregation or the number of Liu's fellow signatories. They remember how the democracy movement in 1989 came within days of overthrowing their predecessors, and now they realize that in a crisis, as envisaged in part 1 of this book, Chinese Christians—especially Calvinists like Wang Yi—will constitute a revolutionary vanguard. Lenin captured control of the Russian Empire with a few hundred Bolsheviks; Fidel Castro landed in Cuba in 1956 with just eighty-two guerrillas. Neither man was backed by a mass movement.

In the meantime, the persecution of Christians is providing yet another illustration of how the communist regime is in decay, reliant on control, not trust. And we see one more demonstration that a totalitarian regime is incapable of strategic compromise: its strategies intensify problems rather than solving them.

6 An Environmental Catastrophe

The state of China's environment is catastrophic. There is extreme pollution of land, air, and water. In many places, for many people, eating, drinking, and breathing are dangerous. Environmental degradation and pollution exact a heavy toll economically, politically, and on public health. Chinese official estimates have calculated the annual cost to the nation at 3.5 percent of GDP.[1] The World Bank has put the cost much higher, at 9 percent.[2]

China is the world's largest current emitter of carbon dioxide. The impact is felt internationally as well as domestically. Japan and South Korea also complain that acid rain from China poisons fisheries, ruins cropland, and erodes buildings within their borders.

A strategic assessment issued by the White House in May 2020 alleged that "China's planned growing emissions will outweigh the reductions from the rest of the world combined. Chinese firms also export polluting coal-fired power plants to developing countries by the hundreds. The PRC is also the world's largest source of marine plastic pollution, discharging over 3.5 million metric tons into the ocean each year. The PRC ranks first in the world for illegal, unreported, and unregulated fishing in coastal nations' waters around the world, threatening local economies and harming the marine environment."[3]

According to the World Bank, in 2007 only 1 percent of China's urban population breathed air considered safe by European Union standards.[4] For children in the country's most polluted cities, that is the equivalent of smoking two packs of cigarettes per day. A 2013 study by the MIT Energy Initiative found that air pollution reduced life expectancy in northern China by an average of five and a half years.[5] Heart and lung diseases are commonplace; cancer mortality rates in China have risen 80 percent over the past thirty years, making cancer the country's leading cause of death. In cities, toxic air is the primary suspect; in the countryside, it is water.[6]

The World Bank has also calculated that seven hundred million people in China drink water contaminated with human and animal waste.[7] An investigation conducted by China's own Ministry of Water Resources found that drinking water in all but three of 118 cities surveyed was polluted, largely by fluoride (which can cause severe pain in the joints) and arsenic (which can cause severe nausea, cancer of the internal organs, or, in the worst cases, death).[8]

A report on soil pollution in the Pearl River delta region showed that 28 percent of the land in the area—including 50 percent in the cities of Guangzhou and Foshan—had excessive levels of heavy metals.[9] Cadmium-tainted rice has been a staple of the food supply in Canton since at least 2009.

For many regions in China, diminishing water supplies pose today's greatest social, economic, and political challenge. The shortage of water is developing inexorably. The Ministry of Water Resources has predicted a "serious water crisis" in 2030, when the population reaches 1.6 billion and China's per capita water resources are estimated to decline to the World Bank's scarcity level.[10] Former Chinese Premier Wen Jiabao warned that water shortages challenge "the very survival of the Chinese nation."[11] As of 2018, over three hundred of 657 cities were already short of water. The region under greatest threat is northern China, which accounts for 43 percent of the country's total use but has only 23 percent of its water resources.[12] In March 2009, Hebei, the province with a population of seventy-five million that surrounds Beijing and supplies much of its water, reported that overexploitation of groundwater had caused more than one-fifth of its land to sink—forty thousand square miles, an area roughly the size of the state of Kentucky.[13]

In 2018, veteran China analyst Charlie Parton wrote: "Clearly if a sudden water crisis were to hit (would a few years of severe drought be sufficient to cause it?), some very hard choices would be forced upon the government between agriculture, power generation, industry and everyday use by the people. Those choices still need to be made now, given that falling renewable water resources render the situation unsustainable. The threat is worse than just to food security, economic prosperity and social well-being: the likelihood of those and other factors leading to large scale unrest is something which must terrify the Party."[14]

Degradation has reduced China's grasslands by 30–50 percent since 1950; of the four hundred million or so hectares of natural grasslands remaining, more than 90 percent are degraded and overgrazed, and more than 50 percent suffer moderate to severe degradation. China reports forest coverage of 18.2 percent, well below the world average of 30.3 percent. More than one-quarter of China's land is now affected by desertification or is degraded due to overgrazing by livestock, overcultivation, excessive water use, or changes in climate.

Forest resources especially have been depleted, triggering a range of devastating secondary impacts such as desertification, flooding, and species loss. The government response to this has been based primarily on large-scale campaigns and administrative actions, rather than policies that change people's economic behavior. A major example is the "Green Wall of China" project intended to create a 2,800-mile (4,500 km) "green belt" to hold back the encroaching desert. First launched in 1978, it calls for the planting of one hundred billion trees along the 2,800-mile border of northern China's encroaching desert by the project's end date of 2050. It is possibly the largest ecological project in history.[15] But some Chinese researchers are sceptical of its chances of success, citing scientific flaws in its design and the failure of similar efforts in the past. In a study published in 2008, Cao Shixiong of Beijing Forestry University calculated that just 15 percent of trees planted on China's drylands since 1949 had survived.[16]

Less controversial has been China's application of renewable energy technologies: it has the highest installed capacity of both solar and wind power generation of any country in the world, and it manufactures a majority of the world's solar panels. But the contribution of solar energy to its electricity consumption is still very modest: in 2017 it was under 2 percent, compared to 58 percent for coal. At this point, its contribution to a cleaner environment is minimal.

Although they are of vital importance, statistics capture only part of reality. Investigative journalists, both foreign and Chinese, and netizens posting on social media have done much to illustrate the impact of pollution on individuals and communities. But, as the *Guardian* newspaper's Green Blood series of articles showed in 2019, environmental journalism is one of the more dangerous occupations: quoting the international Committee to Protect Journalists, it reported that thirteen journalists pursuing environmental stories had been killed in the process of doing their work around the world in the previous ten years. If journalism is dangerous, environmental activism is more so: according to the same *Guardian* series, 207 environmental activists were killed in 2017, most of whom were opposed to agribusiness and mining projects in developing countries.[17] Despite the risks, Chinese journalists have worked bravely to bring the stories of the victims of pollution and those activists who fight for environmental justice to public attention. Some of the most poignant stories have concerned China's "cancer villages"—small communities located near polluting factories such as chemical, pharmaceutical, or power plants, where cancer rates have soared far above the national average. Chinese media, academics, and NGOs have estimated that the country is home to 459 of them, spread across every province except far-western Qinghai and Tibet.[18] Their existence emerged first in 1998, but no ministerial document acknowledged their existence until 2013, when the Ministry of Environmental Protection mentioned them in its latest five-year plan; the ministry was reprimanded and the wording renounced. Officially they do not exist, but their reality is accepted by parts of government: for years no boy from certain villages in the Huai River area was healthy enough to pass the physical examination required to enter the army.[19]

In terms of information policy, the Communist Party of China's response to the degradation of the environment resembled its response to other awkward realities. Generally speaking, it consisted of official silence, denial, censorship, falsification of statistics, punishment of whistle-blowers and activists rather than the true culprits, and the intermittent publication of accurate information in support of government-directed campaigns. There have been periods of comparative openness when more sophisticated tactics were used: certain publications and television programs would be allowed to engage in investigative journalism, provided they never targeted the more senior officials.

The short history of *Under the Dome,* a self-financed documentary film about air pollution in China, is instructive. With a message wholly in line with official policy, it was released online on 28 February 2015, being streamed on three major internet platforms, including one directly under Party control. But it was officially banned on 7 March. In the course of its seven days of officially sanctioned life, it had been viewed over three hundred million times.

In a society where the courts are subordinate to the Party, investigative journalism conducted within tight limits serves the purpose of keeping local officials from totally ignoring the need for protection of the environment, and it gives a semblance of respect for truth and justice. But *Under the Dome* had been far too successful; it had achieved a life of its own, which had to be terminated without delay.

In the realm of law, there has been no lack of legislative activity, regulation making, and standard setting over the years. About thirty laws relating to particular aspects of the environment have been enacted, ninety administrative regulations promulgated, and many environmental standards set. But in the absence of effective enforcement, these have been little more than window dressing. Moreover, for twenty-five years, from 1989 to 2014, the centerpiece of the legal framework, the Environmental Protection Law, was not revised to address the challenges of a rapidly deteriorating environment.

China opened over one hundred thirty environmental courts between 2007 and 2013. Courts can accept cases when disputes are increasing, and turn them away when local power holders are involved and caution appears prudent. Many courts struggled to find enough cases to survive, and even the most active courts did not necessarily tackle China's most pressing environmental problems. An analysis by an American scholar showed that the docket of the provincial court she studied was dominated by "minor criminal cases—crackdowns against powerless rural residents, rather than more ambitious attempts to hold polluters accountable."[20]

But by 2014 events had conspired to persuade the Party leaders that their interests would best be served by stronger efforts to tackle pollution. The number of complaints to the environmental authorities had been increasing strongly—by 30 percent annually between 2002 and 2004 alone, reaching six hundred thousand in 2004.[21] Social media played an important role while the censors permitted: throughout 2011 and 2012, US Embassy officials in Beijing measured and tweeted the true levels of hazardous pollutants in the capital (as opposed to false figures published by the city authorities); Chinese microbloggers spread the news and began to demand that their own government provide similar data; Beijing complied in 2012. Pollution replaced land disputes as the main cause of social unrest in China. The annual number of so-called "mass incidents" (i.e., incidents involving more than one hundred people) rose to 30,000–50,000 by 2013, when a retired senior Party official said: "The major reason for mass incidents is the environment, and everyone cares about it now."

Then in October 2013 Beijing and the rest of northern China suffered an "airpocalypse" when satellite images showed a massive toxic haze that, according to Chinese researchers, covered a span of

1.4 million square kilometers (540,000 square miles), and affected eight hundred million people, 60 percent of the nation's population. Visibility declined to fifty meters. In one of the worst affected areas, a fine particulate matter reading forty times the WHO-recommended upper limit was recorded. Thousands of schools were closed and hundreds of flights grounded. Parents crowded into hospitals with children suffering from respiratory problems.

Other forms of pollution had recently caused sensations. In March of 2013, sixteen thousand dead pigs had been found floating in tributaries of Shanghai's river, the Huangpu, which supplies drinking water to many of the city's twenty-six million residents, leading to concerns about water and food safety in the city. Photos of the city's sanitation workers pulling bloated, decomposing pig carcasses out of the river circulated online and in the media.[22]

Party leaders identified a serious and growing risk of social instability. In 2014, Premier Li Keqiang declared a "war on pollution," outlining an array of targets, policies, and campaigns to address the environmental ills. Soon afterward, the revised Environmental Protection Law was enacted.

The Chinese government could take satisfaction in some of the results of its efforts. Four years later, the Energy Policy Institute at the University of Chicago published a study showing that China's most populated areas were achieving remarkable improvements in air quality, ranging from 21 to 42 percent, with most meeting or exceeding the goals outlined in the National Air Quality Action Plan of 2013.[23]

But the impact of the amended Environmental Protection Law was limited. Its provisions displayed every sign of political caution. For instance, one of its provisions permitted NGOs to bring environmental public interest cases against polluters, but *not* against government agencies. Several lawsuits were brought by NGOs against government entities for violating environmental laws but were duly rejected. In a major test case, five activist lawyers charged the governments of Beijing, Tianjin, and Hebei Province with not doing enough to reduce pollution. Pressure was brought against them, and a "blanket ban on any discussion of the case" was issued. The suit was rejected.[24]

Writing three years after the amended Environmental Protection Law was enacted, Stanley Lubman, who had specialized on China as a scholar and practicing lawyer for over fifty years, commented that "the activities of NGOs, citizens, and prosecutors suggest that environmental litigation generally is in a 'no man's land.' If public interest litigation grows, and with it public opinion favoring the desirability of increasing it, policy could change and limits could be imposed on such litigation. This would be entirely consistent with the People's Republic of China's treatment of legal institutions as *instruments for implementing policy* rather than supporting *the rule of law*."[25]

In late 2017, the government announced long-awaited plans for a national cap-and-trade program for carbon emissions, creating the world's largest carbon market, but it took an extremely cautious approach, driven by fears of undermining economic growth. Experts warned that it would yield no real reduction in emissions until well into the next decade, and they explained that a more effective program would have required a degree of reliance on market forces that the Party is not willing to allow.[26]

How is it that the environment in China has reached a disastrous state? In her work of outstanding scholarship, *The River Runs Black: The Environmental Challenge to China's Future*, Elizabeth C. Economy has written: "China's history suggests a long, deeply entrenched tradition of exploiting the environment for man's needs, with relatively little sense of the limits of nature's or man's capacity to replenish the earth's resources, [but] in the fifteen or so years spanning both the Great Leap Forward and the Cultural Revolution, Mao easily equaled the worst excesses of Imperial China, tearing apart the social fabric of the country, devastating the economy, and ravaging the environment."[27]

Surveying the post-Mao era, Economy wrote: "The dynamic that produced such success in the economic sphere has wreaked havoc on China's natural environment. The burgeoning economy has dramatically increased the demand for resources such as water, land, and energy. . . . Without a strong, independent environmental protection apparatus, the devolution of authority to provincial and local officials has given them free rein to concentrate their energies on economic growth, pushing aside environmental considerations with few consequences from the center."[28]

With roughly four times the population of the United States, China possesses a central environmental protection bureaucracy only one-sixth as large, but it is not only "a strong, independent environmental protection apparatus" that has been missing. The absence of democracy and the rule of law mean that there is no public oversight of local officials, and they are not held accountable to the public. Indeed, there has been no possibility of such safeguards because devolution without democracy and the rule of law was exactly the strategy developed by national leaders after they rejected with armed force the demands of the 1989 democracy movement.

As we saw in chapter 2, in the aftermath of the crushing of that movement, the CPC created conditions under which officials at all levels could loot state property, in order to rebuild the loyalty of those who would continue to rule in its name. As Economy has pointed out, "Even as laws are passed, administrative decrees issued, and regulations set, the politics of resource use conspire to undermine environmental efforts; and the lack of a strong legal infrastructure has enhanced opportunities for corruption and resulted in a systemic crisis for environmental protection enforcement. . . . It seems plausible that the small central environmental protection apparatus and its relatively weak reach are at least partly by design."[29] "At least partly by design" is a scholarly understatement.

In a one-party dictatorship, in which there is no rule of law, no right to free expression, no right to free association, no independent judiciary, a deliberate strategy of weak enforcement, and (despite sporadic anticorruption campaigns) tolerance of crony capitalism, the protection of the environment has always been and will always be doomed to failure, except for campaigns limited in time and place. The laws on the statute books will be flouted by polluting factories; officials will turn a blind eye, either because their promotion prospects depend on the growth of the economy in their area, not on a clean environment, or because they have a financial interest in the polluting factory. Courts, which are subordinate to the Party, will usually not dare to find in favor of environmental activists who bring cases against powerful companies, which are either state owned or well connected to local officials.

Because the Party recognizes that pollution is intrinsically damaging and environmental issues can pose a threat to its hold on power, it has to strike a balance between conflicting priorities. The tolerance of its subjects to its continuance in power depends crucially on a high level of economic growth, but the growing middle class also demands a cleaner environment. NGOs can play a positive role in the struggle for a cleaner environment, but if they grow too powerful, they could be mobilized for political purposes against the Party, as happened in Central and Eastern Europe in the late 1980s. Therefore, they must be kept on a short leash, and no national NGOs can be permitted. News media, laws, and courts could play a positive role also, but they must all be held in subjection to the will of the Party and the interests of Party officials. These are the simple and abiding realities of a one-party dictatorship.

The precise balance struck between the conflicting priorities changes over time. Xi Jinping has staked his political fortunes, and those of the CPC, on a strategy that gives rhetorical prominence to a cleaner environment and promotes legal window dressing. In reality, it reinforces Party dominance over NGOs, the news media, the law, and the courts. He relies on administrative measures and campaigns, carefully and selectively targeted to achieve short-term gains. But he dares not, for instance, impose economic pricing on water, because that would be unpopular and would hurt the vested interests to which the Party long ago sold its soul. For the present, Xi's balancing act keeps him in power, but his rivals know that in a crisis they could exploit the universal recognition of China's environmental catastrophe, as well as the impossibility of effectively tackling it without systemic change, to deliver mortal blows against his political body.

7 *Coronavirus: Cover-up and Costs*

For nations around the world, the COVID-19 coronavirus pandemic has been a test of the health of their body politic, and for their governments it has been a test of transparency, trust, and competence. The eminent authority on constitutional law at Tsinghua University, Xu Zhangrun, has written: "The coronavirus epidemic has revealed the rotten core of Chinese governance; the fragile and vacuous heart of the jittering edifice of the state has thereby been shown up as never before."[1] Viet Thanh Nguyen, a Pulitzer Prize–winning novelist born in Vietnam and raised in the United States, has written of his adoptive country: "If anything good emerges out of this period, it might be an awakening to the pre-existing conditions of our body politic. We were not as healthy as we thought we were. The biological virus afflicting individuals is also a social virus."[2]

On 1 October 2020, the *Scientific American* condemned President Trump's response to the COVID-19 pandemic as "dishonest and inept", and endorsed Joe Biden for President. In its almost 200 years in print the journal had never before made a political statement.[3] The *New England Journal of Medicine*, the world's most prestigious medical magazine, also published an editorial that month, which condemned the Trump administration's handling of the coronavirus pandemic, saying "they have taken a crisis and turned it into a tragedy." In an unprecedented action, it was signed by all thirty-four of the Journal's editors.[4] In November 2020, political analysts commented that this abysmal performance had contributed greatly to Trump's defeat in the presidential election. By contrast, China's use of lockdown on a massive scale seems to have prevented the spread of the virus, in an impressive manner. But it came at great political cost, domestically and internationally.

The story of Li Wenliang, a doctor in the Chinese city of Wuhan who died of the coronavirus on 6 February 2020 at the age of 34, has spread around the globe wherever there is freedom of information. On 30 December, six weeks before his death, he had gone online to warn friends of the strange and deadly virus rampaging through his hospital. For doing that, he was immediately reprimanded and threatened by government authorities, and ordered to cease his warnings. He and seven medical colleagues were condemned on national television (without being named at that stage) for warnings they had issued. As Dali Yang, a professor of Chinese politics at the University of Chicago has commented: "It was truly intimidation of an entire profession."[5] In defiance of the government, Dr. Li started giving interviews to domestic and international media and continued until almost the day of his death. On his deathbed, Dr. Li said that "a healthy society shouldn't have only one voice." He became a hero in China when his health warnings proved to be justified, and a martyr when he died.

Major questions remain over the timeline for the start of the coronavirus epidemic, its development, and the response of the Chinese authorities. I will return to them below, but on 20 January Xi gave the first public warning, and on 23 January, the central government of China imposed a lockdown in Wuhan and other cities in Hubei in an effort to quarantine the center of the outbreak. Thereafter, restrictions of varying intensity were imposed on other areas of China affecting at least 760 million people.[6] The magnitude of these measures convinced a great proportion of the public that the warnings given by Dr. Li and others had been justified, and that the authorities were guilty of delay, denial, and cover-up, allowing the terrible epidemic to develop. A great tide of distrust and indignation surged through social media.

When the news of Dr. Li's death was broadcast, that tide became a *tsunami* of grief and outrage. In a public outcry of unprecedented magnitude, messages expressing these emotions were viewed in China over one billion times.[7] Fewer in number, but equal in political significance, millions of netizens posted messages calling for freedom of speech.[8] Remarkably, these demands were left to circulate uncensored for at least five hours before they were taken down. "Tonight is a monumental moment for our collective conscience," was the judgment of Xu Danei, the founder of a social media analytics company.[9]

The use of the internet to express dissatisfaction or derision has long been a feature of Chinese social media, and every year there are tens of thousands of large-scale physical protests in China, often relating to the environment. But until that night, protesters, both online and offline, had always been careful to confine themselves to a single issue, not linking that issue to a demand for systemic change. After learning of Dr. Li's death, they cast restraint aside. Here is one typical posting: "I am a human being. An independent, lively human being. I deserve to have the most basic human rights. I am a citizen of the People's Republic of China, I deserve to have every right bestowed upon me by the PRC Constitution."

Even before Dr. Li died, China's professors at leading universities had set their own liberty at risk by giving voice to the tide of protest online and in interviews with foreign media. Outstanding among them was Xu Zhangrun, former professor of constitutional law at Tsinghua University, who posted an essay almost nine thousand words long in its English translation, in which he described, denounced, and bewailed the political state of the nation. In 2018 he had been stripped of his rank of professor and banned from teaching for publishing an essay of equal length, in which he had declared: "For thirty years, . . . the political system has seen no substantial or meaningful progress or change." He had warned of the dangers of a return to totalitarianism, one-man rule, a sycophantic bureaucracy, putting politics ahead of professionalism, and the myriad other problems that the system would encounter if it rejected further reforms. As a rare example of an intellectual in China denouncing the nation's contemporary ills, his essay had been widely shared.

Now he was emboldened by what he saw as a "volcanic level of popular fury" to present an equally wide-ranging and hard-hitting essay under the title "Viral Alarm: When Fury Overcomes Fear." He began thus:

> The political life of the nation is in a state of collapse and the ethical core of the system has been hollowed out. The ultimate concern of China's polity today and that of its highest leader is to preserve at all costs the privileged position of the Communist Party and to maintain ruthlessly its hold on power. What they dub "The Broad Masses of People" are nothing more than a taxable unit, a value-bearing cipher in a metrics-based system of social management that is geared towards stability maintenance. Don't

you see that although everyone looks to The One [Xi Jinping] for the nod of approval, The One himself is clueless and has no substantive understanding of rulership and governance, despite his undeniable talent for playing power politics? . . .

Ours is a system in which The Ultimate Arbiter [定於一尊, an imperial-era term used by state media to describe Xi Jinping] monopolizes all effective power. This has led to what I would call "organizational discombobulation" that, in turn, has served to enable a dangerous "systemic impotence" at every level. Thereby, a political culture has been nurtured that, in terms of the actual public good, is ethically bankrupt, for it is one that strains to vouchsafe its privatized party-state, or what they call their "Mountains and Rivers," while abandoning the people over which it holds sway to suffer the vicissitudes of a cruel fate. It is a system that turns every natural disaster into an even greater man-made catastrophe. The coronavirus epidemic has revealed the rotten core of Chinese governance; the fragile and vacuous heart of the jittering edifice of the state has thereby been shown up as never before."

Professor Xu presented his own prescription for restoring the health of the nation:

The way to turn things around, to re-establish the image of China as a responsible major power that can shoulder its global responsibilities, demands that the internal affairs of this country must be sorted out; that can only happen if we as a people join together on the Great Way of Universal Human Values. What is of particular importance is that this nation needs to ground itself substantively in the concept that Sovereignty Resides in the People . . . I believe that the only way for China to end its global and historical isolation and become a meaningful participant in the global system, as well as flourish on the path of national survival and prosperity, is to pursue a politics that embraces constitutional democracy and fosters a true people's republic.[10]

He ended his essay with an impassioned appeal. Beginning with a quotation from the Welsh poet Dylan Thomas, "I will not go gentle into that good night, / Old age should burn and rave at close of day; / Rage, rage against the dying of the light," Xu called on his compatriots to "Rage against this injustice; let your lives burn with a flame of decency; break through the stultifying darkness and welcome the dawn."

Professor Xu's call for constitutional democracy was echoed by Zhang Qianfan, professor of constitutional law at Beijing University, in an article published by the Chinese-language website of the *New York Times*. Under the title "To Prevent and Cure the Virus, China Needs Constitutional Democracy," he wrote: "The Wuhan pneumonia virus has not only caused a national, indeed a global public health crisis, but rather reflected the institutional crisis in China's daily social governance."[11]

Xu Zhiyong, one of China's most prominent human rights lawyers—who, in 2012, had founded the New Citizens Movement, a political movement which tried to facilitate a peaceful transition of China toward constitutionalism—was detained as the expressions of outrage surged. Shortly beforehand he had written a sixty-page letter addressed to Xi Jinping, calling on him to step down. It was released by his friends. Writing half a world away and with an entirely different personal history from my own, he deploys many of the same arguments and voices many of the same criticisms, but expresses them with greater vehemence.[12]

Ren Zhiqiang is a very different man from Xu Zhiyong and Xu Zhangrun. He was born into the hereditary aristocracy of the Communist Party of China, and has been a member of the CPC for decades. He is a friend to some of China's most powerful politicians, most notably Vice President Wang Qishan. He made a fortune from real estate development, while leading a state-run company. But he became a very independent-minded blogger, and his blog on social media used to attract 37 million followers because he dared to criticize the Party. In 2016 he went so far as openly challenge Xi Jinping's view that government media should toe the Party line.[13] Then state-affiliated media accused him of advocating the overthrow of the CPC, and his social media accounts were blocked.

Two months after the coronavirus epidemic was acknowledged by the government, an essay was circulated widely online in private messages that claimed that the actions of a "power-hungry clown" and the Party's strict limits on free speech had exacerbated the epidemic. The writer asserted that a speech made by Xi Jinping on 23 February revealed a "crisis of governance": the Party should "wake up from ignorance" and oust the leaders holding it back, just as it did with the "Gang of Four" in 1976 to end the turmoil of the Cultural Revolution. The clown was not named, but his identity was clearly Xi Jinping. And the author of the article? According to Ren's friends, it was he. Ren vanished and was soon officially reported to be under investigation for "serious violations of discipline and the law." On 22 September 2020, a court in Beijing sentenced him to eighteen years in prison. The court claimed he was guilty of graft, taking bribes, misusing public funds, and abusing his power during and after his time as an executive at a property development company, but his supporters and sympathizers said that his real crime was his attack on Xi and the Party, and his call for radical political change. For Ren, who was sixty-eight years old, an eighteen-year sentence was effectively a life sentence since he would be eighty-six years old at its end, if he survived that long.[14] That Ren should put his freedom, his wealth, and his social position on the line by attacking Xi in such terms suggests that there were deep divisions at the top of the Party. He would not have staked his freedom and fortune if he did not believe that his intervention could affect its outcome. That he failed—in the short term at least—does not prove otherwise. That the Party felt it was necessary to punish a critic so severely demonstrates an extraordinary lack of confidence in its own authority.

A few days after Ren disappeared, a WeChat posting spread widely in China calling for an emergency meeting of the Politburo "to discuss whether Xi Jinping is suitable to continue to be the President of the country, the CCP's General Secretary, and Chairman of the Central Military Commission." The article crisply and clearly outlined a sweeping program of political and economic reforms that amounted to a liberal democratic revolution. It called for a three-person group to organize the meeting consisting of Premier Li Keqiang, Vice Premier Wang Yang, and Vice President Wang Qishan. Alert readers will note the coincidence of the composition of this group with the trio of plotters in chapter 1 of this book, written many months earlier.[15]

Faced with the flood tide of public indignation, censorship could not be enforced with its usual rigor. As a result, some of the most powerful stories about life in quarantined Wuhan and the latest news about the evolution of the outbreak came from mainland newsrooms like that of the magazine *Caixin*, which published results of investigations that showed that the death rate from the virus in Wuhan was much higher than that stated by official sources.

On 27 January and 1 February, the leading social media platform Tencent reported cumulative infection numbers (including both confirmed and suspected cases) ten times higher than the Wuhan authorities had made public. The numbers on Tencent were not taken down for several hours, during which time Chinese netizens snapped screenshots and circulated them around the internet.[16]

Another example of censors going through the motions without exercising effective control was the treatment accorded to an online diary published by Fang Fang, a prominent Chinese writer. On the day Dr. Li died, she posted on her WeChat account the first page of a "Wuhan Diary," in which for the next fifty-seven days she chronicled the sufferings of those around her in the locked-down city. Each day she posted a new installment, and each day it was taken down by the censors—but only after it had been left up long enough to go viral with thousands of re-posts. Fang Fang had already enjoyed 3.5 million followers on social media even before she began chronicling her life during Wuhan's quarantine.[17]

Popular indignation was fueled by accounts of hospitals being flooded with dying patients and appeals by medical workers for protective gear, which were tolerated long enough on social media to be widely circulated before they were taken down.

When a Vice Premier for public health visited Wuhan, residents shouted complaints at her, a highly unusual event. Even more remarkable, a video clip of one resident shouting from her balcony "Everything is fake!" was circulated on social media by the main Party newspaper, the *People's Daily*, tacit acknowledgment that her protest expressed the scepticism of many at the time.[18]

Citizen journalists Chen Qiushi, Fang Bin, and Li Zehua, who tried to report freely about the situation in Wuhan, were more exposed. All three were "disappeared."

Was the tidal wave of popular outrage and extreme denunciations by scholars and activists justified by the facts of the situation? Were Party leaders really guilty of cover-up, denial, and deception? And if so, to what extent? The answers to those questions are of crucial importance to the people of China, but also to the rest of the world, which could have prepared better for the pandemic if it had known its true gravity earlier.

On 30 December, Wuhan Municipal Health Commission issued two urgent announcements concerning "an unknown pneumonia" and the existence of just four cases. That was the day that Dr. Li Wenliang issued to friends his warning of a deadly virus rampaging through his hospital. As we have seen, he was immediately reprimanded and ordered to give no further warnings. In the next three weeks the public was given no further official warning concerning the virus. Then, on 20 January, Xi Jinping publicly declared that "the recent outbreak of novel coronavirus pneumonia in Wuhan and other places must be taken seriously." He did not say that it could be transmitted from human to human. However, on the same day the head of China's National Health Commission gave the first official confirmation that it could be so transmitted.

By 21 January the total number of people officially declared to have died of the coronavirus in Wuhan was only six, there were only 309 confirmed cases in the whole of China, and the Chinese authorities professed to be confident of being able to control the outbreak. Then, on 23 January, out of the blue, the Chinese government began the lockdown which, beginning in Wuhan, was eventually extended to cover 760 million people. The magnitude of the lockdown relative to the number of deaths and confirmed cases announced seemed wildly disproportionate.[19]

How, when, and where had the epidemic (as it was by then being referred to by international media) developed, what had the Chinese authorities known about it and what had they done about it?

As of this writing, the consensus among experts is that the coronavirus originated in bats and was transmitted to humans, possibly via another animal. According to Chinese government data, the first case may have been a man from Hubei Province, in which Wuhan is situated, and the date is recorded as 17 November 2019.[20] What happened between then and mid January to lead the Chinese government to impose the massive lockdown?

As early as late November, US intelligence officials were warning that a contagion was sweeping through China's Wuhan region, changing the patterns of life and business and posing a threat to the population. The warnings came first from the National Center for Medical Intelligence (NCMI), a component of the US Defense Intelligence Agency, whose mission is to monitor, track, and assess a full range of global health events that could negatively impact the health of US military and civilian populations. Reports such as this are the result of analysis of satellite imagery intelligence, human intelligence, and signals intelligence. In early January 2020, after weeks of vetting and analysis, including by area and subject specialists, a detailed account of findings appeared in the US president's daily brief of intelligence matters. The intelligence briefings said China's leadership knew the epidemic was out of control.

A study co-led by Lucia Dunn, economics professor at Ohio State University, and Mai He, pathology professor at Washington University School of Medicine in St. Louis, Missouri, has stated that infection numbers revealed on Tencent in late January imply that the coronavirus began to spread in October or even late September 2019, which would be consistent with the NCMI findings.[21] Scientists at the University of London analyzed the genome of more than seven thousand five hundred SARS CoV-2 viruses from people who had COVID-19. They concluded that the virus spread from animal to human in late 2019, with the first case as early as 6 October.[22] The account of the NCMI warnings, published on 9 April by investigative reporters of ABC News, was refuted immediately by the Pentagon. But it was refuted in terms that failed to convince.[23] The picture that the account gave of developments in China is supported by the studies referred to in this paragraph, by a surge in traffic outside five hospitals in Wuhan from late August to December coinciding with a surge in online searches for words associated with the symptoms of coronavirus on the Chinese search engine Baidu, and by evidence of a mass exodus from the city.[24]

Beginning in mid December, people left Wuhan in their thousands, tens of thousands, and then hundreds of thousands, until by 23 January the cumulative total had reached millions. According to the city's mayor, speaking on national television, five million people left Wuhan in the three weeks before the city was locked down on 23 January with just seven hours' notice of the transportation lockdown.[25] According to Wuhan city statistics, some three million of these can be explained by people returning to their home cities or villages to celebrate the Lunar New Year, as they do each year, but that leaves two million more unaccounted for.

An investigation by the Beijing-based magazine *Caixin*, which manages to undertake investigations with a degree of independence, revealed that the results of tests carried out in December by several labs in genomic companies indicated that a highly infectious virus had broken out in Wuhan.

In the following days, genomics company executives paid a visit to Wuhan to discuss their findings with local hospital officials and disease control authorities. According to *Caixin*, "there was an intensive and confidential investigation underway, and officials from the hospital and disease control centre had acknowledged many similar patients." The results from the lab tests were fed into an infectious disease control system that was designed to alert China's top health officials and political leaders about outbreaks. It is inconceivable that the alerts were not conveyed to the highest political level; that is, Xi Jinping and the Politburo.[26]

As a member state of the World Health Organization, China is bound by the International Health Regulations of 2007, of which article 6 says that "each State Party shall notify the World Health Organization . . . within 24 hours . . . of all events which may constitute a public health emergency of international concern within its territory. . . . " Annex 2 of those same rules provides that countries must notify the WHO of any unusual or unexpected public health events such as occurrences of severe acute respiratory syndrome (SARS), caused by a close genetic cousin of the coronavirus that causes COVID-19.

But instead of acknowledging the outbreak, warning people of it, and advising them on how to protect themselves, the authorities withheld the information from their own people and from the world at large.

When the Wuhan Municipal Health Commission informed the WHO of the outbreak on 31 December, it insisted that it had no evidence of human-to-human transmission. The next day, the Hubei Provincial Health Commission issued an order to the genomics company that had sequenced the virus's genetic code in December finding suggestions of a highly infectious virus similar to the SARS of 2002–2004. The company was to stop lab testing of samples from Wuhan related to the new disease and destroy all existing samples. Test results and information about the tests were not to be made public, and any future results were to be reported only to the authorities.[27]

Relying on its own sources of information, the government of Taiwan concluded at that time that a contagious new respiratory illness had broken out in China and on 31 December began monitoring incoming passengers from Wuhan.[28]

There is abundant evidence that the suppression of information in the weeks that followed was a policy dictated at the national level, not the local level. On 3 January 2020, China's top health authority, the National Health Commission (NHC), ordered institutions not to publish any information related to the unknown disease and ordered labs to transfer any samples they had to designated testing institutions, or to destroy them. The order, which *Caixin* saw, did not specify any designated testing institutions.[29]

When Dr. Li Wenliang and others sounded the first alarm, they were quickly denounced on national television (and not only on local Wuhan channels). Social media censors received orders to block online discussion of the virus. Their instructions were to delete posts that mentioned a list of coronavirus-related terms, including "Wuhan unknown pneumonia" and "unknown SARS."[30]

On 6 January the US Centers for Disease Control and Prevention (CDC) offered to send a team to assist the Chinese authorities; it never received permission to enter the country.

On 14 January the head of China's NHC laid out a grim assessment of the situation in a confidential teleconference with provincial health officials. A memo of the conference warned: "The risk of transmission and spread is high. All localities must prepare for and respond to a pandemic." The commission issued a sixty-three-page document on response procedures. But the document was labeled "internal," and "not to be publicly disclosed."[31] To its own people and to the world community, the government was still in denial of human-to-human transmission, leading the WHO to issue a statement stressing that Chinese authorities had recorded no cases of human-to-human transmission.

Yet only six days later, China would finally acknowledge that transmissibility, and nine days later it would begin a lockdown that would extend to 760 million of its own people. That admission and that action would come too late for the more than 800,000 who would die outside the country in the next six months, or to mitigate the suffering that would be caused by the greatest depression in the world economy since 1929.

Xi Jinping is on public record as claiming that by 7 January he was leading a national effort to contain the epidemic. That means he was personally responsible from at least that date for the policy of cover-up and then restricted disclosure.

Caixin focused a second investigation on testing the veracity of official statistics on deaths from the coronavirus in the city. To do so, it looked into the operation of crematoria in Wuhan. It found that they had been working nineteen hours a day throughout the peak period of the epidemic. At that rate, and given their capacity, they must have cremated a total number of bodies far exceeding the officially published number of deaths in the city.[32]

Taking *Caixin's* findings as her starting point, the editor of *China Change,* an online publication based in the United States, carefully estimated the true number of deaths and confirmed cases in Wuhan. In making her calculations, Yaxue Cao also drew on leaked official documents and an abundance of eyewitness accounts, many of which were posted on social media. She also drew attention to striking inconsistencies in publicly available information. For instance, she pointed out that the megacity of Wuhan has one of the best-resourced health systems in China, with over one hundred thousand health-care workers, which should have been able to cope with the limited number of cases acknowledged by the city (a cumulative total of fifty thousand cases over four months), whereas state media reported that forty thousand extra health-care workers were drafted in from all over the country. Cao quoted the comment of a Weibo user, "Living in this land, you only have to have elementary school math to separate lies and facts."

The disparity between official figures and reality was sometimes precisely measurable, based on leaked documents. For instance, according to a leaked internal briefing, more than eleven hundred health-care workers in Wuhan had been infected by 18 January, whereas the Wuhan Health Commission reported on 21 January that there had been only fifteen such cases.[33]

Whereas Wuhan Municipal Health Commission reported a total of 50,008 coronavirus cases and 2,575 deaths as of 9 April 2020, Cao put the total number of cases at between 400,000 and 600,000, and the death toll between 22,000 and 30,000, about ten times greater than the NHC's numbers.[34] On 17 April, the Commission revised its figure for deaths upward to 3,869, but this is still about seven times less than Cao's estimate.[35]

In another very detailed study published in early April, entitled *Estimating the True Number of China's COVID-19 Cases,* Derek Scissors, a resident scholar at the American Enterprise Institute, estimated conservatively that the true number of cases (not deaths) outside of Wuhan City and Hubei Province was one hundred or more times greater than that shown by official statistics. He believed that the migrant outflow from Wuhan caused 2.9 million cases as compared to the fifteen thousand cases announced by the Chinese authorities. He showed that it would not have been hard for the authorities to hide this number of cases in the far larger number of Chinese respiratory illnesses of all kinds, which could easily exceed 100 million. This is how he concluded his article: "Getting to 2.9 million cases starts with information offered by state media, uses the lowest available infection rate, applies days in circulation with a deliberately reduced figure to reflect a superior Chinese virus response, then stirs in the 1.39 billion people. Or you can believe that 1.2 million travelers from ground zero of a pandemic, some freely circulating for weeks, resulted in national contagion of a little over 15,000 cases."[36]

The lack of statistical transparency in China was illustrated by the complete absence of published figures for testing for the coronavirus. This was in total disregard of the WHO's insistence that "diagnostic testing for COVID-19 is critical to tracking the virus, understanding epidemiology, informing case management, and to suppressing transmission."[37] It is also in dramatic contrast with the strategies pursued by neighboring Taiwan and South Korea, both of which performed outstandingly well in dealing with the epidemic. Having studied the SARS epidemic of 2002–2004, they understood the importance of testing and tracing. As of 8 September 2020, there had been seven deaths and 495 confirmed cases in the twenty-three million people on Taiwan, and 341 deaths and 21,432 cases in the fifty-two million people of South Korea.[38] These countries have shown that democratic, open societies can handle such a challenge with superb efficiency, without massive lockdowns, without economic damage, and without infringing the human rights of their citizens.

When the authorities began to ease the lockdown in China in March, they redoubled their efforts to control the narrative of the epidemic at home and abroad. At home, the instruments of totalitarian control enabled them to recover control of the published narrative, but it was a hollow victory. The damage done by the cover-up, denial, and lying in the early phases of the epidemic to the authority of the Party and its leader Xi Jinping cannot be undone. Millions of people have made the connection between the systemic denial of freedom of expression and the damage done to society by its consequences. An entire generation of young people from whom the history of the 1989 democracy movement and its crushing has been hidden has learned firsthand about the regime's treatment of historical truth. But that is not all. A regime that depends upon fostering a belief that it is the Master of the Universe, that it can control everything, even the natural world, has been shown to be at the mercy of a pandemic that spread across the world to cause an economic catastrophe. How the effects of all this play out politically will depend to a large degree on how well China is able to recover from the economic shock, but the damage is irreparable.

The same is true internationally, with the difference that China's rulers cannot control the narrative abroad as they do at home. As the pandemic raged through first Europe and then the United States, its effects were felt not only in the public health and economic fields but also in geopolitics. In America, distrust and hostility were reinforced. In Europe, which had been gradually awakening before the pandemic to the dangers posed by predatory investment and economic coercion by China, the coronavirus pandemic accelerated the process. This was most starkly illustrated in the United Kingdom, where before the coronavirus the British government had been willing to damage its "special relationship" with the United States by allowing Huawei to supply much of its non-core 5G telecommunications network. In the midst of the crisis, the government signaled that it would reconsider policy and yield to US warnings and the strong body of opinion among "back-bench" Conservative Members of Parliament, who were fiercely opposed to this policy.[39]

The Party's diplomatic and propaganda machines worked hard to counter this trend. Large quantities of testing kits and protective masks were delivered to Europe, but the initiative backfired when, in country after country, millions of them were proven to be defective. Foreign Ministry Spokesman Zhao Lijian, dubbed the "wolf warrior" diplomat,[40] floated the idea that the virus had not originated in China but been brought there by US military personnel; he posted this to his three hundred thousand followers on Twitter, but the canard failed to fly abroad.[41] The failure of these efforts was acknowledged internally when a report, presented in April by the Ministry of State Security to the Party's most senior leaders, concluded that global anti-China sentiment was at its highest since the 1989 Tiananmen Square crackdown.[42]

The incompetence displayed by some liberal democracies in handling the coronavirus has been a valuable gift to China's rulers, helping them deflect criticism of their own performance and their political system. President Trump was the supreme example of this, and the disarray of the US federal government led to the unnecessary and tragic loss of lives on a very large scale. But there was nothing comparable to the *tsunami* of grief and outrage that was generated in China by the silencing and then death of Dr. Li Wenliang, and the American people had the opportunity to pass judgment on Trump and his administration in the presidential election in November 2020.

The historical significance for China of the coronavirus pandemic is that it exposed for all to see just how a totalitarian regime handles such a challenge. The overall priority is survival of the regime, and every other consideration is subordinate to that. Because its survival depends not on trust but on control, mastery of the narrative is crucial. The aura of omnipotence and omniscience must be preserved; the popular belief that the Party can control everything, including fatal diseases, must be sustained. Because truth has no value in and of itself to the regime, officials have not the slightest compunction about engaging in cover-up, denial, and lying. They can distinguish between truth and falsehood, but truth has no moral superiority because morality is just another factor in the political calculus.

Saving lives matters, of course, but the lives of the people have no value in and of themselves, or as Xu Zhangrun put it in the words quoted above: "The ultimate concern of China's polity today and that of its highest leader is to preserve at all costs the privileged position of the Communist Party and to maintain ruthlessly its hold on power. What they dub 'The Broad Masses of People' are nothing more than a taxable unit, a value-bearing cipher in a metrics-based system of social management that is geared towards stability maintenance."

It is important to recognize that the rulers of a totalitarian regime act in this way not because of strategic choices they make as the crisis unfolds. Rather, they are prisoners of a system which dictates that at every stage their overriding priority is the survival of the regime they serve. Their only power of decision is over how best to safeguard the Party's dictatorship. For governments, institutions, or commentators around the world to hope that the

Chinese communist regime may be brought to act in future in a way that is fundamentally different is utter folly.

When an unknown contagion spread in Wuhan in the fall of 2019, and the number of cases brought it to the attention of the city's public health officials, they no doubt sought to identify it, monitor it, and report it through confidential channels to the national level in a timely manner. But the more serious the situation looked, the more sensitive information about it became, and the tighter the controls they imposed to prevent information about it becoming public. Whereas in a liberal democracy, news media are incentivized to expose and report news that is unwelcome to their rulers, in a totalitarian system the opposite is true. Moreover, the people of Wuhan were not seen as an ally in the effort to trace, monitor, and control the virus, but a population to be controlled like the virus—until the efforts at suppression were overwhelmed by the forces of nature. Some very senior Chinese disease control officials displayed a sense of international professional responsibility: they took the risk of informing their foreign counterparts. International scientists agree that Chinese scientists detected and sequenced the then-unknown pathogen with astonishing speed, but political leaders were viscerally opposed to sharing information internationally, unless and until they could do so from a position of strength, having brought the epidemic under control, in reality or in presentational terms. For them, there could be no question of accepting help from a political rival such as the US government. As the forces of nature threatened to overwhelm them, they brought into play the instruments of centralized control that permitted them to lock down, to varying degrees, 760 million people, hide the true number of cases and deaths, and proclaim that their handling of the epidemic demonstrated the superiority of their political system.

As of this writing, the story is far from over. In China, as elsewhere, there is fear of a second wave of infections, and the challenge of dealing with the economic impact of the lockdown, and the social consequences flowing therefrom, has only just begun. According to the IMF, policy makers in China have reacted very strongly to the outbreak of the crisis, using monetary and fiscal policy to reduce the impact of the virus on vital sectors of the economy and to support recovery. By April 2020 they had announced fiscal measures of around 3 percent of GDP and had more room for both monetary and fiscal policies, if need arose. Even allowing for the impact of the lockdown, the IMF expected the economy to grow by 1.2 percent in 2020, and by a much faster rate, 9.2 percent, in 2021.

The massive lockdown, the reassertion of censorship, and police controls have enabled the regime to weather the storm so far and embolden it to claim to have shown the world how to cope with the pandemic. But an economy already hugely overburdened by debt has taken on more, and a highly vulnerable financial system has been put under greater strain. A large number of people have lost their jobs in a society without an adequate welfare system. China's export markets have been badly hit, and the domestic property market is unlikely to make a strong recovery. Trust between rulers and ruled, already in short supply before, has been further eroded, and the regime's aura of omniscience and omnipotence greatly dimmed. That is as true for Xi Jinping personally as it is for the regime as a whole, indeed more so. His public appearances and travel in early and mid January showed no indication that he took aggressive actions to contain the outbreak after he had been notified of a new mysterious virus in Wuhan.[43] Instead of making public appearances to assure the nation he was leading the effort to control the virus, he was virtually invisible for four weeks when the crisis in Wuhan was at its height, and he waited two months before visiting that city. When he did so, his visit was stage-managed to an embarrassing degree, as was revealed by a video posted on social media.[44]

Now displays of bravado by the regime multiply, but those who look into the future with deeper knowledge know that China's problems have not been solved, they have been intensified. The physical virus may have been contained, for now, but the political sickness has spread further and deepened.

8   *America and the Fate of Xi*

Under Xi's leadership, the Communist Party of China is set on a collision course with the United States. Some in China's elite understand this, but the totalitarian nature of the regime makes a radical change of course impossible.

Republican Senator Marco Rubio is in the vanguard of an awakening to the real nature of the threat the CPC poses to the world order that the United States and its allies have built since 1945. In October 2018, he told a gathering of some of America's largest, most innovative companies that China is "the most comprehensive threat to our country that it has ever faced." He saw an imbalance in relations between America and China that, if left unaddressed, would "inevitably lead to very dangerous conflict." In a later speech, he said: "This century will be defined by the relationship between the United States and China. And it will either be the story of an unfair and unbalanced relationship that led to the decline of a once great beacon of liberty and prosperity. Or it will be the story of a stable, balanced, and sustainable relationship that allowed us to further and protect our national interest and the common good of our people."[1] Rubio has been giving strong warnings on China since at least 2015. Neoconservative commentators and analysts like William Kristol and Robert Kagan had argued as early as 1996 for "an overall strategy for containing, influencing, and ultimately seeking to change the regime in Beijing," but their calls had fallen on deaf ears in the climate of optimism which then prevailed under President Clinton.[2] Under President Obama, disillusion with the political fruits of America's engagement began to set in, but, as noted earlier, his "pivot to Asia" remained largely symbolic. Under Trump the awakening spelled out by Rubio became evident across the American political spectrum, in Congress, the executive branch of government, the news media, universities and think tanks, and in business.

At about the same time as Rubio gave his warning, US Vice President Mike Pence summed up the sea change in the US stance toward China in a major, set-piece speech:

America had hoped that economic liberalization would bring China into a greater partnership with us and with the world. Instead, China has chosen economic aggression, which has in turn emboldened its growing military.

Nor, as we had hoped, has Beijing moved toward greater freedom for its own people. For a time, Beijing inched toward greater liberty and respect for human rights. But in recent years, China has taken a sharp U-turn toward control and oppression of its own people. Today, China has built an unparalleled surveillance state.[3]

In November 2019, when the *New York Times* published details of a 403-page collection of internal Party documents on its policy on Xinjiang, it commented that the documents revealed "the paranoia of totalitarian leaders who demand total fealty in thought and deed and recognize no method of control other than coercion and fear."[4]

Both Republican and Democratic lawmakers have condemned the Party's policies in Xinjiang as "de facto cultural genocide."

Daniel Tobin, a China specialist at the US National Intelligence University, told Congress in March 2020: "The ambitions articulated by Xi Jinping at the 19th Party Congress [in 2017] underscore that Washington and its allies face a global, strategic rivalry driven as much by ideology and values embodied in competing domestic governance systems as by perceptions of changing power dynamics. While this rivalry differs in many respects from the Cold War, one of the most important differences is that it is a competition to define the rules and norms that will govern an integrated, deeply connected world rather than a world divided into competing camps."[5]

The fundamental reconsideration of American strategy indicated by Vice President Pence's speech in 2018 was set out more fully two years later in a sixteen-page policy document issued by the White House with the President's authority entitled *United States Strategic Approach to the People's Republic of China*.[6]

The Awakening of America has resulted in a new global struggle that is being fought not with armed force but with economic power and cyber weapons. Hostilities have not yet reached full scale, but major offensives have been launched.

For Xi Jinping, control, not trust, is the key to security abroad as it is at home. Control, not political revolution, is the objective. Xi is implacably opposed to reform of China's political system but knows that the regime he heads does not enjoy true popular support. The unspoken deal with the people, "We let you make money, you let us rule," on which the regime has long relied for popular tolerance of its rule is losing its potency as the economy falters, and for it he has substituted chauvinism.

As soon as Xi became the Party leader in 2012, he abandoned the cautious, low-profile strategy devised by Deng Xiaoping for dealing with the outside world. He made clear the regime's hostility to universal values and its determination to further restrict the flow of ideas, values, and information into China.

His decision to adopt a more assertive strategy appears to have been based on the following reasoning. The global financial crisis of 2008 had inflicted extreme and lasting damage on the United States and its liberal democratic allies, who were already in relative decline vis-à-vis China. The combination of Leninist control and a dynamic private sector was enabling China to rise fast as liberal democracy declined, and Leninist control was being reinforced by the application of new technologies.

Xi believed the "China model" could marshal the resources needed to achieve world leadership in those technologies that would be decisive in the competition for global supremacy in the mid twenty-first century, including next-generation information technology and telecommunications, advanced robotics, and artificial intelligence. These technologies form part of a ten-part program known as "Made in China 2025." By 2025, China aims to achieve 70 percent self-sufficiency in these high-tech industries, and by 2049—the hundredth anniversary of the People's Republic of China—it seeks a dominant position in global markets. By then, the world will have progressed to a fourth industrial revolution, at the heart of which will be 5G technology, which is expected to be up to a hundred times faster than current wireless technology and will lead to a whole new Internet of Things, in which all things will be connected. For Xi, attainment of the goals of "Made in China 2025" would mean the nation was realizing his China Dream. For liberal democrats, it evokes a vision of a world dominated by an unreformed totalitarian regime.

How strong is Xi Jinping's reasoning?

It is grounded on some major developments in the real world. The global financial crisis indeed shook the advanced industrial economies to their foundations. There was continuing deadlock in Washington between Republicans and Democrats; the Arab Spring had yielded only one new democracy, in little Tunisia; European democracies seemed only too ready to subordinate their liberal values to their supposed economic interests in dealing with China. Obama's reluctance to apply American hard power around the world looked like weakness. China had been acquiring advanced technologies needed to achieve its goals by fair means and foul for years without the United States and its allies daring to resist or retaliate. China's growing assertiveness, such as the militarization of the South China Sea, had prompted from the United States nothing more than a "Pivot to Asia" strategy that was largely symbolic.

But if Xi believed the crisis had inflicted extreme and lasting damage on the US economy, he was mistaken. After a short, sharp recession, 2009 saw the beginning of the longest period of economic growth in the history of America. By contrast, China saw its growth rate decline from 12 percent in 2009 to a little over 6 percent in 2019. As we saw in chapter 3, "The Looming Economic Crisis," a decade of credit growth left the nation with a debt mountain of such proportions that economists at home and abroad fear China may suffer the next financial crash. Like all major economies, the United States and China are suffering from the deep recession caused by the coronavirus pandemic, but having entered this recession with an economy deemed by Xi Jinping to be "unbalanced, uncoordinated and unsustainable," China is less able to withstand the shock.[7]

If the economic premise of Xi's reasoning was defective, the political premise that liberal democracy would continue to sleepwalk in the face of the rise of China was proved wrong when Trump succeeded Obama. What has caused the sea change in US attitudes toward China?

The US and other governments do not object to China's economic growth, nor to the technological progress at which its "Made in China 2025" is aiming. They object to some of the methods the regime is using to pursue these ambitions of growth and advanced technology, and some of the uses to which they are being put.

Under Xi's leadership, China's acquisition of advanced technology makes use of the forced transfer of intellectual property from foreign companies to Chinese joint-venture partners. Foreign companies complain that to invest or do business in China, they must enter into joint ventures with Chinese firms under terms that require them to share sensitive intellectual property and advanced technological know-how.

Foreign governments also complain that the Chinese state engages both covertly and openly in practices, such as state subsidies and protectionism, that either contravene its obligations as a member of the World Trade Organization or breach the spirit of WTO rules while technically conforming to them. China has in effect engineered a huge asymmetry: it is free to invest in foreign countries, but foreign companies selling to and operating in China are either barred outright—like Google, Facebook, and Twitter—or highly constrained by investment requirements and other regulations. Its subsidies skew markets and lead to overproduction and the dumping of cheap products in the global market.[8]

The final component of the strategy on which Xi relies to enable China to achieve a dominant position in high technology is state-sponsored theft, including classic espionage and cyber theft, of industrial and commercial secrets from major partners in trade and investment, on a scale unprecedented in world history.

The Chinese telecommunications manufacturer, Huawei, provides one important illustration of Xi's strategy in practice. It is widely recognized as the global leader in the application of 5G technology. The African Union installed Huawei servers in its headquarters, in Addis Ababa, only to discover that those servers had been sending sensitive data back to China every evening. (Under Chinese law, all Chinese companies must accept instructions from the state.) Huawei is constructing a global network of undersea internet cables and next-generation mobile networks that some experts believe could give China effective control of the digital commanding heights.[9] This would have far-reaching implications for the possibility of data theft, surveillance, the invasion of privacy, and social and political control.

China's track record on cyber theft prompted Obama to seek and obtain from President Xi in September 2015 mutual assurances that "neither country's government would conduct or knowingly support cyber-enabled theft of intellectual property, including trade secrets or other confidential business information, with the intent of providing competitive advantages to companies or commercial sectors."[10] China broke its word. In the seven years from 2011 to 2018, more than 90 percent of the cases by the US Department of Justice that alleged economic espionage by or to benefit a state involved China. According to the report, the objective of the Chinese government was "Rob, replicate, and replace. Rob the American company of its intellectual property, replicate the technology, and replace the American company in the Chinese market and, one day, the global market." This strategy required the

Chinese government to pass on fruits of its espionage to Chinese companies, whether state-owned or private.[11]

The sea change in Washington owed something to a change of political leadership. When Donald Trump came to office in 2017, US policy changed rapidly. Numerous currents that had been gathering strength beneath the surface in different fields of American life emerged. The president himself proved keen to maintain a friendly relationship with Xi, but under his leadership the administration adopted much tougher policies, starting with the tariff war. Departments of the executive branch that had chafed at the bit for years under the ultra-cautious Obama found they had freedom to act on the information they had been gathering and the judgments they had formed.

In Congress a bipartisan consensus quickly formed in favor of a much more robust stance toward China, led by people like Senator Rubio. Even US corporations, which for thirty years had brought massive influence to bear on successive administrations to subordinate concern over human rights to their interest in trade and investment, began to take the view that the Chinese state had taken advantage of them, failed to reciprocate their goodwill, and systematically developed a one-sided relationship.

The proposition that economic reform would eventually lead to political reform became harder to defend as economic reform stalled and political repression intensified. A more assertive policy in the East China and South China Seas, especially the militarization of the islands China controls or has created, antagonized China's major partners in trade and investment—the United States and Japan—and its neighbors in East and Southeast Asia. In September 2015, Xi gave assurances to Obama that China would not pursue a policy of militarization of islands in the South China

Sea, but satellite images released only thirteen months later showed, for the first time, evidence of military point-defense capabilities (short-range and close-in weaponry) on various China-controlled features in the Spratly Islands.[12] Xi's rejection of the July 2016 judgment of the tribunal held in The Hague over the Scarborough Shoal dramatized his defiance of international law.

Since June 2019, China's relations with the United States and its allies have deteriorated dramatically over Hong Kong. The Basic Law of the Hong Kong Special Administrative Region of China is a national law of China that serves as the de facto constitution of the Hong Kong Special Administrative Region. It was enacted under the Constitution of China to implement the Sino-British Joint Declaration of 1984, a legally binding international treaty. Both the Basic Law and the joint declaration laid out the basic policies of China on Hong Kong, including the "one country, two systems" principle, under which the governance and economic system practiced in mainland China were not to be extended to Hong Kong before 2047. The pledges made by China include the right to freedom of expression, an independent judiciary, and the rule of law. In May 2020, the National People's Congress imposed a "national security law" on Hong Kong. This was widely interpreted by Hong Kong citizens and the governments of the United States and its allies as a violation of the "one country, two systems" principle, and as the termination of the high degree of autonomy for Hong Kong stipulated in the Sino-British Joint Declaration and the Basic Law. A US law requires the executive branch to report annually on the state of autonomy in Hong Kong, and therefore whether Hong Kong should continue to enjoy privileged access to the US market.[13] On 27 May 2020, Secretary of State Mike Pompeo declared Hong Kong "no longer autonomous," putting its special designation into uncertainty.[14] Britain reacted by declaring that it would grant a right to live and work in the United Kingdom to any of the nearly 3 million Hong Kong citizens (40% of the population) who were eligible for a British National Overseas passport.[15]

The decision by Beijing to impose a national security law on Hong Kong came after a year of confrontation between the Hong Kong government and the defenders of the territory's autonomy. In June 2019 the Hong Kong government tried to introduce legislation that would allow extraditions to mainland China. Critics said the Beijing-endorsed bill would allow the Chinese government to crack down on political opponents by subjecting them to the mainland's legal system. In a single day, two million people, 30 percent of the population, joined in a mass demonstration against the bill, forcing the government to suspend the legislation. When the government refused to declare that it would formally withdraw the bill, Hongkongers widened their demands to include election of the chief executive of the government by universal suffrage. Xi Jinping warned: "Anyone who attempts to split any region from China will perish, with their bodies smashed and bones ground to powder."[16] The intransigence of the central government led to violent confrontations between protesters and police, and to a sweeping victory for pro-democracy candidates in local elections. The defiance of the Hong Kong David in the face of the Goliath of the central government drew the attention of the world. The actions of China's Communist leaders in Hong Kong demonstrated in a most dramatic way the truth of Robert Conquest's definition of a totalitarian state as one that recognizes no limits to its authority in any sphere of public or private life and that extends that authority to whatever length feasible.

Just as Beijing's disregard for the doctrine of "one country, two systems" in Hong Kong contributed to the change in attitudes in the US Congress, so did its strategy toward Taiwan. Rhetorically, Beijing has long looked forward to the day when both territories would "return to the motherland." But in fact, Xi Jinping's refusal to engage in political reform at home and his reinforcement of oppression have led to the inexorable growth of alienation from his regime of the people of both territories.

The US Taiwan Relations Act requires the United States to have a policy "to provide Taiwan with arms of a defensive character," and "to maintain the capacity of the United States to resist any resort to force or other forms of coercion that would jeopardize the security, or the social or economic system, of the people on Taiwan." The readiness of the US Congress (and the executive branch) to fulfill America's obligations toward Taiwan has been strengthened by the robust, multi-party democracy and the rule of law in Taiwan developed and sustained since 1987.

The handling of the coronavirus epidemic by China's rulers powerfully reinforced American distrust of them. The awakening of America to the threat from China prompted institutions and individuals across the board from Congress to the executive branch to think tanks and universities to develop initiatives and strategies for responding to it. What began as a trade war quickly moved beyond that. National security considerations led to the blocking of Huawei to the US telecommunications market, and the tightening of restrictions on Chinese acquisition of sensitive technologies through exports or the purchase of companies. Universities began to question whether they should permit Confucius Institutes, which are ultimately controlled by the CPC, to operate on their campuses. In 2018 a bill was introduced into the US Congress to address human rights abuses in Xinjiang; one of its clauses sought to impose targeted sanctions on officials credibly alleged to be responsible for such abuses.

Most important was the move from a trade war to an economic war. Vice President Pence was correct to show, in the speech quoted earlier, that it was China that had opened hostilities by adopting a strategy of "economic aggression." Now America began to think and act in terms of economic warfare. It was based on recognition of where the true fighting strength of the United States and other liberal economies lies, above all in the markets for capital and currencies. The United States and the United Kingdom offer the greatest markets for capital in the world, and the US dollar is by far the most important global reserve currency. The US government had demonstrated in the cases of Russia, Iran, and North Korea that it possessed the power and the will to use denial of access to these markets to inflict great, even mortal, damage on companies and banks.

In June 2019, Senator Rubio and colleagues introduced legislation that would increase oversight of Chinese companies listed on American stock exchanges and make mandatory the delisting of those that fail to comply with the new requirements within three years. Days later, Rubio queried US index compiler MSCI about its addition of domestic Chinese stocks to its global indexes, saying it risked exposing American investors to corporate fraud. Other voices demanded that the US Treasury restrict US pension funds and other such asset managers from investing in Chinese companies, or at least blacklist state-owned ones. Such moves would represent a major new front of an economic war with China.

Beijing could not effectively reciprocate in kind because it invests comparatively tiny sums of Chinese money in overseas stocks due to its capital controls. If China responded by selling US Treasury bills, notes, and other bonds, any subsequent fall in the price of those securities would devalue China's remaining holding of them, and there would be no satisfactory alternative investment for its funds. China's holdings accounted for no more than 7 percent of outstanding US Treasuries in 2019, and the US bond market is liquid enough to absorb even aggressive selling.

The Chinese leadership could also face internal pressure in the case of such dramatic capital market conflict. If the most extreme sanctions were to gain traction, those who have gained most from China's economic rise would suddenly find their assets effectively frozen offshore or remitted back onshore. It surely would play badly for Xi if the Chinese elites were thus left substantially poorer and shackled within the nation's financial system.

As Joe Biden prepared to take office after winning the presidential election in November 2020, the evidence of his own pronouncements as the Democratic candidate and the Democrats' foreign policy document for the presidential and Congressional election campaigns showed that the incoming administration would not soften American policy towards China. A key passage from the policy paper read: "We will work with our allies to mobilize more than half the world's economy to stand up to China and negotiate from the strongest possible position."[17]

As the extent of the US reappraisal of its China policy became ever more evident, signs appeared that members of the Chinese elite, both within the CPC and in business, were asking far-reaching questions about Sino-American relations, and even about the fundamental policies of the Party.

What was the true balance of forces—political, economical and military—between China and the United States?

Given that no state ruled by an 'authoritarian' regime—let alone a totalitarian one—had yet escaped the middle-income trap, except some oil-rich economies, how realistic were the goals of Xi's China Dream?

If the US pursued decoupling of the two economies, how self-reliant could China become? What would be the impact on the "Made in China 2025" program? A Leninist state could direct funds at high-priority projects, as the Soviets had done with their Sputnik program, but none had ever created a comprehensive, enabling environment for innovation such as exists in the United States.

The Party could assert its authority over even the largest private sector companies like Alibaba, whose founder Jack Ma had suddenly and inexplicably taken early retirement, but how strongly would they support Xi if his policies led the United States to deny them access to its capital markets?

China had garnered a rich harvest of advanced technologies and data by the various means, legitimate and otherwise, as described previously, but had the Great Awakening of America rendered that strategy counterproductive?

What was the ultimate objective of the emerging US strategy? Was it simply a fairer deal in economic relations and reciprocity in cultural exchanges and treatment of journalists? Or was it regime change such as President Reagan had achieved in the Soviet Union in the 1980s?

These are the kinds of questions that were surely being asked behind closed doors when Zhang Weiying, liberal-minded professor of economics at Peking University, gave the lecture described in chapter 3. And these questions were reflected in the fundamental questions he raised, albeit in cautious terms.[18]

Since Xi had very publicly centralized authority in his own hands, questions about the formulation and handling of Sino-American relations were questions about his own judgment and competence. But the questions went well beyond Sino-American relations. As Professor Zhang said, the trade war not only reflected conflict between China and the United States, but between China and the larger Western world. It also went beyond trade to reflect the clash over value systems, he said. For "value systems," read "political systems"; prudence inhibited him from putting it that way, but that was what he meant.

Chinese intellectuals like Zhang understand that fundamentally, in the realm of politics, there is no "Chinese exceptionalism." To understand China's totalitarian regime, it is helpful to study how the totalitarian regime of the Soviet Union worked. The penultimate premier of the Soviet Union, Nikolai Ryzhkov, wrote in his memoirs that the Politburo judged all public phenomena in terms of benefit to one side or another in a worldwide, unappeasable conflict.[19] We should bear in mind that no totalitarian regime has ever made a lasting peace with liberal democracy. We only achieved peace with Nazi Germany by inflicting a military defeat, and with the Soviet Union through its collapse under a combination of external pressure and internal failure.

As Xi's rivals in the Chinese leadership (and has there ever been a political system in which the leader has no rivals, secret or overt?) analyzed China's conflict with America, they must have reflected on the process that got them to this situation. Of course, Xi had not invented the Leninist system, but it was he who had shaped the strategy of reinforcing it, of explicitly rejecting "universal values" and casting aside the caution and self-restraint that Deng Xiaoping had insisted upon as guiding principles for the conduct of China's foreign relations. Although he had not stalled the transition to the market economy, he *had* abandoned the reform program adopted at the third plenary session of the Eighteenth Central Committee in 2013. It was not he who had initiated the campaigns of cyber theft, industrial espionage, forced transfer of intellectual property, protectionism, or even the militarization of the South China Sea, but he had held China on its course long after the risk of collision with the United States became evident. Xi's rivals understand that trust between China and the United States cannot be rebuilt without the removal of Xi from power, as a prelude to changing China's political system.

In the fall of 1967, Richard Nixon wrote in *Foreign Affairs* magazine, "The world cannot be safe until China changes. Thus our aim, to the extent that we can influence events, should be to induce change." This has remained the assessment and the aim underlying US policy towards China ever since. What has changed from time to time is the degree of optimism or pessimism which America has felt about achieving its aim, and the means it has adopted in pursuing that aim.

When in 2000 the US government gave its agreement to China's entry into the World Trade Organization (WTO), President Clinton said:

By joining the WTO, China is not simply agreeing to import more of our products; it is agreeing to import one of democracy's most cherished values: economic freedom. The more China liberalizes its economy, the more fully it will liberate the potential of its people— their initiative, their imagination, their remarkable spirit of enterprise. And when individuals have the power, not just to dream but to realize their dreams, they will demand a greater say. . . . The path that China takes to the future is a choice China will make. We cannot control that choice; we can only influence it. . . . Now of course, bringing China into the WTO doesn't guarantee that it will choose political reform. But accelerating the progress—the process of economic change will force China to confront that choice sooner, and it will make the imperative for the right choice stronger.[20]

Regrettably, in about 2008, the leaders of the Communist Party of China—not China as a nation because the people were not consulted—confronted that choice, and chose to preserve their dictatorship, by abandoning further transition to a market economy. By the time of Biden's entry into the White House, the consequences of that choice, and of Xi's subsequent ratcheting up of politicoeconomic hostility towards America were plain for all to see. Nixon's words, "The world cannot be safe until China changes," had taken on a new urgency. The challenge to America and its democratic allies now was to develop a strategy, combining overt and covert means to help create the conditions in which Xi's rivals in China would remove him from office and launch a transition to democracy, making a clear distinction at all times between on the one hand the Chinese nation and its people, for whom we harbor no hostility, and on the other those in the Communist Party of China who seek to defend totalitarian dictatorship.

9   *The Great Unfinished Business*

Since the late nineteenth century, China has been engaged in a search for modernization that has taken it through extremes of social and political form. Only one other country, the Soviet Union, has experienced this in modern times.

In this time, China has experienced the rule of emperors, of strong men at the national or local level, and of a one-party dictatorship. The only form of government the Chinese have not experienced for any length of time is multiparty democracy, except on the island of Taiwan.

At the start of the modern era, China was still ruled by an imperial system more than two thousand years old. It was the impact of European and American power, values, and ideas from the mid nineteenth century that set in train the search for a modern identity. In the hundred years that followed, the competition between political ideas, and between cultural and social values, was as intense as the struggles for power. After the overthrow of the last imperial dynasty in 1912, an attempt was made to establish a democratic republic, but it failed within a year. It was succeeded by decades of government by warlords, authoritarian rule under Generalissimo Chiang Kai-shek, dictatorship in the areas controlled by the Communist Party, and Japanese rule in northeastern and eastern China.

Although liberal democracy was never established as a form of government, many educated Chinese were strongly attracted by its ideals, until they were silenced by the Communist Party after 1949.

The Party then imposed the Soviet model of Marxist-Leninist, one-party dictatorship. This has only been disrupted once, for a few years, by the anarchy of the Cultural Revolution. Within this broad framework, Chairman Mao led the Party in an attempt in 1958–62 to make a Great Leap from socialism to full communist collectivization of every area of life. When that ended in starvation, disease, and death for forty-five million people, there was a reversion to state socialism. Since Mao's death in 1976, the Party has developed a hybrid of a Leninist political system and a semi-market economy, in which lightly regulated capitalism is mixed with a large state-owned sector.

When the Party launched a Reform Era under Deng Xiaoping in 1979, it abandoned Marx but clung to Lenin for dear life. The four decades since then have largely modernized the economy and society but left the political system unreformed. As we saw in chapter 7, Xu Zhangrun, a professor of law at Tsinghua University, declared in 2018 that for thirty years, the political system had seen no substantial or meaningful progress or change, and he warned of the dangers of one-man rule and the many other problems that the system would encounter if it rejected further reforms.[1]

A people that began to search for a radically new form of society in the mid nineteenth century is now being denied the freedom to continue that exploration.

The Party claims that by imposing the Leninist political system in 1949 it has completed China's political modernization. That is as absurd as it is false. Its dictatorship has suppressed the issues, not resolved them, and is now the biggest stumbling block to restoring the greatness of the nation. The defects of the political system are at the heart of the moral, ecological, and social crises from which the nation suffers.

If China is to escape the middle income trap, it must encourage innovation throughout society and the economy. But the suppression of free thinking and individualism militate against this in every sphere. The education system does not educate people, it trains unquestioning minds. Culture is stifled and stunted. Political scientists have shown that no country that is not a democracy has ever progressed from middle-income to high-income status, except for oil-rich states, of which China is not one.

Since 1949, there have been periods, usually brief, when for one reason or another the people felt themselves free to give expression to political ideas radically opposed to the Party line.

In 1957, seven years after coming to power, Mao insisted that the Party should encourage the public to comment freely on its rule. After initial hesitation, intellectuals spoke out with devastating candor and made clear that the Party's attempt to brainwash them had failed; the most vehement critics were the students who had been educated under communist rule. The Party was so alarmed that it launched the Anti-Rightist Campaign, in which educated people in general were targeted. Five hundred thousand were sent into internal exile, or imprisoned, or condemned to death.

In April 1976, when Mao and his extreme leftist supporters in the leadership were riding high and denouncing the pragmatic approach to modernization espoused first by the late Prime Minister Zhou Enlai and then by Deng Xiaoping, millions of people from every walk of life demonstrated their preference for Zhou's legacy for days on end in major cities throughout the country.

In the winter of 1978–79, two years after Mao's death, when Deng was emerging as the paramount leader of the Party and nation, young people launched the democracy movement.

In 1987 and again in 1989, two general secretaries of the CPC in succession were dismissed because they favored political reform.

In 1989, the biggest popular movement for democracy and the rule of law that the world has ever seen swept the country. It was mercilessly suppressed by armed force, but it had shown the extent of popular support for political reform.

In December 2008, a group of 303 intellectuals, leaders of workers' and farmers' groups, and a few government officials published *Charter 08*, a document inspired by *Charter 77*, which had been published in Czechoslovakia thirty-one years earlier. The document called for an end to one-party rule and its replacement by a system based on human rights and democracy. The transition was to be brought about by peaceful means. The lead signatory was Liu Xiaobo, China's best-known human rights campaigner.

Its foreword begins:

A hundred years have passed since the writing of China's first constitution. . . . The Chinese people, who have endured human rights disasters and uncountable struggles across these same years, now include many who see clearly that freedom, equality, and human rights are universal values of humankind and that democracy and constitutional government are the fundamental framework for protecting these values. By departing from these values, the Chinese government's approach to "modernization" has proven disastrous. It has stripped people of their rights, destroyed their dignity, and corrupted normal human intercourse. So we ask: Where is China headed in the twenty-first century? Will it continue with "modernization" under authoritarian rule, or will it embrace universal human values, join the mainstream of civilized nations, and build a democratic system?

A later passage reads:

The political reality, which is plain for anyone to see, is that China has many laws but no rule of law; it has a constitution but no constitutional government. . . . The stultifying results are endemic official corruption, an undermining of the rule of law, weak human rights, decay in public ethics, crony capitalism, growing inequality between the wealthy and the poor, pillage of the natural environment as well as of the human and historical environments, and the exacerbation of a long list of social conflicts, especially, in recent times, a sharpening animosity between officials and ordinary people. . . . As these conflicts and crises grow ever more intense, and as the ruling elite continues with impunity to crush and to strip away the rights of citizens to freedom, to property, and to the pursuit of happiness, we see the powerless in our society—the vulnerable groups, the people who have been suppressed and monitored, who have suffered cruelty and even torture, and who have had no adequate avenues for their protests, no courts to hear their pleas—becoming more militant and raising the possibility of a violent conflict of disastrous proportions.[2]

No mention of *Charter 08* was permitted in the Chinese news media. Liu was arrested, brought to trial a year later, and sentenced to eleven years in prison. He was awarded the Nobel Peace Prize in 2010, and he died in captivity in July 2017.

As we saw in chapter 7, the death of the Wuhan whistle-blower, Dr Li Wenliang, in February 2020 provoked millions of netizens to call for freedom of expression.

These episodes show that there are broad and deep currents among the Chinese people for political change, currents that surface when political conditions permit. They demonstrate the falsity of the assertion by the Party under Xi Jinping that universal values have no place in Chinese society. Very powerful evidence of the falsity of Xi's claim is provided by Taiwan's successful transition from authoritarian government to a robust, multiparty democracy, ruled by law, and the impassioned and courageous demands of Hongkongers for the establishment of democracy and preservation of the rule of law in their territory.

It has been well documented that even in recent decades, until Xi Jinping came to power, members of China's academic and business elites made use of the very limited space permitted for free expression to continue to debate the future of China's political system, with some of them advocating liberal democracy.[3] Even the Central Party School itself published detailed studies of how a transition to a limited form of democracy and the rule of law might be effected.[4] As we have seen, at the height of the coronavirus epidemic, China's two leading authorities on constitutional law called for constitutional democracy.[5]

Soon afterwards, Professor Cai Xia, a professor emerita who had taught for fifteen years at the Party school for senior officials—an institution of great prestige and influence—made a devastating denunciation of Xi Jinping in terms never before used by a person of similar standing in the Party against any leader in the history of communist rule in China. Professor Cai, who was well-known for her liberal views, told members of private web chat group that Xi "has become a total mafia boss who can punish his underlings how-ever he wants. . . . This Party has become a political zombie. . . . He has turned ninety million Party members into slaves, tools to be used for his personal advantage."[6] An audio recording of her remarks was later circulated online.

Professor Cai did not just advocate the removal of Xi Jinping. She called for the rooting out of both the existing political system and the ideology of Marxism-Leninism. "This system is going nowhere. It is useless to try and change it. Fundamentally speaking, this system must be abandoned. . . . The second point is that our theory is fundamentally problematic. . . . Much of this theoretical stuff must be uprooted."[7] Professor Cai had taken the precaution of moving from China to the United States a few months before mak-ing her attack. To do otherwise would have sacrificed her freedom.

In an interview with *The Guardian* in June 2020, Cai went fur-ther, saying: "The party has no ability to correct errors. . . . Wrong decisions continue to be made until the situation is out of control. In this vicious cycle, there is no way to stop the country from slid-ing toward disaster." Democracy must replace dictatorship. "People yearn for freedom and freedom is only possible when peo-ple's rights are protected, right? To protect these rights, you need a system based on democracy and rule of law. . . . China is bound to go through political transformation, toward democracy, political freedom, rule of law and constitutionalism. This is the inevitable trend of modern human political civilisation."

Cai claimed that the overwhelming majority of Party members "know in their hearts what is going on" and believe that there must be reform. "Within the CCP the proportion is 70%, and among middle- and high-level officials the proportion may be even higher."[8]

That three senior professors in the most prestigious institutions in China, Cai Xia, Xu Zhangrun, and Zhang Qianfan, and the extremely well-connected and respected billionaire Ren Zhiqiang (see chapter 7 for references to Xu, Zhang, and Ren), chose within weeks of each other to denounce with such vehemence the supreme leader of the Party and the system in which they themselves had long flourished is a very ominous sign for the regime. They would not have done so unless they were sure that they were voicing the views of a large and powerful body of opinion in the middle and upper ranks of the Party, as Cai has claimed.

This demonstrates the urgency, the existential need for a resumption of China's search for a political modernisation. This need is evident in other ways also. As we saw in chapter 4, "No Trust, No Truth," the one-party dictatorship breeds distrust between rulers and ruled, and within the ranks of the ruled. If the rulers trusted their subjects, they would not suppress civil society. If they were truly confident of their support, they would permit free elections, and they would not feel compelled to censor every medium of expression. On the contrary, they live in fear of liberal ideas, in fear of peaceful dissent, and in fear of the emergence of any autonomous organization, such as workplace, religious, or ecological movements. Xi Jinping himself has made clear that the Party fears for its very life.[9] Consider these points, taken from official Chinese publications:

- Expenditure on internal security has exceeded that on external security since 2011.
- The rise of all major religions in China demonstrates that the regime is losing the struggle for the souls of the nation.
- Hostility toward the regime is intensifying in Tibet, Xinjiang, Hong Kong, and Taiwan.

- China is suffering from the greatest brain drain in the history of the world, and, uniquely in the history of migration, it is principally the rich and powerful, not the poor and oppressed who are emigrating. All who can, send their children to study abroad, above all in the United States. In the words of Professor Cai: "To protect their livelihoods, those who have the means to flee outside of China and move their assets offshore have already done so."

In an article entitled "Immobilism and Decay," published in 1966, Robert Conquest, the most far-sighted British expert on the Soviet Union, saw "the USSR as a country where the political system is radically and dangerously inappropriate to its social and economic dynamics. This is a formula for change—change which may be sudden and catastrophic."[10] What was true of the Soviet Union then is even more true of China today.

In 1978, only 1.4 percent of the college-age population was in higher education; by 2015, it was 20 percent. According to official statistics, the adult literacy rate has risen from 65 percent to over 95 percent. Almost all adults have completed nine years of basic education. Despite the Great Firewall and censorship, the Chinese of today are much better informed than ever before.

China is now a network society, with profound consequences for the diffusion of information and the diversification of values and opinions. In 1978, only 0.38 percent of Chinese had telephones; today, there are mobile phones for 95 percent of the population. Over nine hundred million people have access to the internet.

An estimated one hundred million people are able to use the English language. More than one hundred twenty million travel abroad annually. In 1977 China sent only a few dozen people to study abroad; since then, over four million have done so, of whom 2.2 million have returned home after completing their studies. They have learned firsthand about alternative political, economic, and legal systems.

In 1978, China was a country with almost no private property or even money in private hands: by 2017, it had two hundred eighty billionaires (second only to the United States), 1.6 million millionaires (just behind Germany), and a middle class numbering three hundred million. Most people work in the private sector. As a result, the Chinese are economically more independent than ever since 1949.

Since 1978, over five hundred fifty million people have migrated from the countryside to towns and cities, raising the urban population from under 20 percent to about 60 percent today. In 1978, the main means of transport was the bicycle, and there were no private cars; today there are one hundred seventy million cars and sixty million motorcycles, and China is Audi's second-largest market in the world. China is now the world's largest market for luxury goods.

People have become more assertive in the defense or promotion of their rights and interests. In 2010, the last year with published figures, there were one hundred eighty thousand unofficial demonstrations involving more than ten thousand people, a twentyfold increase in the twenty-seven years since 1993. Although there is no rule of law in China, there are many laws and many lawyers: the number of lawyers has grown from virtually none in 1978 to over three hundred thousand today. Millions more have gained an understanding of law far greater than that of earlier generations.

The tension between, on the one hand, a society that has changed and continues to change at a pace and on a scale without precedent in history and, on the other hand, a political system that is paralyzed, grows ever more intense. The life story of one man, Jack Ma, illustrates the tension: starting without privileges, capital or connections, he built his company Alibaba to the point where he could take it to the New York Stock Exchange and achieve the biggest initial public offering in the history of the world, yet he has no vote for the mayor of his home town.

Political modernization is the great unfinished business of contemporary China. There are those in the elite who understand this and believe that only a democratic revolution offers the possibility for China to achieve true greatness. If circumstances offers them the opportunity, they will seize it. The shaping of those circumstances does not depend on China alone: it depends also on men and women in the United States and its liberal democratic allies displaying courage and wisdom in their public actions. These qualities that have been in short supply in recent years. But a great diversity of people in places such as Hong Kong and Taiwan, the US Congress, the authors of *Charter 08* and the leaders of Christian congregations in mainland China have shown that they are far from extinct. It will also require skill, imagination, and resolve in devising strategies for covert action to complement public policy in creating the conditions that will embolden those inside China who seek radical change to move when the time is ripe.

3 *After the Coup,*
a Revolution

10 *Launching the Revolution*

This Part begins Where Part 1 Ended.

A few hours after the conclusion of the Politburo meeting at which Xi Jinping was obliged to resign, Vice President Wang Qishan opens a broadcast to the nation by announcing Xi's resignation and the new appointments proposed by the Politburo. He explains that Xi has accepted responsibility for the financial crisis that has engulfed China's markets, thanks him for his service to the nation, and wishes him a peaceful retirement. He then introduces Li Keqiang as general secretary designate. Li speaks with the whole Politburo behind him. As agreed with them, he seeks to say enough to persuade the people that they are going to be politically empowered, but not so much that the Central Committee feels it is being forced to sign up to a detailed blueprint. By his candor, directness, and brevity (the speech lasts just six minutes), he suggests the character of a new era.

He acknowledges the gravity of the double crisis, military and economic, the nation has faced, taking it to the brink of war with the United States and putting its financial system at risk. He summarizes the measures agreed with the US to defuse both confrontations, stabilize the financial markets, and guarantee bank deposits.

He explains the reasons for the resignation of President Xi and the new appointments agreed by the Politburo. Then he continues:

"Although these two confrontations were triggered by tactical decisions taken by former President Xi, they reflect deeper problems that we must urgently address. They can be summed up in a single idea: lack of trust. Lack of trust is the poison in every vein of our nation's body. To regain our health and strength, we must purge it.

"There is a lack of trust between the government and the people, between the ethnic majority and the minorities, between those who practice a religion and those who do not, and between our country and those nations that practice liberal democracy. Trust is lacking in our economic and social life. True social stability within our borders can only be built on trust, not control. The key to reconciliation with the people of Taiwan is trust, not coercion. The true foundation for peace with other nations is trust.

"But from what source has this poison infected our body? The source is in the failure since the Reform Era began in 1979 to accompany economic reform with political reform. As individuals, you are entrusted to take economic decisions but not political ones. As individuals, Chinese people have built some of the largest companies in the world, but they have no right to elect or dismiss the mayor of the smallest city in our country.

"Globalization, in economic activity, culture, and ideas, is the very essence of the modern world. And since 1979, China has engaged in the economic dimension of that process. We have become the world's number one trading nation and have benefited enormously from inward and outward flows of investment. Our people can study abroad, travel abroad, and engage in the global economy, but our system does not trust them to search the global internet for knowledge and ideas, or debate what foreign ideas or institutions China should or should not adopt. Foreigners can research and write the history of China under Mao, but our system does not trust Chinese people to do so. Where there is no trust there can be no truth. Lack of trust and lack of truth give rise to contradictions that are absurd and humiliating, and have no place in the life of a great nation.

"In short, our country has achieved great material progress, which has led to far-reaching social changes, but there is tension between a society that has changed and a political system that has not. Without political change, we cannot restore trust or respect for truth.

"For over one hundred years, our country has been grappling with the challenges of modernization. Our great revolutionary leader Sun Zhongshan set out Three Principles of the People: nationalism, democracy, and the livelihood of the people.[1] We have achieved much in pursuit of nationalism and the livelihood of the people. Now is the time to build democracy in China.

"I believe this is the will of the people. In 1989, the biggest popular movement for democracy and the rule of law that the world has ever seen swept our country. On a single day, 18 May, six million people joined demonstrations in 132 cities across the country. In 2020, upon the death of Li Wenliang, the Wuhan doctor who was silenced and reprimanded for warning of the coronavirus, millions of people went online to demand freedom of expression, and messages expressing grief and outrage were viewed one billion times. I believe the longing for freedom, democracy, and the rule of law is growing ever stronger.

"For too long, you, the vast mass of our people, have been treated as political eunuchs. Now is the time for you to become citizens. Under a new constitution, you must be empowered to elect and dismiss those who rule our nation.

"Political modernization is the great unfinished business of our nation. This is a matter for the whole nation, not one party alone, but we must proceed in an orderly manner. First, deliberation by the Central Committee of the Communist Party, which must reach its conclusions within forty-eight hours, and then a wider consultation.

"The Party's Central Committee will meet in thirty minutes' time. Between now and then, orders will be issued to end censorship of all communications media. By then, the Great Firewall of China will have been dismantled. An invitation will be sent to Professor He Weifang, professor of law at Peking University, to head a commission that will review the Social Credit System in order to make it conform with the rule of law.[2] China will rejoin the community of free nations.

"My fellow countrymen of every ethnic group, we are embarking on a revolution as great as any in our recorded history. We face uncertainties but also opportunities. I appeal to you for patience in the days to come, and I exhort you to vigilance against those who might exploit the situation for their own ends, by disrupting social order.

"Let us so work together that in the years to come we shall look back and say: on this day was hope born again, and we did not fail those who came before us, nor shall we fail those who will come after us.

"To those who live in the regions on the periphery of our nation, on Taiwan, in Hong Kong, in Xinjiang and Tibet, I declare that we will work to rebuild trust with you. To start this process, I envisage four major initiatives, as follows:

- The head of the government on Taiwan should be invited to Beijing to discuss the future of cross-strait relations.
- An election by universal suffrage for the office of chief executive of the Hong Kong government should be held within twelve months from now.
- The strategy being employed to strip the Uyghurs of Xinjiang of their cultural and religious identities must be abandoned.
- His Holiness the Dalai Lama should be invited to Beijing to discuss the future of the Tibetan Autonomous Region.

"To all who believe in and practice religious faiths, I promise that our new constitution will guarantee true freedom of religion and separation of the state and religion.

"To all members of the international community, I say: since 1945, nations have worked hard to build a world order based on trust, law, and respect for shared values. It is far from perfect. The depression caused by the coronavirus pandemic has greatly weakened it. China has a great part to play in rebuilding and improving it. We are ready to join you in that endeavor. We extend our hand to you in friendship: grasp it."

Half an hour later, the Central Committee convened, and Li Keqiang gave the opening address:

"Comrades,

I speak to you on behalf of the Politburo of our Party. In the past week, our nation and our Party faced a crisis that was both international and domestic. The situation was so urgent that there was no time to convene the Central Committee, despite the importance of the issues.

"I now seek your endorsement of the action we took to resolve the confrontations we faced with the United States and your consideration of the way forward for our nation and our Party.

"For reasons that I shall explain, my colleagues and I in the Politburo are unanimous in believing that the crisis we faced was not the fault of any one individual. The causes lie too deep for that. But nor was it inevitable. It could have been avoided, but Comrade Xi Jinping committed such mistakes of strategic direction, and was so proud, blind, and stubborn in adhering the mistaken course for over a decade, that our nation came within days of disaster. The Politburo was unanimous in demanding his resignation. He submitted it and has promised that he will not seek to reverse this outcome. We should take this into account in handling his case.

"However, this particular crisis has its roots in problems that lie deep in our political life and cannot be solved by simply a change of leadership. This crisis is a time of danger, but we can make of it an opportunity to renew the strength and vitality of our country.

"Comrades, as I reminded the nation in my broadcast just now, for over one hundred years, our country has been grappling with the challenges of modernization in economic, social, and political terms. It is a story of achievements, mistakes, and tragedies. We have made great material progress, although its benefits have not been shared fairly. We have made substantial social progress in education, health standards, communications, and other fields. Our country has become a world leader in the application of digital technology. But our political system has not changed in line with economic and social conditions. As a result, we face many problems we have long recognized but have not effectively addressed.

Why? We can see the solutions, but we cannot adopt them because we are trapped in a political system that forces us to rely on control rather than trust.

"Let us acknowledge some of the most important examples.

"Our economic growth has slowed; the key to faster growth lies in structural reform, in relaunching the transition to a full market economy. Economic reform has ground to a halt and must be relaunched, but it is being blocked for fear it would undermine the political power of our Party. Our private sector is the great dynamo of our economy, but we in the Party block its expansion because we fear loss of control. The deep recession at home and abroad caused by the coronavirus pandemic has greatly exacerbated the economic problems that were already apparent.

"The blocking of economic reform has prevented the emergence of transparent, well-regulated financial markets. Instead, investors and entrepreneurs are forced to resort to opaque, ill-regulated shadow banking, which, as we have seen in the last few weeks, is vulnerable to external shocks. This is the origin of the contagion that threatens the stability of our banks and other financial institutions, even as we meet.

"Since the global financial crisis of 2008, we have maintained our rate of growth largely by expanding the supply of credit to the economy. Much of it has been used for nonproductive purposes, like property speculation. As a result, we have accumulated a huge debt mountain. Why have we allowed the growth of this debt mountain, which the measures taken to respond to the coronavirus depression have compounded? Because we have relied on ever-rising prosperity to buy our people's tolerance of our regime. We did not have the legitimacy that comes from being elected. The whole system became infected with debt, but for too long we did not dare to face the consequences of a major, sustained strategy to reduce the debt mountain: deflation, bankrupt companies, and large-scale unemployment. Why? Because our relationship with the people was based on control, not on trust.

"For too long we have pursued economic growth without due regard to its impact on the environment. The result is disastrous pollution of the air we breathe, the water we drink, and the earth on which we grow our crops. We have passed many laws and regulations to combat this, but in restricting the role of nongovernmental organizations we have suppressed those forces that should work with the state to enforce their implementation. We have restricted them because we do not trust them, and we fear loss of control if they grow too powerful.

"A political system that relies on control rather than trust is hostile toward cultural and religious diversity. We see the results of this in the tensions that exist in Tibet and Xinjiang, where millions of people have been stripped of their cultural and religious identities, and the alienation elsewhere in China of tens of millions of Muslims and Christians.

"A political system that relies on control rather than trust has failed to reunite Taiwan to the motherland. Indeed, it has progressively alienated our kinsmen who live there.

"The same is true of the people of Hong Kong. When we regained sovereignty over Hong Kong in 1997, we pledged in an international treaty that for the next fifty years we would adhere to a strategy of "one country, two systems." The people of Hong Kong demanded constitutional safeguards for the freedoms they enjoyed but were refused them. What was only a few years ago one of the most law-abiding cities in the world became an urban battleground. A great international financial marketplace became the site of a collision between the two systems, with disastrous consequences for China's international relations.

"China has long been mired in a deep moral crisis. On that there is widespread agreement. Anticorruption campaigns have only addressed the symptoms, not the causes. Why? Because, as all of us in this hall understand very well, after the events of 1989 Party leaders adopted a strategy of decentralizing the rights of control over state property without clarifying the rights of ownership. Rights of control were separated from rights of ownership, and where ownership is uncertain, control is key. This created endless opportunities for the abuse of power. Party members, high and low, have been caught in this system. They have had no choice. It brought material advantage to many, but we all know that our Party has lost the trust and respect of the people. The result has been political decay and sickness. This is essentially an issue of our political system.

"In the thirty or more years after 1979, we enjoyed a highly productive relationship with the United States and its allies. The attitude of the Americans toward China was one of positive engagement. But since 2010, their attitude has swung from positive engagement to distrust and even hostility. Why? Because we took their goodwill for granted. We pursued certain policies, particularly on the acquisition of intellectual property which, while they accelerated our rate of technological progress, forfeited the goodwill of the world's most powerful nation and its allies. In this field also, we underestimated the value of trust.

"After World War II, the South China Sea returned to its traditional role of an international sea route through which one-third of the world's maritime trade passes peacefully. Then, beginning in 2013, we adopted a strategy of island-building and militarization.

Why? We did it to mobilize nationalist sentiment. Lacking the trust of the people that comes from the ballot box, we relied on chauvinism to generate support for our regime. Comrades, China is not trusted or respected by the international community. We have no true allies or friends: we rely on our economic strength to buy collaboration. In recent days, these assumptions and this strategy have brought us to the brink of war with a superpower.

"Comrades, we are trapped in a political system that is exacerbating our problems instead of enabling us to resolve them. The strategy of economic and social reform without political reform was laid down in 1978, at the start of the Reform Era. It was not a strategy that Karl Marx would have endorsed: he argued that the political superstructure is determined by the economic substructure.[3] He would have warned that the contradiction inherent in the strategy would manifest itself in the long run, which is just what has happened. A political system based on this contradiction is inherently unsustainable. Because of it, we have repeatedly made bad choices, and now it is driving us towards disaster.

"If the negative consequences of all these strategies were so clear, why did those of us in the Politburo who now denounce them not oppose them years ago?

"Some of us here today played a decisive role in the biggest-ever collaborative project between China and the World Bank, which produced *China 2030*, a wide-ranging, far-reaching report that indicated, in suitably diplomatic language, that we would have to embrace pluralism if China is to avoid the "middle-income trap" that ensnared Latin America and North Africa. We had become convinced that the model of economic without political reform has not only outlived its usefulness, it has become counterproductive. Dangerously so.

"On becoming general secretary, Comrade Xi recognized that we faced a struggle to survive like the one the Soviet Communist Party had faced under Mikhail Gorbachev, but did he take the opportunity to lead us in a strategic reassessment? On the contrary, in Directive no. 9 of 2013 he made clear that there must be no discussion of political reform. He proceeded to centralize power in his own hands to a degree not seen since the days of Mao Zedong. At the Nineteenth Party Congress, he had his Thought incorporated into the Constitution. At the National Party Congress of March 2018, he had the term limit on the post of president of the republic abolished, opening the way to him retaining that title for life.

"Those who had identified the problems in our political system, and there were many of us, hoped he would lead us in the direction of reform soon, but we discovered that his intentions were the very opposite of that. We realized that he was in denial of key trends in the development of our country and the world at large. We became convinced that his refusal of reform would intensify our problems, and set us on a collision course with the United States and its allies. But we found that he was deaf to all appeals to reconsider, and his centralization of power made it impossible to resist him. We feared that his policies would lead us to a crisis. Some of us prepared for that eventuality. That is why we were able to move decisively and quickly when the crisis came.

"At this moment our Party faces a choice: either we lead a radical reform of our nation's political system or the nation will collapse into chaos. In the last twenty-four hours, reports have been flowing to the Center that show discipline is starting to crumble within the police and in the ranks of those who enforce foreign exchange controls. We have just forty-eight hours in which to decide the guiding principles for a new constitution for our republic. If any of you think that force can be used to impose control, listen to what our security and military colleagues think of that idea: they will tell you it's totally unrealistic. As one who lived through the 1980s, and as one who studied the institutions and values of liberal democracy, I can tell you that so long as I play any role in the leadership of this Party, the People's Liberation Army will never be ordered to open fire on Chinese demonstrators voicing demands for democracy and freedom. Trust, not control, will shape our future.

"Many of us in the Party have long felt trapped in a system that prevents us from realizing our ideals, and we recognize that our Party must lead the reform if it is to recover its sense of purpose and play a leading role in the future of our country. In doing so, our Party will regain the trust of our people and will be true to the aspirations of those who brought it into existence a century ago.

"There are millions of Party members who are well qualified by experience and knowledge to play a leading role in the government of our country under a new, democratic system.

"As I said in my address to the nation just now, for over one hundred years, our country has been grappling with the challenges of modernization. Sun Zhongshan set out Three Principles of the People: nationalism, democracy, and the livelihood of the people. Now is the time to for us to design and construct a democratic system of government for China.

"There are those who say that because China has had two thousand years of autocracy, and seven decades of what is in truth one-party rule, and therefore lacks any tradition of democracy, the people are not ready for it. They say that because this is a huge and complex country, any transition to a democratic system is bound to bring chaos. They argue that the precedents from history are discouraging. They are too pessimistic. Over the past four decades we have undergone a great social revolution, in ways that set the objective conditions for democracy to succeed:

- Standards of literacy have risen greatly.
- We have built a legal system, and many of our people have gained an understanding of its operation; we have trained many lawyers and judges.
- Millions of our younger generations have studied abroad and learned how democracies operate.
- We have become a networked society in which over half our people hold in their hands the means to become fully informed and active citizens, if only we will guarantee freedom of expression.
- Citizen activism, although repressed for too long, has manifested itself in the great growth of nongovernmental organizations.
- Property ownership, a positive factor in the building of democratic systems in many countries, has become wide-spread.

"Consider too that our traditions and our history have bred in us a deep respect for order. Finally, bear in mind that our fellow Chinese in Taiwan have given us a fine example of transition from an authoritarian regime to a robust democracy. We must recognize the uncertainties and the difficulties, but we should not be defeatist.

"This is a matter for the whole nation, and not one party alone, however great has been our Party's contribution to the building of a modern China. I announced in my broadcast just now the abolition of all censorship, the dismantling of the Great Firewall of China, and the reform of the Social Credit System, to make it conform to the rule of law. Without those actions the nation would never believe we were sincere in our pledge of wider consultation.

"I also declared to the nation that we should take a number of initiatives to rebuild national unity. I now propose to you that the head of the government on Taiwan should be invited to Beijing to discuss the future of cross-strait relations, that an election for the office of chief executive of the Hong Kong government by universal suffrage should be held within twelve months, that the strategy being employed to strip the Uyghurs of Xinjiang of their cultural and religious identities must be abandoned, and that His Holiness the Dalai Lama should be invited to come to Beijing, or send his representatives, to discuss the future of the Tibetan Autonomous Region.

"The policies we have pursued on religion since 2012 have been deeply mistaken. They have alienated tens of millions of our people who are patriotic and would be law-abiding if they could practice their religion freely. We must guarantee them that freedom by separating the state from religion.

"We need to proceed in an orderly manner. So, Vice President Wang Qishan will now present for your consideration principles that we believe should shape a new state constitution, and a process for a wider consultation on this great matter. Important aspects of reform remain to be settled, but one thing is essential: our Party must sacrifice its monopoly over the political system of our country. True competition between political parties must be at the heart of our new system. That is essential if we are to transform ourselves into citizens, citizens empowered with democracy and the rule of law. With democracy and the rule of law, we will gain trust abroad and true stability at home.

"Political modernization is the great unfinished business of our nation. If we succeed, we will earn ourselves a place in the history of China and make a contribution to the community of nations.

"Let us get to work."

Li's speech was heard at first in stunned silence. By the time he was halfway through, murmurs of approval could be heard. He could not relax: knowing the strength of vested interests in the status quo, particularly in the state sector and at the regional level, he realized a strenuous battle lay ahead, first within the hall, then in the arena of public opinion. But he had seized the initiative by abolishing censorship and promising an end to one-party rule. He had begun this battle fifteen days before, excited but nervous; he was even more excited, and even more nervous now, as he turned over the microphone to Wang Qishan.

Afterword

One Life, Two Questions

An abiding interest in two questions has shaped my life: how do countries get out of poverty, and what makes for good government?

During sixty years of adult life, my interest in those questions has led me into diplomacy, development banking, and the development of capital markets in countries making the transition from a command economy to a market economy.

I have lived and worked in countries ruled by a colonial government, a military junta, a one-party socialist dictatorship, and various types of liberal democracy with market economies. I have learned, to different degrees of proficiency, two Asian languages (Gurkhali and Mandarin Chinese), and three Romance languages (French, Spanish, and Latin). But it was China, one of the most puzzling and dramatic countries on earth, that first awakened my interest in the escape from poverty and the challenges of governance. I chose to study Mandarin for two years, volunteered for two diplomatic postings in Beijing, and wrote a book about how and why Deng Xiaoping won the struggle for the succession to Mao Zedong and Zhou Enlai.

For sixty years I have tracked China's search for a modern identity, a search that began in the late nineteenth century and is far from complete. In that time, I have seen China plumb the depths of political tragedy and scale the heights of economic success. I am impelled to write this book now because I believe that China's search for a modern identity is about to enter a new and perilous phase in which there will be a crisis, there may be chaos, and there could—just possibly—emerge a new and better political order.

I pride myself on my objectivity, but I did not approach this writing as an agnostic on the fundamental issues of politics and economics. I came to it with a mind formed by my six decades of wide-ranging experience.

My objectivity is sustained by the fact that, unlike many writers whose livelihood or career prospects depend on continuing access to China, I am completely independent: I have not the slightest need to consider self-censorship.

I began my China watching on the China–Hong Kong border in 1958, peering through a pair of binoculars. I was commanding a small detachment of Gurkha soldiers in the Sha Tau Kok Observation Post, set high on a hillside overlooking a valley through which ran a flimsy fence of wire netting that divided the British Empire from Red China. In the hills that faced us there was no doubt an observation post where the People's Liberation Army was watching us.

By day, the valley slumbered, but every night a stealthy drama was played out across the border. Scores or even hundreds of people from the mainland would try to evade the border guards and slip into Hong Kong. They were trying to escape from a society that had been thrown into turmoil by Mao Zedong's Great Leap Forward. They had been promised a great leap into prosperity and a modern industrial society, but the outcome was social upheaval, starvation, disease, and forty-six million premature deaths, as collectivization threw investment, production, and distribution into total chaos, and drove a resentful people to subvert the system.

On my visits to the city of Kowloon, I observed how those few refugees who succeeded in escaping coped with life in the colony. I admired the way they lived with dignity in their make-shift shelters on the streets or on the hillside overlooking the city. They built new lives, starting with nothing.

No two societies in the world presented a greater contrast in governance than the People's Republic of China and the British Crown Colony of Hong Kong. China under Mao was rushing headlong from socialism to communism. Starting with its leading role in the Korean War, the People's Republic had isolated itself from most of the world in every aspect of life. The power of the Communist Party of China was not subject to any constraint from a political opposition, a free press, or a constitution that protected the property, life, or liberty of the individual. By contrast, in Hong Kong, the role of government was extremely limited; it was a politics-free zone, a free enterprise economy par excellence, an entrepôt completely open to international trade, where the rule of law prevailed. The situation might have been designed by a social scientist to test the effects of the two systems of government. On the one side of the border, at that time, a Chinese society was suffering from turmoil and famine. On the other, people displayed extraordinary resilience, enterprise, family and social solidarity, and were exceptionally law-abiding.

My experience in Hong Kong, and the role Britain then still played east of Suez, led me to volunteer to study Mandarin when I joined the Foreign Service after university. I began my two years' study in Hong Kong in 1965, and the following year Mao Zedong launched his next visionary adventure, the Cultural Revolution. My Chinese teachers, fellow students, and I watched with horror as China descended into violent anarchy and civil strife. Families, friendships, schools, and workplaces were torn apart. A two-year posting to our diplomatic mission in Beijing followed my language studies, and I learned what could happen even in a society that was heir to an ancient civilization when there is no law and politics take command. On my first excursion out of Beijing, driving across the North China plain to Tianjin, I gazed at the villages, little changed in millennia, and parties of men laboring to dig irrigation ditches, and asked myself, How do nations get out of poverty? Is it money, is it education, or is it ideas? My degree in English literature did not offer me even the most rudimentary answer, but I decided that I wanted to join an organization that had the mission and the means to work with poor countries to help them escape from poverty. The World Bank was clearly the organization I should aim for.

After my return from Beijing, I resigned from the Foreign Service and took myself, in 1971, to the Massachusetts Institute of Technology for the Sloan Fellows program to learn something about economics, law, and management science. Upon graduating, I found a way into the World Bank in Washington, DC. Thus I moved from a society in the grip of anarchy to one governed by a constitution, one that had succeeded in uniting under the rule of law a nation of immigrants from every corner of the globe.

In the four years I spent in the United States, its Constitution was subjected to two great tests of its strength: the Pentagon Papers legal case, followed by the Watergate political affair. In the first, the *New York Times* and the *Washington Post* tested the freedom of expression enshrined in the constitution by their determination to publish, against the will of the federal government, the Pentagon Papers, thousands of top-secret documents showing that the United States had entered the Vietnam War for wholly different reasons than the declared ones, and that presidents and commanding generals knew that victory was unlikely. The government applied for an injunction to prevent publication. The US Supreme Court refused to grant it.

A year later, the Watergate affair began to surface. The press exercised its freedom guaranteed by the constitution to publish the fruits of its investigations, and the value of the separation of powers enshrined in the constitution was demonstrated as the three branches of government, judicial, legislative, and executive, interacted with each other and with public opinion. This interaction forced the most powerful person in the world, the president of the United States, to resign from office.

At the same time, my work in the East Asia and Pacific Department of the World Bank brought me face to face with the spectacular growth of the export-oriented, market economies of East Asia—South Korea, Taiwan, Hong Kong, and Singapore—while Mao's China and Brezhnev's Union of Soviet Socialist Republics stagnated under variants of autarkic socialism. That contrast taught me something about how countries get out of poverty.

Robert McNamara was a great president of the World Bank, but he ran it by numbers—as he had run everything from Ford Motors to the Vietnam War. After three years, I could see that my "soft science" understanding of the dynamics of Asian societies was not valued there, so I returned to diplomacy and to Beijing. From January 1976 to January 1979, I witnessed the greatest turning point in China's history since the communists' victory in 1949: the struggle for the succession to Prime Minister Zhou Enlai and Chairman Mao Zedong, both of whom died in 1976. As the world knows, that struggle was won by the reform faction of the Party led by Deng Xiaoping, who emerged in late 1978 as the supreme leader of China, and then launched the strategy of economic but not political reform. The outcome of the struggle was of course not decided through a democratic process, yet public opinion played a crucial role. I was struck by what it showed about the values held by many Chinese and their resolve to shape the future.

At the start of my tour of duty as the British Embassy's principal analyst of China's internal politics, I had taken a decision, known only to myself, that I would work on the assumption that in terms of political values and instincts the similarities between Chinese people and "us" were primary, and the differences were secondary. Events over my three-year posting confirmed me in this view.

The most spectacular illustration of their values and their resolve to shape their own future took place on Beijing's Tiananmen Square in April 1976, four months after the death of Zhou Enlai, in the week leading up to the festival of Qingming, when Chinese by tradition honor the dead. For four days, the square was filled by half a million people who came, spontaneously and against the orders of the Party, to pledge loyalty to the vision of economic modernization left them by Zhou, and to oppose the violent, visionary communism of the ailing, but still living Mao and his cronies. In their speeches, and in hundreds of poems and declarations that individuals pinned on bushes and pasted on stonework around the square, currents of language, thought, and feeling that had been flowing underground for years broke to the surface. Similar demonstrations were happening in dozens of cities across China, almost certainly planned by reformers loyal to the legacy of Zhou Enlai and led by Deng Xiaoping, his heir-apparent. After four days, Mao and his allies in the Politburo ordered the public places to be cleared of demonstrators and the wreaths they had brought. Those who resisted were clubbed to the ground, and the stones on which they stood were spattered with their blood. The protestors had lost the battle that day, but for the first time since 1949, Mao had faced a mass outpouring of popular sentiment opposed to him, and not only in Beijing but in major cities across China.

Deng Xiaoping was removed from office. My ambassador called me into his office and asked me: "What do you make of this, Roger?" I replied: "Deng will get back. He will rule China." My ambassador laughed derisively.

The leftists had won a tactical victory, but five months later Mao died, and the Gang of Four were arrested. The blood shed by the brave young men and women in April had not been shed in vain. Over the next two years, we watched as the reformers gradually won control of the CPC, and therefore the state. The struggle had not just been waged among the elite, acting behind closed doors: the reformers had won the public to their side by revealing through the media those of their reform intentions that would most appeal to the public, and then discreetly mobilizing the mass demonstrations at Qingming in such a way as to make them look entirely spontaneous. There was an element of cynical manipulation in this, but it was also interaction between the reformers and the public.

The cynical element became apparent after Deng Xiaoping emerged supreme. He and his allies had mobilized support by giving the impression that they were more in favor of political liberalization than they actually were. For some weeks before his final victory, a movement in favor of democracy was allowed to emerge, led by youthful activists who set up "democracy walls" and published unofficial magazines that advocated democracy and the rule of law. As soon as Deng had established friendly relations with the United States, he moved ruthlessly to suppress the movement.

I experienced the rise and fall of the 1978–79 democracy movement in a very personal way. In October 1978, I watched hundreds of people on Tiananmen Square file past posters on which a poet had written a set of his poems, each one of which was political dynamite. The most explosive, "The Fallen Idol," began:

"The tyrant of this era has fallen
From the pinnacle of unrighteous power,
From the tip of a rusty bayonet,
From the bent backs of a generation,
And a billion gasping, bleeding souls,
He has fallen,
He is dead."

The tyrant was not named, but the readers recognized him as Chairman Mao, whom they had been forced to worship as an idol. As the poet wrote elsewhere, in mass movements to collectivize social and economic life, Mao had "moved billions of people around / As though whipping billions of tops."

And this was only one of nine poems posted there. In others, the poet showed God liberating society from the grip of dictatorship, and he described that dictatorship in vivid detail that made it recognizable to any Chinese. He showed a total disregard for Mao Zedong Thought, which had the status of Holy Scripture. Words like "freedom," "democracy," and "human rights" that had long since disappeared from view leaped off his posters.

These poems electrified the capital and sent shock waves across the country. In the months that followed, many other men and women in cities across China would dare to give voice to demands for human rights and democracy, expressing themselves in unofficial public gatherings, wall posters, and a host of unofficial publications. The poems encouraged young democracy activists who had started to put up their own posters on a drab stretch of brick wall about a mile to the west of Tiananmen Square. For four months in the winter of 1978–79, voices would come from that wall that would be heard around the world and earn it the name of Democracy Wall. In the few months when it was allowed to flourish, I spent many hours at Beijing's Democracy Wall, reading posters. In less public places, I met discreetly with democracy activists. The boldest of them was Wei Jingsheng. In his posters and articles, he argued that China could not achieve the Four Modernizations proposed by Zhou Enlai (agriculture, industry, science and technology, and national defense) without a Fifth—democracy. He fully expected the Party to act against him and other democracy activists, so I asked him:

"Why do you persist?"

"Because I know that democracy is the future of China and if I speak out now there is a possibility that I can hasten the day when the Chinese people will enjoy democracy."

He opened his mouth, pointed to his tongue, and said, "Two years ago it was pointless for us to speak or write as we do now, for we would have been arrested as soon as the words had left our tongues."

He was a member of the generation of Red Guards whom Mao had sent out from Tiananmen Square to fight for his collectivist vision of China's future but who had returned thirsting for the very things Mao had called on them to destroy. They wanted individual freedom, and they had a consuming passion for liberal ideas and foreign knowledge. And they were determined to go to study in the United States and other liberal democracies, and not return.

Wei Jingsheng publicly denounced Deng as a "political swindler" who had won the struggle for the succession to Mao and Zhou on a false manifesto, pretending to be in favor of political liberalization when he was nothing of the sort. He was soon proved right: shortly after Deng made the first visit to the United States since the communist victory in 1949, he ordered the repression of demands for political reform to begin. Wei was arrested and sentenced to fifteen years in prison. It so happened that the day of his arrest was my birthday, and the news reached me as I sat at my desk on a college campus in California, writing a book about the struggle for China's future in which Wei would feature.

The developments I had witnessed in China during that great turning point of its history had validated for me the hypothesis on which I had determined to work at the outset, that in terms of political values and instincts the similarities between Chinese people and "us" were primary, and the differences were secondary.

When my second posting to Beijing ended, I took a year of unpaid leave to write a book about how and why Deng Xiaoping had won the struggle for the succession to Mao Zedong and Zhou Enlai, and the direction in which he would lead China. No serving member of the British Diplomatic Service had ever published a book on the politics of a country to which he had been posted, but I thought it worth a try. The US Navy Postgraduate School invited me to spend a year as an Adjunct Professor of China Studies, and there I wrote *Coming Alive: China After Mao*. Our Foreign Secretary Lord Carrington and his ministerial colleagues approved it for publication, with a few minor changes, and I returned to the Diplomatic Service in early 1980.

Over the next twenty years, my professional life was not directly concerned with China, but it taught me much about the interaction between politics and economics, and developed my ideas about how nations get out of poverty and what is good government. As a diplomat, I worked on the response of the liberal democracies to the Soviet invasion of Afghanistan, and to the rise of the populist forces in Central and Eastern Europe that led to the eventual collapse of the Soviet empire. Coming so soon after the 1978-79 democracy movement in China, the rise of Solidarity in Poland convinced me that grassroots resistance to totalitarian socialism was growing in Europe as well as Asia. I became convinced of the coming of a new era. I held the post of economic and financial counselor in our embassy in Paris as the British government under Margaret Thatcher started to roll back the state, helping to promote the role of the market in the European Economic Community, rejuvenating our economy, and leading a trend to privatization that spread across the world.

Those were years when, in the realms of ideas and of global economic competition, the classic freedoms of expression, association, and religion; open borders; free markets; and private ownership were gradually gaining ground against dictatorship, autarky, the command economy, and state ownership. After Paris, I resigned from the Diplomatic Service to become director of public affairs of the London Stock Exchange, at a time when Soviet power was weakening but the USSR had not yet collapsed. Reformers from countries like Hungary and Bulgaria came to ask if we would help them build stock exchanges of their own, at some point in the future when political circumstances might permit it. They were convinced that the Soviet Empire was going to crumble, that its component nations would undergo a transition from the command economy to a market economy, and that they would want to set up free capital markets. I shared their conviction.

Having been present at the birth of the era of "reform and opening" in China, I had watched from a distance as Deng had launched the transition to a market economy ten years before the Berlin Wall came down. Although that transition was gradual and hesitant, and was not accompanied by political reform, the trend in the economic sphere was clear enough for me to arrange a visit to China by the chairman of the London Stock Exchange, the first by any major exchange. At the end of our stay in Beijing, we were received in a beautiful pavilion in the former Imperial City by a member of the Party's Politburo, Tian Jiyun. Tian, who was not afraid to display a sense of humor in public, explained that he was responsible for the work of developing a capital market in China, then in its infancy, but that he knew little about the matter, adding, "If, on your return to London, you will send me papers on the subject, I will become your propaganda agent here in China."

When, a year later, in May 1989, Chinese student demonstrators filled Tiananmen Square demanding democracy and freedom, I was not there to observe them. Instead, I was standing on the stage of the National Opera House in Hồ Chí Minh City (Saigon), explaining to an auditorium filled to overflowing the purpose of a stock exchange and what it could do for Vietnam's economy. While the Chinese students were demanding political freedom, I was explaining to the Vietnamese how a free capital market operates.

In the collapsing Soviet Empire, and in many other countries starting to make a transition from the command economy to the market economy, I saw a business opportunity in advising governments how to create the legislation and the institutions, such as stock exchanges and investment funds, required by capital markets. I created a company to seize that business opportunity, and over the next ten years, from 1990 to 2000, we worked in countries that ran through the alphabet from A for Albania to Z for Zambia.

We did not witness the coming of utopia. Indeed, I learned much about human wickedness. In every country in which we worked, we saw at close range the newly emerging elite professing their commitment to democracy and free markets but struggling to shape the new system to their own advantage, skew regulations, or fight for control of new institutions. In a single year while we were working in Russia, the press reported a total of forty bankers who lost their lives in contract killings, as rival groups competed for financial power. Sometimes the violence came rather close to me. In St. Petersburg, my hosts assigned me bodyguards and drove me in unmarked cars. In Novosibirsk, where I spent two months one winter initiating the first international investment fund for Siberia, the heavy mob broke into my flat after I declined to pay them protection money. In Moscow, the chief executive of a stock exchange apologized for being late for our meeting, explaining that he had been attending the funeral of his counterpart in another city, who had been assassinated. Just after meeting the founder of an exchange who wanted us to work with him, I learned he had just lost the services of his chauffeur, whose knees had been shot through on the orders of a rival exchange; I declined what could have been a lucrative contract.

The decade I spent working with these newly established "democracies" making the transition to the market economy brought home to me two concepts. One is that there are essential linkages between democracy, the rule of law, an independent judiciary, and a free press. Another is the extreme difficulty of developing all these good things until they function robustly. But my experiences reminded me, time and again, the truth of the oft-quoted words of Winston Churchill: "Democracy is the worst form of government, except for all those other forms that have been tried from time to time."[1]

When in later years I returned to the study of China, I was thankful for that diversity of experience which had equipped me with a broader frame of reference than if I had continued as a single-track China specialist. That experience enabled me to bring to bear a judgment forged at the front line of economic and political change.

Acknowledgments

Working on this book has made me realize to what extent a book like this is a collective product, to which many people have contributed without knowing it. I owe a debt beyond measure to all those whose thoughts and words have helped me write it. Some of them are reflected in the bibliography or the endnotes, or are named below; many more are not. Errors of judgement and fact are my responsibility alone.

I owe very special thanks to a smaller group of people whose interventions have been crucial to the publication of this book. Steve Levine, who taught Chinese history and politics at the University of Montana for many years, gave me much valuable editorial advice, as he has given many others over the years; he also recommended me to his literary agent, Peter Bernstein, whom I knew to be held in the highest regard by authors of China books. I was thrilled when Peter offered to represent this book. It was his idea that I should not only predict the end of tyranny in China, but show how it might happen, an idea I took up with enthusiasm. Fraser Howie, who has worked in China's capital markets since 1992, helped me greatly in fleshing out that idea. When the book was written, Peter searched with skill and vigor for a publisher until

Reed Malcolm at the University of California Press saw merit in it, an act of recognition for which I shall be eternally grateful. It has been a delight to work with him and his many able colleagues.

In the liberal democracies, there is a strong community of people like me who have been fascinated by China for most or all of their adult lives, a community greatly facilitated nowadays by the internet and online communities such as Pangolin. I have been deeply touched by the generosity of spirit shown to me by my fellow "China junkies" in helping me in this project. My prospects of attracting a publisher, no easy matter in the crowded field of China books, were greatly increased by the endorsements generously given to my proposal by a dozen or so distinguished specialists in the field. Other friends and contacts have read and commented helpfully upon my manuscript, in whole or in part.

My respect for the Chinese people, as distinct from the political system to which they have been subject since 1949, has shaped this book, and indeed my life. Among those known to me personally, I pay tribute to my teachers in the School of Chinese at the University of Hong Kong, under whom I studied Mandarin, 1965–67, headed by Professor Ma Meng; Huang Xiang, poet and freedom fighter (fighting with words, not guns); Wei Jingsheng, the most courageous and articulate leader of the 1978–79 democracy movement, and Wu Ningkun, author of *A Single Tear,* the classic account of a patriot who returned to China in the early 1950s to serve his country and was rewarded by decades of persecution.

In my sometimes solitary work of researching and writing, there are others from my past who have inspired me in a variety of ways that have a bearing on my work, direct or indirect. I take this opportunity of paying tribute to John Northam, my supervisor in English literature studies at Clare College, Cambridge; Charlie

Moule, Lady Margaret's Professor of Divinity at the University of Cambridge; Percy Cradock, under whom I served when he was Ambassador in Beijing; and Leon Brittan, vice president of the European Commission, a friend since Cambridge days. None of them are around to read these words on the printed page, but they may have some way of keeping themselves informed of my doings.

For several years now, I have participated in China lunches organized by Guy de Jonquières, former world trade editor and international business editor at the *Financial Times*. He brings together people whose careers have been in academia, the aerospace industry, banking, diplomacy, environmental NGOs, journalism, and the intelligence community. I have greatly benefited from our lively exchanges.

My dear friend Jonathan Mirsky, who reviewed over 100 books on China and Tibet for the *New York Review of Books* between 1969 and 2018, shared with me his passionate interest in and extensive knowledge of Chinese politics over many a long lunch at "Forters" and elsewhere in the course of two decades, and sustained my morale when it showed signs of sagging.

I thank Lesli Wheeler for her excellent work in formatting my typescript.

I am grateful to Lucy Edwards and Victoria Wei Qi, who—working as my advisers, fixers, and interpreters—enabled me to meet fifty-eight people in a thirty-day visit to Beijing and Shanghai in April–May 2017.

My daughters, Juliette, Alice, and Rebecca, three women of courage and character, have been my dear companions in Washington, DC; Beijing; the Carmel Valley in California; Paris; and London.

My wife, Mariota, has given me unstinting, unwavering love and support, for which no words of thanks are adequate.

Notes

Preface

1. Eugene Lyons, "The Realities of a Vision," in *Dilemmas of Change in Soviet Politics,* ed. Zbigniew Brzezinski (New York: Columbia University Press, 1969), 52.

2. Leon Aron, "Everything You Think You Know about the Collapse of the Soviet Union Is Wrong," *Foreign Policy,* 20 June 2011, https://foreignpolicy .com/2011/06/20/everything-you-think-you-know-about-the-collapse-of-the-soviet-union-is-wrong.

Chapter One. The Coup

1. Nigel Stevenson, "Luckin Coffee Scandal Highlights Murky Standards of China Inc.," *Nikkei Asian Review,* 16 April 2020, https://asia.nikkei.com /Opinion/Luckin-Coffee-scandal-highlights-murky-standards-of-China-Inc.

2. Kellie Mejdrich, "Congress Clears Bill to Ban Trading in Chinese Firms that Thwart U.S. Auditors," *Politico,* 2 December 2020, https://www.politico .com/news/2020/12/02/congress-clears-bill-to-ban-trading-in-chinese-firms-that-thwart-us-auditors-442362.

3. Justin Sink and Jenny Leonard, "White House Cuts Off Savings Fund's Investment in China Stocks," *Bloomberg News,* 12 May 2020, www.bloomberg .com/news/articles/2020-05-12/white-house-cuts-off-savings-fund-s-investment-in-china-stocks.

4. "Memorandum on Protecting United States Investors from Significant Risks from Chinese Companies," US presidential memorandum, 4 June 2020,

www.whitehouse.gov/presidential-actions/memorandum-protecting-united-states-investors-significant-risks-chinese-companies/.

5. Donald J. Trump administration, *United States Strategic Approach to the People's Republic of China*, 20 May 2020, www.whitehouse.gov/wp-content/uploads/2020/05/U.S.-Strategic-Approach-to-The-Peoples-Republic-of-China-Report-5.20.20.pdf.

6. Bob Davis and Lingling Wei, "The Soured Romance between China and Corporate America," *Wall Street Journal*, 5 June 2020, www.wsj.com/articles/the-soured-romance-between-china-and-corporate-america-11591365699.

7. "Chinese president Xi Jinping can't bear being compared to Winnie the Pooh anymore, so the cartoon cub is now banned in China," *South China Morning Post*, 18 July 2017, https://yp.scmp.com/news/china/article/106802/chinese-president-xi-jinping-cant-bear-being-compared-winnie-pooh-anymore.

8. At the undergraduate level, Li Keqiang chose to study law under Professor Gong Xiangrui, a well-known expert on Western political and administrative systems, and the author of a textbook on Western constitutional law. Li and his classmates, under Gong's guidance, translated important legal works from English into Chinese, including a history of the British constitution and Lord Denning's *The Due Process of Law*. He won an open election to become president of the head of the Executive Committee of the Student Assembly. Cheng Li, *Chinese Politics in the Xi Jinping Era: Reassessing Collective Leadership* (Washington, DC: Brookings Institution Press, 2016), 126–27, and the Wikipedia entry on Li Keqiang.

9. For his Ph.D., Li chose to study under "Mr. Stock Market," the economist Li Yining, who was boldly advocating the privatization of state-owned industries and the opening of stock exchanges when these ideas were still anathema to the more conservative members of China's leadership. See "Li Yining," Wikipedia, accessed 28 February 2019, https://en.wikipedia.org/wiki/Li_Yining.

10. After studying chemical engineering as an undergraduate, Xi was awarded a doctorate for a thesis on China's "rural marketization," which attracted allegations of plagiarism and ghost writing. See "Plagiarism and Xi Jinping," *Asia Sentinel*, 24 September 2013, www.asiasentinel.com/politics/plagiarism-and-xi-jinping.

11. In one month, June to July 2015, A shares on the Shanghai Stock Exchange lost a third of their value.

12. World Bank and Development Research Center of the State Council, the People's Republic of China. 2013. *China 2030: Building a Modern, Harmonious, and Creative Society*. Washington, DC: World Bank, https://openknowledge .worldbank.org/handle/10986/12925.

13. "Everybody Loves Chinese Vice-Premier Wang Qishan," Public Intelligence, 23 January 2011, https://publicintelligence.net/everybody-loves-chinese-vice-premier-wang-qishan.

14. "Wang Qishan Still Attending Top Communist Party Meetings and in Line For China's Vice-Presidency," *South China Morning Post*, 1 December 2017, www.scmp.com/news/china/policies-politics/article/2122382/wang-qishan-still-attending-top-communist-party.

15. Kirkland & Ellis, "The U.S. Probe of Chinese Banks—What Counterparties Need to Know," *Bloomberg Law*, 6 September 2019, www.kirkland.com /publications/article/2019/09/insight_the-us-probe-of-chinese-banks_what-counter.

16. According to the website of the US Treasury's Office of Foreign Assets Control (OFAC): "[OFAC] administers and enforces economic and trade sanctions based on US foreign policy and national security goals against targeted foreign countries and regimes, terrorists, international narcotics traffickers, those engaged in activities related to the proliferation of weapons of mass destruction, and other threats to the national security, foreign policy or economy of the United States." See the OFAC About page, www.treasury.gov/about /organizational-structure/offices/pages/office-of-foreign-assets-control.aspx.

17. President Trump signed the Hong Kong Human Rights and Democracy Act 2019 into law in November 2019; he signed the revised Uyghur Human Rights Policy Act of 2020 in June 2020.

18. Timothy Garton Ash, "Revolution in Hungary and Poland," *New York Review of Books*, 17 August 1989, www.nybooks.com/articles/1989/08/17 /revolution-in-hungary-and-poland/.

19. Zhao Ziyang, *Prisoner of the State: The Secret Journal of Premier Zhao Ziyang* (New York: Simon and Schuster, 2009).

Chapter Two. Totalitarian China

1. Robert Conquest, *Reflections on a Ravaged Century* (New York: W.W. Norton, 1999), 74.

2. Boris Meissner, "Totalitarian Rule and Social Change," in *Dilemmas of Change in Soviet Politics*, ed. Zbigniew Brzezinski (New York: Columbia University Press, 1969), 75.

3. Perry Link, "China: The Anaconda in the Chandelier," *ChinaFile*, 11 April 2002, www.chinafile.com/library/nyrb-china-archive/china-anaconda-chandelier.

4. Reuters, "China boosts domestic security spending by 11.5 percent," 4 March 2012, www.reuters.com/article/2012/03/05/us-china-parliament-security-idUSTRE82403J20120305.

5. Chen, Yu-Jie, Ching-Fu Lin, and Han-Wei Liu, "'Rule of Trust': The Power and Perils of China's Social Credit Megaproject," *Columbia Journal of Asian Law* 32, no. 1 (April 2018): 1–36, https://ssrn.com/abstract=3294776.

6. Frank Hersey, "China to Have 626 Million Surveillance Cameras within 3 Years," *Technode*, 22 November 2017, https://technode.com/2017/11/22/china-to-have-626-million-surveillance-cameras-within-3-years.

7. Xinhua News Agency, accessed July 2019, www.xinhuanet.com/fortune /2019-07/17/c_1124761947.htm.

8. *Shenzen Daily*, accessed September 2019, www.sznews.com/news /content/2019-09/18/content_22478357.htm; SINA Finance, accessed July 2019, https://finance.sina.com.cn/roll/2019-07-07/doc-ihytcitm0295272 .shtml; https://credit.suzhou.com.cn/news/show/22296.html; Echo Huang, "Garbage-Sorting Violators in China Now Risk Being Punished with a Junk Credit Rating," *Quartz*, 8 January 2018, https://qz.com/1173975/garbage-sorting-violators-in-china-risk-getting-a-junk-credit-rating/; Sohu Inc., accessed 2019, www.sohu.com/a/320082697_100191050.

Chapter Three. The Looming Economic Crisis

1. Cited in "Herbert Stein," Wikipedia, https://en.wikipedia.org/wiki /Herbert_Stein#cite_note-5.

2. *People's Republic of China: Financial System Stability Assessment*, Country Report no. 17/358, International Monetary Fund, December 2017, www.imf .org/en/Publications/CR/Issues/2017/12/07/people-republic-of-china-financial-system-stability-assessment-45445.

3. Bloomberg News, "China's Xi Declares 'Critical Battle' to Quell Financial Risks," 20 December 2017, www.bloomberg.com/news/articles/2017-12-20/china-says-monetary-policy-will-be-prudent-and-neutral-next-year.

4. The theory is named after economist Hyman Minsky.

5. Kenneth Rogoff, "China is the Leading Candidate for Being at the Center of the Next Big Financial Crisis," *Finanz und Wirtschaft*, 19 January 2018, www.fuw.ch/article/rogoff-china-is-the-leading-candidate-for-being-at-the-center-of-the-next-big-financial-crisis/.

6. Matt Sciavenza, "A Chinese President Consolidates His Power", *Atlantic*, 19 November 2013, www.theatlantic.com/china/archive/2013/11/a-chinese-president-consolidates-his-power/281547/.

7. Xi Jinping's explanation concerning the "CCP Central Committee Resolution concerning Some Major Issues in Comprehensively Deepening Reform," accessed 2019, www.xinhuanet.com/politics/2013-11/15/c_118164294.htm.

8. Rhodium Group, China Dashboard, Asia Society, June 2020, https://chinadashboard.asiasociety.org/spring-2020/page/overview.

9. Daniel C. Lynch, *China's Futures: PRC Elites Debate Economics, Politics, and Foreign Policy* (Stanford, CA: Stanford University Press, 2015), preface, loc. 90 of 9361, Kindle.

10. Nectar Gan, "Economist Zhang Weiying Slams 'China Model' that 'inevitably leads to confrontation with the West," *South China Morning Post*, 26 October 2018, www.scmp.com/news/china/politics/article/2170447/economist-slams-china-model-inevitably-leads-confrontation-west.

11. Lynch, *China's Futures*, chap. 2, loc. 723 of 9360, Kindle.

12. Edward Wong, "China's Growth Slows, and Its Political Model Shows Limits," *New York Times*, 10 May 2012, www.nytimes.com/2012/05/11/world/asia/chinas-unique-economic-model-gets-new-scrutiny.html.

Chapter Four. No Trust, No Truth

1. Wen Jiabao, "Jiangzhenhua, chashiqing" [Examine the Facts and Tell the Truth], *China Newsnet*, 14 April 2011, http://china.com.cn/policy/cxc/20l1-04/J 8/content_2238158 1_2.htm.

2. Fredrik Fällman, "Public Faith? Five Voices of Chinese Christian Thought," *Contemporary Chinese Thought* 47, no. 4 (2016): 223-34, https://doi.org/10.1080/10971467.2015.1262610.

3. He Huaihong, *Social Ethics in a Changing China—Moral Decay or Ethical Awakening?* (Washington, DC: Brookings Institution, 2015), xxi.

4. See New China News Agency, "An Outline of the Implementation of Citizen Moral Construction in the New Era," 27 October 2019, having "recently been issued by the Central Committee of the CPC and the State Council," www.xinhuanet.com/2019-10/27/c_1125158665.htm.

5. Frank Dikötter, *Mao's Great Famine: The History of China's Most Devastating Catastrophe, 1958-63* (London: Bloomsbury, 2010), x.

6. Dikötter, *Mao's Great Famine*, chap. 7.

7. Dikötter, 322.

8. Dikötter, 325.

9. Minutes of Mao's talk, Gansu, 18 March 1959, Gansu Provincial Archives, 91-18-494, p. 19, cited in Dikötter, *Mao's Great Famine*, 134.

10. Li Ma and Jin Li, *Surviving the State, Remaking the Church: A Sociological Portrait of Christians in Mainland China* (Eugene, OR: Pickwick Publications, 2018), chap. 2, loc. 585 of 5140, Kindle.

11. Quoted in He Huaihong, *Social Ethics*, xx.

12. Arthur Kleinman et al., *Deep China: The Moral Life of the Person, What Anthropology Psychiatry Tell Us about China Today* (Berkeley: University of California Press, 2011), 5-10 and 285-88.

13. Ma Jian, conversation with the author, September 2016.

14. Li Ma and Jin Li, *Surviving the State*, chap. 2, loc. 589 of 5140, Kindle.

15. Minxin Pei, *China's Crony Capitalism* (Cambridge, MA: Harvard University Press, 2016).

16. See works listed in the bibliography by Ci Jiwei, He Huaihong, Arthur Kleinman, Minxin Pei, Gerda Wielander, and Yan Yunxiang.

17. He Huaihong, *Social Ethics*.

18. He Huaihong, xxi.

19. Minxin Pei, *China's Crony Capitalism*.

20. Article on *Caixin* from 9 March 2015, cited in Elizabeth C. Economy, *The River Runs Black: The Environmental Challenge to China's Future*, 2nd ed. (Ithaca, NY: Cornell University Press, 2010), 48.

21. Economy, 48.

22. Cai Fanghua, "The Unbearable Coldness of Being Chinese," *China Youth Daily*, 6 December 2015, accessed 2015, http://chublicopinion.com/2015/12/06/the-unbearable-coldness-of-being-chinese.

23. Willy Wo-Lap Lam, *Chinese Politics in the Era of Xi Jinping: Renaissance, Reform, or Retrogression?* (New York: Routledge, 2015), xvii.

24. Qi Lin, "The Dating Game by Jiangsu TV," *China Daily*, 24 April 2010, accessed 5 January 2012.

25. "Enter the Dragon: Chinese Theatre in the 21st Century," *BBC Radio*, 6 August 2015, 45 min, www.bbc.co.uk/programmes/b04lpqnj.

26. Nigel Andrews, "Jia Zhangke: Life in Interesting Times," *Financial Times*, 1 December 2017, www.ft.com/content/1fd0ca04-d393-11e7-a303-9060cb1e5f44.

27. Yan Lianke, "On China's State-Sponsored Amnesia," *New York Times*, 1 April 2013.

28. Jiayang Fan, "Yan Lianke's Forbidden Satires of China," *New Yorker*, 15 October 2018, www.newyorker.com/magazine/2018/10/15/yan-liankes-forbidden-satires-of-china.

29. Jiayang Fan, "Yan Lianke's Forbidden Satires."

30. C. K. Tan, "China Spending Puts Domestic Security ahead of Defense," *Nikkei Asian Review*, 14 March 2018, https://asia.nikkei.com/Spotlight/China-People-s-Congress-2018/China-spending-puts-domestic-security-ahead-of-defense.

31. Simon Leys, "The Art of Interpreting Nonexistent Inscriptions Written in Invisible Ink on a Blank Page," *New York Review of Books*, 11 October 1990, republished at www.chinafile.com/library/nyrb-china-archive/art-interpreting-nonexistent-inscriptions-written-invisible-ink-blank.

32. Milovan Djilas, quoted in Robert Conquest, *Reflections on a Ravaged Century* (New York: W. W. Norton, 1999), 81.

33. "Foreign Spies Stealing U.S. Economic Secrets in Cyberspace," Office of the National Counterintelligence Executive, Washington, DC, www.ncix.gov/publications/reports/fecie_all/Foreign_Economic_Collection_2011.pdf.

34. Leon Aron, "Everything You Think You Know about the Collapse of the Soviet Union Is Wrong," *Foreign Policy*, 20 June 2011, https://foreignpolicy.com/2011/06/20/everything-you-think-you-know-about-the-collapse-of-the-soviet-union-is-wrong.

35. Aron, "Everything You Think."

Chapter Five. Who Rules?

1. CPC Document 19, "The Basic Viewpoint on the Religious Question during Our Country's Socialist Period," Central Committee of the Chinese Communist Party, 31 March 1982. translation uploaded with permission from Donald E. MacInnis, *Religion in China Today: Policy and Practice* (Maryknoll, NY: Orbis Books, 1989), 8–26. www.religlaw.org/content/religlaw/documents /doc19relig1982.htm.

2. David Aikman, *Jesus in Beijing* (Washington, DC: Regnery Publishing, 2004), loc. 374 of 6939, Kindle.

3. Sarah Cook, *The Battle for China's Spirit: Religious Revival, Repression and Resistance under Xi Jinping* (Washington, DC: Freedom House, 2017), 48.

4. Ian Johnson, "The Eastern Jesus," *New York Review of Books*, 24 October 2019.

5. Fredrik Fällman, "Public Faith? Five Voices of Chinese Christian Thought," *Contemporary Chinese Thought* 47, no. 4 (2016): 229, https://doi.org /10.1080/10971467.2015.1262610.

6. Wang Yi, "Shénme shì jiàohuì de liángxīn zìyóu, hé xìntú de yánlùn zìyóu" 什么是教会的良心自由, 和信徒的言论自由 [What is Freedom of Conscience in the Church? And Freedom of Speech for Disciples?], accessed 3 January 2020, www.360doc.com/content/15/0717/19/22274473_485555425.shtml.

7. Early Rain Covenant Church, "Wǒmen duì jiātíng jiàohuì lìchǎng de chóngshēn (jiǔshíwǔ tiáo)" 我们对家庭教会立场的重申 (九十五条) [Reaffirming Our Stance on the House Churches: 95 Theses], August 2015, accessed 25 August 2020, http://weibo.com/p/1001603881634431670754.

8. Early Rain Covenant Church, "Reaffirming Our Stance."

9. See, for example, results of interviews conducted in Phil Entwistle, "Faith in China: Religious Belief and National Narratives amongst Young, Urban Chinese Protestants," *Nations and Nationalism* 22, no. 2 (2016): 347–70, https://doi.org/10.1111/nana.12162.

10. Dr Ezra Jin, senior pastor of Zion Church, Beijing, "Emerging Urban Churches in China," privately distributed essay, 2017, 11.

11. Carsten T. Vala, *The Politics of Protestant Churches and the Party-State in China, God above Party?* (New York: Routledge, 2018), 52.

12. Republic of Korea census 2005, quoted in "Christianity in Korea," Wikipedia, https://en.wikipedia.org/wiki/Christianity_in_Korea#cite_ref-14.

13. Paul Y. Chang, *Protest Dialectics: State Repression and South Korea's Democracy Movement, 1970–1979* (Stanford, CA: Stanford University Press, 2015), 24–25.

14. Vala, *Politics of Protestant Churches*, 110, 125.

15. For much of the information about Christian churches in contemporary China in this chapter, I have drawn on the excellent book by Carsten T. Vala, *The Politics of Protestant Churches and the Party-State in China, God above Party?*, which brings together the fruits of his own extensive fieldwork in China, and that of numerous other scholars whom he cites. Ian Johnson's *The Souls of China: The Return of Religion after Mao* (London: Allen Lane, 2017) has also been inspirational and informative: it offers deep, vivid, and insightful reportage on four faith communities.

16. David C. Schak, "Protestantism in China: A Dilemma for the Party-State," *Journal of Current Chinese Affairs* 40, no. 2 (2011): 85.

17. Vala, *Politics of Protestant Churches*, 137, 143.

18. Vala, 59–61.

19. Vala, 130.

20. "Christianity in China," BillionBibles.com, accessed 25 August 2020, www.billionbibles.com/china/how-many-christians-in-china.html; "Annual Report on Persecution of Chinese House Churches by Province: From January 2006 to December 2006," China Aid Association, January 2007, https://docs.google.com/file/d/0B_YUgSyiG6aIZXU2clEoWF9NWlE/edit.

21. Ezra Jin, *Emerging Urban Churches*, 19–20.

22. "ChinaAid Special Report: Chinese Government Launches New Campaign to Eradicate House Churches," China Aid Association, April 2012, www.chinaaid.org/2012/04/chinaaid-special-report-chinese.html.

23. By 2019, China had been relegated in the index compiled by Reporters Without Borders to fourth worst country in the world for press freedom, a rank it maintained in 2020. See https://rsf.org/en/ranking_table.

24. Under religious regulations, no child under eighteen may attend religious services or any kind of religious event. No one under 18 may receive religious education of any kind from anyone.

25. See the annual persecution reports of the China Aid Association on its website, www.chinaaid.org.

26. Cook, *Battle for China's Spirit*, 42.

27. In 2010, the International Congress on World Evangelization (also called the Lausanne Congress for its initial meeting in Switzerland) brought four thousand leaders of evangelical Protestant churches from nearly two hundred countries to South Africa.

28. Minnie Chan, "Christianity in Wenzhou Rose from Humble Beginnings to One Million Adherents," *South China Morning Post*, 23 July 2014, www.scmp.com /news/china/article/1557358/christianity-wenzhou-rose-humble-beginnings-one-million-adherents.

29. Ian Johnson, "Decapitated Churches in China's Christian Heartland," *New York Times,* 21 May 2016, www.nytimes. com/2016/05/22/world/asia /china-christians-zhejiang.html.

30. Xu Yangjingjing, "Why Chinese Christians Are Camping Out to Save Their Church and Cross from Demolition," *Washington Post*, 4 April 2014, www .washingtonpost.com/news/worldviews/wp/2014/04/04/why-chinese-christians-are-camping-out-to-save-their-church-and-cross-from-demolition/.

31. Johnson, "Decapitated Churches."

32. Johnson, "Decapitated Churches."

33. Johnson, "Decapitated Churches."

34. Voice of America, "Crackdown on Christian Churches Intensifies in China," 7 September 2018; Nina Shea and Bob Fu, "Inside China's War on Christians," *Wall Street Journal,* 30 May 2018.

35. Christopher Bodeen, "Group: Officials Destroying Crosses, Burning Bibles in China," Associated Press, 10 September 2018, www.washingtonpost .com/world/asia_pacific/group-officials-destroying-crosses-burning-bibles-in-china/2018/09/10/55d68366-b4af-11e8-ae4f-2c1439c96d79_story.html.

36. China Aid Persecution Report for 2018, www.chinaaid.org, 30.

37. Christian Shepherd, "For a 'House Church' in Beijing, CCTV Cameras and Eviction," Reuters, 30 August 2018, https://uk.reuters.com/article/uk-china-religion/for-a-house-church-in-beijing-cctv-cameras-and-eviction-idUKKCN1LF0J2.

38. Bodeen, "Group: Officials Destroying Crosses."

39. www.helplinfen.com/2011/04/persecution-photos.html, accessed 2018.

40. Benjamin Haas, "China Church Demolition Sparks Fears of Campaign against Christians," *Guardian*, 11 January 2018, www.theguardian.com/world

/2018/jan/11/china-church-demolition-sparks-fears-of-campaign-against-christians.

41. See Maya Wang, *Eradicating Ideological Viruses: China's Campaign of Repression against Xinjiang's Muslims*, Human Rights Watch, 9 September 2018, www.hrw.org/report/2018/09/09/eradicating-ideological-viruses/chinas-campaign-repression-against-xinjiangs.

42. Robert Conquest, *Reflections on a Ravaged Century* (New York: W.W. Norton, 1999), 74.

Chapter Six. An Environmental Catastrophe

1. Elizabeth Economy, "China Wakes Up to Its Environmental Catastrophe: Cleaning Up the Environment Is an Urgent Task for China's Leaders, Who Face a Backlash from Enraged Citizens," *Bloomberg News*, 13 March 2014.

2. *Cost of Pollution in China: Economic Estimates of Physical Damages*, World Bank and State Environmental Protection Administration of China, 2007.

3. United States Strategic Approach to the People's Republic of China, 20 May 2020, www.whitehouse.gov/wp-content/uploads/2020/05/U.S.-Strategic-Approach-to-The-Peoples-Republic-of-China-Report-5.20.20.pdf.

4. Joseph Kahn and Jim Yardley, "As China Roars, Pollution Reaches Deadly Extremes," *New York Times*, 25 August 2007.

5. Jonathan Kaiman, "China's Reliance on Coal Reduces Life Expectancy by 5.5 Years, Says Study," Guardian, 9 July 2013, www.theguardian.com/environment/2013/jul/08/northern-china-air-pollution-life-expectancy.

6. Jonathan Kaiman, "Inside China's 'Cancer Villages,'" *Guardian*, 4 June 2013, www.theguardian.com/world/2013/jun/04/china-villages-cancer-deaths.

7. Agence France Presse, "Poor Pay Most for Water Corruption, Says Anti-Graft Watchdog," 25 June 2008, www.seeddaily.com/reports/Poor_pay_most_for_water_corruption_says_anti-graft_watchdog_999.html.

8. *Cost of Pollution in China*," 82.

9. Elizabeth Economy, "The Environmental Problem China Can No Longer Overlook," Diplomat, 17 July 2015, https://thediplomat.com/2015/07/the-environmental-problem-china-can-no-longer-overlook/.

10. "China's Water Shortage to Hit Danger Limit in 2030," Xinhua News Agency, 16 November 2001, cited in Elizabeth C. Economy, *The River Runs*

Black: *The Environmental Challenge to China's Future*, 2nd ed. (Ithaca, NY: Cornell University Press, 2010), 69.

11. Charlie Parton, *China's Looming Water Shortage*, Chinadialogue, April 2018, http://chinadialogue-production.s3.amazonaws.com/uploads/content/file_en/10608/China_s_looming_water_crisis_v.2_1_.pdf.

12. Parton, *China's Looming Water Shortage*.

13. "Official: Beijing's Major Water Supplier Faces Serious Water Shortage," Xinhua News Agency, 21 March 2009.

14. Parton, *China's Looming Water Shortage*.

15. Evan Ratliff, "The Green Wall of China," *Wired*, 1 April 2003, www.wired.com/2003/04/greenwall/.

16. Shixiong Cao, "Why Large-Scale Afforestation Efforts in China Have Failed to Solve the Desertification Problem," *Environmental Science and Technology* 42, no. 6 (2008): 1826–31, https://pubs.acs.org/doi/10.1021/es0870597.

17. Mark Schapiro, "What Happens to Environment Journalists Is Chilling: They Get Killed for Their Work," *Guardian*, 18 June 2018, www.theguardian.com/commentisfree/2019/jun/18/environment-journalists-killed.

18. Kaiman, "Inside China's 'Cancer Villages.'"

19. Mark Hertsgaard, "Our Real China Problem," *Atlantic Monthly*, November 1997, www.theatlantic.com/issues/97nov/china.htm.

20. Rachel E. Stern, "The Political Logic of China's New Environmental Courts," *China Journal* (University of Chicago) 72 (July 2014): 53–74, www.journals.uchicago.edu/doi/10.1086/677051.

21. www.chinadialogue.net/article/show/single/en/733-How-participation-can-help-China-s-ailing-environment, accessed 2017.

22. Jennifer Duggan, "Dead Pigs Floating in Chinese River," *Guardian*, 17 April 2014, www.theguardian.com/environment/chinas-choice/2014/apr/17/china-water.

23. "China Declared a War on Pollution and Four Years Later It's Winning," *Epic News*, 12 March 2018, https://epic.uchicago.edu/news-events/news/china-declared-war-pollution-and-four-years-later-its-winning.

24. Stanley Lubman, "Can Environmental Lawsuits in China Succeed?" China File, 14 December 2017, www.chinafile.com/reporting-opinion/viewpoint/can-environmental-lawsuits-china-succeed.

25. Lubman, "Can Environmental Lawsuits" (emphasis in the original).

26. James Temple, "China Is Creating a Huge Carbon Market—but Not a Particularly Aggressive One," *Technology Review*, 18 June 2018, www.technology review.com/s/611372/china-is-creating-a-huge-carbon-market-but-not-a-particularly-aggressive-one/.

27. Economy, *River Runs Black*, 54–55.

28. Economy, 59.

29. Economy, 277.

Chapter Seven. Coronavirus

1. Xu Zhangrun, "Viral Alarm: When Fury Overcomes Fear," trans. Geremie R. Barmé, China File, 10 February 2020, www.chinafile.com/reporting-opinion/viewpoint/viral-alarm-when-fury-overcomes-fear.

2. Viet Thanh Nguyen, "The Ideas that Won't Survive the Coronavirus," *New York Times*, 10 April 2020, www.nytimes.com/2020/04/10/opinion/coronavirus-america.html.

3. The Editors, "*Scientific American* Endorses Joe Biden," *Scientific American*, 1 October 2020. https://www.scientificamerican.com/article/scientific-american-endorses-joe-biden1

4. The Editors, "Dying in a Leadership Vacuum," *New England Medical Journal*, 8 October 2020. https://www.nejm.org/doi/full/10.1056/NEJMe2029812.

5. Associated Press, "China didn't warn public of likely pandemic for 6 key days," 15 April 2020, https://apnews.com/68a9e1b91de4ffc166acd6012d82c2f9.

6. Raymond Zhong and Paul Mozur, "To Tame Coronavirus, Mao-Style Social Control Blankets China," *New York Times*, 15 February 2020, www .nytimes.com/2020/02/15/business/china-coronavirus-lockdown.html.

7. "Zhòngdà wǎng qíng zhuān bào - guānyú lǐwénliàng qùshì yǐnfā de wǎngmín qíngxù fǎnyìng yǔ jiànyì de bàogào" 重大网情专报－关于李文亮去世引发的网民情绪反应与建议的报告 [Major Internet News Report - Report on the Emotional Reactions and Suggestions of Netizens Triggered by the Death of Li Wenliang], *Pingcong*, February 2020, accessed 9 September 2020, https://pincong.rocks/article/14038.

8. "Netizens Demand Free Speech after Death of Disciplined Wuhan Doctor," China Digital Times, 6 February 2020, https://chinadigitaltimes.net/2020 /02/netizens-demand-free-speech-after-death-of-disciplined-wuhan-doctor/.

9. Li Yuan, "Widespread Outcry in China over Death of Coronavirus Doctor" *New York Times*, 7 February 2020, www.nytimes.com/2020/02/07 /business/china-coronavirus-doctor-death.html.

10. Xu Zhangrun, "Viral Alarm."

11. Zhang Qianfan, "Fángzhì bìngdú, zhōngguó xūyào xiànzhèng mínzhǔ" 防治病毒,中国需要宪政民主 [To Prevent the Virus, China Needs Constitutional Democracy], *New York Times* Chinese edition, 11 February 2020, accessed 9 September 2020, https://cn.nytimes.com/opinion/20200211/zhang-qianfan-constitutional-cure-coronavirus-china-democracy.

12. Xu Zhiyong, "Dear Chairman Xi, It's Time for You to Go," trans. Geremie R. Barmé, China File, 26 February 2020, accessed 8 September 2020, www.chinafile.com/contributors/xu-zhiyong.

13. "Punching High," *Economist*, 25 February 2016, www.economist.com /china/2016/02/25/punching-high.

14. Chris Buckley, "China's 'Big Cannon' Blasted Xi. Now He's Been Jailed for 18 Years," *New York Times*, 22 September 2020, www.nytimes.com/2020 /09/22/world/asia/china-ren-zhiqiang-tycoon.html.

15. "Leadership: The Wide Spread of a WeChat Posting Calling for a Politburo Meeting to Remove Xi Jinping," China Scope, 23 March 2020, http:// chinascope.org/archives/22328.

16. Mai He and Lucia F. Dunn, "Evaluating Incidence and Impact Estimates of the Coronavirus Outbreak from Official and Non-Official Chinese Data Sources," *SSRN Papers*, posted 20 February 2020, https://papers.ssrn .com/sol3/papers.cfm?abstract_id=3540636.

17. Hemant Adlakha, "Fang Fang: The 'Conscience of Wuhan' amid Coronavirus Quarantine," *Diplomat*, 23 March 2020, https://thediplomat.com/2020 /03/fang-fang-the-conscience-of-wuhan-amid-coronavirus-quarantine; Helen Davidson, "Chinese Writer Faces Online Backlash over Wuhan Lockdown Diary," *Guardian*, 10 April 2020, www.theguardian.com/world/2020 /apr/10/chinese-writer-fang-fang-faces-online-backlash-wuhan-lockdown-diary.

18. Vivian Wong, "As Death Toll Mounts, Governments Point Fingers over Coronavirus," *New York Times*, 6 March 2020, www.nytimes.com/2020/03/06 /world/coronavirus-news.html.

19. *Coronavirus Disease (COVID-19) Weekly Epidemiological Update and Weekly Operational Update*, WHO COVID-19 Dashboard, Situation Report no. 2,

22 January 2020, www.who.int/docs/default-source/coronaviruse/situation-reports/20200122-sitrep-2-2019-ncov.pdf?sfvrsn=4d5bcbca_2.

20. Josephine Ma, "Coronavirus: China's First Confirmed Covid-19 Case Traced Back to November 17," *South China Morning Post*, 13 March 2020, www .scmp.com/news/china/society/article/3074991/coronavirus-chinas-first-confirmed-covid-19-case-traced-back.

21. Mai He and Lucia F. Dunn, "Evaluating Incidence and Impact Estimates," https://papers.ssrn.com/sol3/papers.cfm?abstract_id=3540636.

22. "Emergence of genomic diversity and recurrent mutations in SARS-CoV-2," Science Direct, republished from *Infection, Genetics and Evolution* 83, September 2020, 104351, www.sciencedirect.com/science/article/pii /S1567134820301829?via%3Dihub.

23. Josh Margolin and James Gordon Meek, "Intelligence Report Warned of Coronavirus Crisis as Early as November," ABC News, 9 April 2020, https:// abcnews.go.com/Politics/intelligence-report-warned-coronavirus-crisis-early-november-sources/story?id=70031273.

24. BBC News, "Coronavirus: Satellite Traffic Images May Suggest Virus Hit Wuhan Earlier," 9 June 2020, www.bbc.co.uk/news/world-us-canada-52975934.

25. https://news.cgtn.com/news/2020-01-27/5-million-people-left-Wuhan-before-the-lockdown-where-did-they-go—NACCu9wItW/index.html, cited in Derek Scissors, "Estimating the True Number of China's COVID-19 Cases," American Enterprise Institute, April 2020. See www.aei.org/foreign-and-defense-policy/why-do-you-believe-china-about-covid-19.

26. www.caixinglobal.com/2020-02-29/in-depth-how-early-signs-of-a-SARS-like-virus-were-spotted-spread-and-throttled-101521745.html, accessed March 2020.

27. www.caixinglobal.com/2020-02-29/in-depth-how-early-signs-of-a-SARS-like-virus-were-spotted-spread-and-throttled-101521745.html, accessed March 2020.

28. Tsai Ing-wen, "President of Taiwan: How My Country Prevented a Major Outbreak of COVID-19," *Time*, 16 April 2020, https://time.com/collection /finding-hope-coronavirus-pandemic/5820596/taiwan-coronavirus-lessons/.

29. www.caixinglobal.com/2020-02-29/in-depth-how-early-signs-of-a-SARS-like-virus-were-spotted-spread-and-throttled-101521745.html, accessed March 2020.

30. "Coronavirus Timeline," Hudson Institute, 31 July 2020, www.hudson
.org/research/15920-coronavirus-timeline.

31. Associated Press, "China Didn't Warn Public of Likely Pandemic for 6
Key Days," 14 April 2020, https://apnews.com/5aa3549e8b70fdbb0a93453968
8ec794.

32. Bao Zhiming, "Wuhan Opens Ashes Collection, Hankou Funeral Home
Deceased Relatives Line Up," *Caixin*, 26 March 2020, https://m.china.caixin
.com/m/2020–03–26/101534558.html.

33. Yaxue Cao (@YaxueCao), "From Chinese social media today: 2 photos
of the same ChinaCDC chart," Twitter, 5 February 2020, https://twitter.com
/YaxueCao/status/1225204383895429120.

34. Yaxue Cao, "No Access to the CIA Report? Let's DIY: Estimating Total
Infections and Death Toll in Wuhan, the Epicenter of Covid-19," *China Change*,
12 April 2020, https://chinachange.org/2020/04/12/no-access-to-the-cia-report-
lets-diy-estimating-total-infections-and-deaths-toll-in-wuhan-the-epicenter-
of-covid-19/.

35. Yaxue Cao, "No Access?"

36. Derek Scissors, "Why Do You Believe China (about COVID-19)?", *AEI-
deas* (blog), 27 March 2020, www.aei.org/foreign-and-defense-policy/why-
do-you-believe-china-about-covid-19/.

37. "Taiwan," Worldometer, accessed 8 September 2020, www.worldometers
.info/coronavirus/country/taiwan.

38. "South Korea," Worldometer, accessed 8 September 2020, www
.worldometers.info/coronavirus/country/south-korea.

39. Kitty Donaldson, "Johnson Huawei Plan at Risk; U.K. Set to Rethink China
Ties," *Bloomberg*, 16 April 2020, www.bloomberg.com/amp/news/articles/2020–
04–16/johnson-s-huawei-plan-at-risk-as-u-k-set-to-rethink-china-ties.

40. The highest-grossing film in Chinese history, released in 2017, is entitled *Wolf Warrior 2*. It shows heroic Chinese soldiers battling against mercenar-
ies who are led by a racist American. A promotional poster for the film featured
the slogan, "Anyone who insults China—no matter how remote—must be
exterminated."

41. Ben Westcott and Steven Jiang, "Chinese Diplomat Promotes Conspiracy Theory that US Military Brought Coronavirus to Wuhan," *CNN*, 14 March
2020, https://edition.cnn.com/2020/03/13/asia/china-coronavirus-us-lijian-
zhao-intl-hnk/index.html.

42. Reuters, "Internal Chinese Report Warns Beijing Faces Tiananmen-Like Global Backlash over Virus," 4 May 2020, www.reuters.com/article/us-health-coronavirus-china-sentiment-ex/exclusive-internal-chinese-report-warns-beijing-faces-tiananmen-like-global-backlash-over-virus-idUSKBN22G19C.

43. Minxin Pei, "How Has the Coronavirus Crisis Affected Xi's Power: A Preliminary Assessment," *Chinese Leadership Monitor*, 1 June 2020, www.prcleader.org/pei-1.

44. "Xi Jinping's 'Fake Wuhan Show,'" China Scope, discussed on Radio France International, 11 March 2020, www.rfi.fr/cn/中国/20200311-习近平视察武汉几个怪异的细节; http://chinascope.org/archives/22128.

Chapter Eight. America and the Fate of Xi

1. Marco Rubio, "American Industrial Policy and the Rise of China," *American Mind*, 10 December 2019, https://americanmind.org/essays/american-industrial-policy-and-the-rise-of-china/.

2. William Kristol and Robert Kagan, "Toward a Neo-Reaganite Foreign Policy," *Foreign Affairs* 75, no. 4 (July/August 1996): 18–32.

3. "Remarks by Vice President Pence on the Administration's Policy Toward China," speech given at the Hudson Institute, Washington, DC, October 4, 2018, www.whitehouse.gov/briefings-statements/remarks-vice-president-pence-administrations-policy-toward-china/.

4. "What Chinese Officials Told Children Whose Families Were Put in Camps," *New York Times*, 16 November 2019, www.nytimes.com/interactive/2019/11/16/world/asia/china-detention-directive.html.

5. Daniel Tobin, "How Xi Jinping's 'New Era' Should Have Ended U.S. Debate on Beijing's Ambitions," Testimony before the U.S.–China Economic and Security Review Commission, 13 March 2020, www.uscc.gov/sites/default/files/testimonies/SFR%20for%20USCC%20TobinD%2020200313.pdf.

6. *United States Strategic Approach to the People's Republic of China*, May 2020, White House, www.whitehouse.gov/wp-content/uploads/2020/05/U.S.-Strategic-Approach-to-The-Peoples-Republic-of-China-Report-5.20.20.pdf.

7. "Xi Jinping's Explanation Concerning the 'CCP Central Committee Resolution Concerning Some Major Issues in Comprehensively Deepening Reform,'" www.xinhuanet.com//politics/2013-11/15/c_118164294.htm.

8. James Mcbride and Andrew Chatzky, "Is 'Made in China 2025' a Threat to Global Trade?" Council on Foreign Relations, 13 May 2020, www.cfr.org /backgrounder/made-china-2025-threat-global-trade.

9. Senator Tom Cotton and Senator John Cornyn, "Keep the Chinese Government away from 5G Technology," *Washington Post,* 2 April 2019.

10. "President Xi Jinping's State Visit to the United States," White House, Office of the Press Secretary, 25 September 2015, https://obamawhitehouse .archives.gov/the-press-office/2015/09/25/fact-sheet-president-xi-jinpings-state-visit-united-states.

11. "China's Non-Traditional Espionage against the United States: The Threat and Potential Policy Responses," report by US Department of Justice to Senate Intelligence Committee, 18 December 2018, 5, www.justice.gov/sites /default/files/testimonies/witnesses/attachments/2018/12/18/12-05-2018_ john_c._demers_testimony_re_china_non-traditional_espionage_against_the_ united_states_the_threat_and_potential_policy_responses.pdf.

12. Ankit Panda, "It's Official: Xi Jinping Breaks His Non-Militarization Pledge in the Spratlys," *Diplomat,* 16 December 2016, https://thediplomat .com/2016/12/its-official-xi-jinping-breaks-his-non-militarization-pledge-in-the-spratlys/.

13. Hong Kong Human Rights and Democracy Act of 2019, S. 1838, Cong. Rec. vol. 165, no. 186, 116th Cong. (2019), www.congress.gov/congressional-record/2019/11/20/house-section/article/H9100-1.

14. Adam Shaw, "Pompeo Officially Declares Hong Kong 'No Longer Autonomous,' Slams China Intervention," *Fox News,* 27 May 2020, www.foxnews.com /politics/pompeo-hong-kong-autonomous-china-intervention.

15. Patrick Wintour and Helen Davidson, "Boris Johnson Lays Out Visa Offer to Nearly 3M Hong Kong Citizens," *Guardian,* 3 June 2020, www.theguardian .com/world/2020/jun/03/britain-could-change-immigration-rules-for-hong-kong-citizens.

16. BBC News, "Hong Kong Protests: President Xi Warns of 'Bodies Smashed,'" 14 October 2019, www.bbc.co.uk/news/world-asia-china-50035229.

17. 2020 Democratic Party Platform, https://www.demconvention.com /wp-content/uploads/2020/08/2020-07-31-Democratic-Party-Platform-For-Distribution.pdf.

18. Nectar Gan, "Economist Zhang Weiying Slams 'China Model' that 'Inevitably Leads to Confrontation with the West,'" *South China Morning*

Post, 26 October 2018, www.scmp.com/news/china/politics/article/2170447
/economist-slams-china-model-inevitably-leads-confrontation-west.

19. Robert Conquest, *Reflections on a Ravaged Century* (New York: W.W. Norton, 1999), 113.

20. President Clinton's speech on China Trade Bill at the Paul H. Nitze School of Advanced International Studies of the Johns Hopkins University, 9 March, 2000. https://www.iatp.org/sites/default/files/Full_Text_of_Clintons_Speech_on_China_Trade_Bi.htm

Chapter Nine. The Great Unfinished Business

1. "Xu Zhangrun's China: 'Licking Carbuncles and Sucking Abscesses,'" China Change, 1 August 2018, https://chinachange.org/2018/08/01/xu-zhangruns-china-licking-carbuncles-and-sucking-abscesses/.

2. *Charter 08* (Chinese and English text), US Congressional – Executive Commission on China, 10 December 2008, www.cecc.gov/resources/legal-provisions/charter-08-chinese-and-english-text.

3. Daniel Lynch, *China's Futures: PRC Elites Debate Economics, Politics, and Foreign Policy* (Stanford, CA: Stanford University Press, 2015).

4. See, for example, *Storming the Fortress: A Research Report on China's Political System Reform after the 17th Party Congress*, Central Party School, Beijing, 2007, reported on by Chris Buckley, "Elite China Think-Tank Issues Political Reform Blueprint," 18 February 2008, Reuters, www.reuters.com/article/us-china-politics-idUSPEK20590720080219.

5. See the passages on Xu Zhangrun and Zhang Qianfan in chapter 7.

6. "Former Party Professor Calls CCP a 'Political Zombie,'" China Digital Times, 12 June 2020, https://chinadigitaltimes.net/2020/06/translation-former-party-professor-calls-ccp-a-political-zombie.

7. "Former Party Professor."

8. Lily Guo, "'He killed a party and a country': A Chinese Insider Hits Out at Xi Jinping; An Edited Transcript of an Interview with Cai Xia," *Guardian*, 18 August 2020, www.theguardian.com/world/2020/aug/18/cai-xia-chinese-insider-hits-out-at-xi-jinping-he-killed-a-party-and-a-country.

9. "Leaked Speech Shows Xi Jinping's Opposition to Reform," posted by Sophie Beach, China Digital Times, 27 January 2013, https://chinadigitaltimes.net/2013/01/leaked-speech-shows-xi-jinpings-opposition-to-reform/.

10. Robert Conquest, "Immobilism and Decay," *Problems of Communism* (September–October 1966): 35–37.

Chapter Ten. Launching the Revolution

1. Sun Zhongshan, known to the English-speaking world as Sun Yatsen, was instrumental in the overthrow of the Qing dynasty in 1912. He is a unique figure among twentieth-century Chinese leaders for being widely revered in both mainland China and Taiwan.

2. Professor He Weifang is a leading authority on and advocate of the rule of law. See his book *In the Name of Justice: Striving for the Rule of Law in China* (Washington, DC: Brookings Institution Press, 2012).

3. Friedrich Engels to J. Bloch in Königsberg, 21 September 1890, reprinted in *On Historical Materialism* (Moscow: Progress Publishers, 1972), 294–96.

Afterword

1. Winston S. Churchill, speech to the House of Commons, London, 11 November 1947.

Select Bibliography

Becker, Jasper. *Hungry Ghosts: Mao's Secret Famine*. New York: Henry Holt, 1996.

Buswell, Robert E., and Timothy S. Lee, eds. *Christianity in Korea*. Honolulu: University of Hawai'i Press, 2006.

Cao, Jiwei. *Moral China in the Age of Reform*. Cambridge: Cambridge University Press, 2014.

Chang, Jung, and Jon Halliday. *Mao: The Unknown Story*. London: Random House, 2005.

Chang, Paul Y. *Protest Dialectics: State Repression and South Korea's Democracy Movement, 1970-1979*. Stanford, CA: Stanford University Press, 2015.

Chau, Adam Yuet, ed. *Religion in Contemporary China: Revitalization and Innovation*. New York: Routledge, 2011.

Chen Guidi and Wu Chuntao. *Will the Boat Sink the Water? The Life of China's Peasants*. Translated by Zhu Hong. New York: PublicAffairs, 2006.

Conceison, Claire. "China's Experimental Drama: The Badass Theater of Meng Jinghui." *TDR: The Drama Review* 58, no. 1 (Spring 2014): 64-88.

Sarah Cook, *The Battle for China's Spirit: Religious Revival, Repression and Resistance under Xi Jinping*. Special report. Washington, DC: Freedom House, 2017.

DeLisle, Jacques, Avery Goldstein, and Guobin Yang, eds. *The Internet, Social Media and a Changing China*. Philadelphia: University of Pennsylvania Press, 2016.

Dikötter, Frank. *Mao's Great Famine: The History of China's Most Devastating Catastrophe, 1958-63*. London: Bloomsbury, 2010.

———. *The Tragedy of Liberation: A History of the Chinese Revolution, 1945-57*. London: Bloomsbury, 2013.

———. *The Cultural Revolution: A People's History, 1962-1976*. London: Bloomsbury, 2016.

Economy, Elizabeth C. *The River Runs Black: The Environmental Challenge to China's Future*. 2nd ed. Ithaca, NY: Cornell University Press, 2010.

Fenby, Jonathan. *Will China Dominate the 21st Century?* 2nd ed. Cambridge, UK: Polity, 2017.

Friedman, Edward, Paul Pickowicz, and Mark Selden. *Chinese Village, Socialist State*. New Haven, CT: Yale University Press, 1991.

Gao Zhisheng. *Unwavering Convictions: Gao Zhisheng's Ten-Year Torture and Faith in China's Future*. Durham, NC: Carolina Academic Press, 2017.

Garside, Roger. *Coming Alive: China After Mao*. New York: McGraw-Hill, 1981.

He Weifang. *In the Name of Justice: Striving for the Rule of Law in China*. Washington, DC: Brookings Institution Press, 2012.

He Huaihong. *Social Ethics in a Changing China—Moral Decay or Ethical Awakening?* Washington, DC: Brookings Institution Press, 2015.

Huang Xiang. *A Bilingual Edition of Poetry out of Communist China*. Translated by Andrew Emerson. Lewiston, NY: Edward Mellen Press, 2004.

Johnson, Ian. *The Souls of China: The Return of Religion after Mao*. New York: Pantheon Books, 2017.

Kleinman, Arthur, Yunxiang Yan, Jing Jun, Sing Lee, Everett Zhang, Pan Tianshu, Wu Fei, and Jinhua Guo. *Deep China: The Moral Life of the Person, What Anthropology and Psychiatry Tell Us about China Today*. Berkeley: University of California Press, 2011.

Lam, Willy Wo-Lap. *Chinese Politics in the Era of Xi Jinping: Renaissance, Reform, or Retrogression?* New York: Routledge, 2015.

———. *The Fight for China's Future: Civil Society vs. the Chinese Communist Party*. New York: Routledge, 2019.

Lardy, Nicholas R. *Markets over Mao: The Rise of Private Business in China*. New York: Columbia University Press, 2014.

———. *The State Strikes Back: The End of Economic Reform in China?* New York: Columbia University Press, 2019.

Li, Cheng. *Chinese Politics in the Xi Jinping Era: Reassessing Collective Leadership*. Washington, DC: Brookings Institution Press, 2016.

Li, Zhisui. *The Private Life of Chairman Mao: The Inside Story of the Man Who Made Modern China*. London: Chatto & Windus, 1994.

Liao Yiwu. For a Song and a Hundred Songs: A Poet's Journey through a Chinese Prison. Translated by Wenguang Huang. Newburyport, MA: New Harvest/Houghton Mifflin Harcourt, 2013.

Lifton, Robert Jay. *Thought Reform and the Psychology of Totalism*. London: Victor Gollancz, 1961.

Link, Perry. *Liu Xiaobo's Empty Chair: Chronicling the Reform Movement Beijing Fears Most*. New York: New York Review of Books, 2011.

Liu Xiaobo. *No Enemies, No Hatred: Selected Essays and Poems*. Edited by Perry Link, Tienchi Martin-Liao, and Liu Xia. Cambridge, MA: Belknap Press, 2012.

Lu Hong. *China Avant-Garde Art 1979–2004*. Shijiangzhuang, Hebei, China: Hebei Fine Arts Publishing House, 2006.

Lynch, Daniel C. *China's Futures: PRC Elites Debate Economics, Politics, and Foreign Policy*. Stanford, CA: Stanford University Press, 2015.

MacFarquhar, Roderick, ed. *The Hundred Flowers*. London: Stevens & Sons. 1960.

MacFarquhar, Roderick and Michael Schoenhals. *Mao's Last Revolution*. Cambridge, MA: Belknap Press, 2008.

Magnus, George. *Red Flags: Why Xi's China Is in Jeopardy*. New Haven, CT: Yale University Press, 2018.

Mahbubani, Kishore. *Has China Won? The Chinese Challenge to American Primacy*. New York: PublicAffairs, 2020.

Mao Zedong. *Jiandang he dageming shiqi Mao Zedong zhuzuoji*. Unpublished manuscript. December 1920–July 1927, CCP Archive and Study Office and CCP Hunan Committee, 422. Cited in Chang and Halliday, *Mao*.

Miles, James A. R. *The Legacy of Tiananmen*. Ann Arbor: University of Michigan Press, 1996.

Nye, Joseph S. *The Future of Power*. New York: PublicAffairs, 2011.

Obrist, Hans Ulrich. *Ai Weiwei Speaks with Hans Ulrich Obrist*. London: Penguin Books, 2011.

Pantsov, Alexander V., with Steven I. Levine. *Mao: the Real Story*. New York: Simon & Schuster, 2012.

Pei, Minxin. *China's Trapped Transition: The Limits of Developmental Autocracy*. Cambridge, MA: Harvard University Press, 2006.

———. *China's Crony Capitalism: The Dynamics of Regime Decay*. Cambridge, MA: Harvard University Press, 2016.

Pettis, Michael. *Avoiding the Fall: China's Economic Restructuring*. Washington, DC: Carnegie Endowment for International Peace, 2014.

Pils, Eva. *Human Rights in China: A Social Practice in the Shadows of Authoritarianism*. Cambridge, UK: Polity, 2017.

Ringen, Stein. *The Perfect Dictatorship: China in the 21st Century*. Hong Kong: Hong Kong University Press, 2016.

Seymour, James D. *The Fifth Modernization: China's Democracy Movement 1978–1979*. Stanfordville, NY: Human Rights Publishing Group, 1980.

Shambaugh, David, *China Goes Global: The Partial Power*. Oxford: Oxford University Press, 2013.

———. *China's Future,* Cambridge, UK: Polity, 2016.

Shapiro, Judith. *China's Environmental Challenges*. Cambridge, UK: Polity, 2016.

Shen Tong. *Almost a Revolution*. Boston: Houghton Mifflin, 1990.

Smith, Karen, Hans Ulrich Obrist, and Bernard Fibricher. *Ai Weiwei*. London: Phaidon Press, 2009.

Spence, Jonathan D. *The Search for Modern China*. London: Hutchinson, 1990.

Sun, Yan. *Corruption and Market in Contemporary China*. Ithaca, NY: Cornell University Press, 2004.

Tong, James. "The 1989 Democracy Movement in China: A Spatial Analysis of City Participation," *Asian Survey* 38, no. 3 (March 1998): 310–27.

Unger, Jonathan, ed. *The Pro-Democracy Protests in China: Reports from the Provinces*. Armonk, NY: M. E. Sharpe, 1991.

US Office of the National Counterintelligence Executive. *Foreign Spies Stealing U.S. Economic Secrets in Cyberspace: Report to Congress on Foreign Economic Collection and Industrial Espionage, 2009–2011*. Washington, DC: Office of the National Counterintelligence Executive, 2011.

Vala, Carsten T. *The Politics of Protestant Churches and the Party-State in China: God above Party?* New York: Routledge, 2017.

Walter, Carl, and Fraser Howie. *Privatizing China: Inside China's Stock Markets*. Singapore: John Wiley & Sons, 2000.

———. *Red Capitalism: The Fragile Financial Foundation of China's Extraordinary Rise*. Hoboken, NJ: Wiley-Blackwell, 2012.

Wei Jingsheng. *The Courage to Stand Alone: Letters from Prison and Other Writings*. London: Penguin Books, 1997.

Wielander, Gerda. *Christian Values in Communist China*. New York: Routledge, 2013.

Wu Ningkun, in collaboration with Li Yikai. *A Single Tear: A Family's Persecution, Suffering, Love and Endurance in Communist China*. New York: Little, Brown, 1993.

Wu, Emily, and Larry Engelmann. *Feather in the Storm: A Childhood Lost in Chaos*. New York: Pantheon Books, 2006.

Xu Zhiyuan. *Paper Tiger: Inside the Real China*. London: Head of Zeus, 2015.

Yan, Haiping. *Theater and Society: An Anthology of Contemporary Chinese Drama*. Armonk, NY: M. E. Sharpe, 1998.

Yan Lianke. *The Explosion Chronicles*. London: Chatto & Windus, 2016.

Yang, Fenggang. *Religion in China: Survival and Revival under Communist Rule*. Oxford: Oxford University Press, 2012.

Yang Guobin. *The Power of the Internet in China: Citizen Activism Online*. New York: Columbia University Press, 2011.

Yang Jisheng. *Tombstone: The Great Chinese Famine, 1958–62*. Translated by Stacy Mosher and Guo Jian. New York: Farrar, Straus and Giroux, 2012.

Zhang Liang, comp., *The Tiananmen Papers*. Edited by Andrew J, Nathan and Perry Link, with afterword by Orville Schell. London: Little, Brown, 2001.

Zhao Ziyang. *Prisoner of the State: The Secret Journal of Premier Zhao Ziyang*. New York: Simon & Schuster, 2009.

Zheng Yi. *Scarlet Memorial: Tales of Cannibalism in Modern China*. Translated by T. P. Sym. Boulder, CO: Westview Press, 1996.

Index

access to, 167, 175
sanctions on, 47
Internet of Things, 145
investigative journalism, 110-12
Iran, 153
Islam, 74, 104. *See also* Muslims

Japan, 51, 52, 107, 149, 160
"jasmine revolutions," 91
Jiang Hong, 66-67
Jiangxi Province, 96
Jiang Zemin, 73
JieChu, 5
Jilin Province, 96
Jin Mingri, Pastor Ezra, 82, 97-99
Jin Tianming, Pastor, 89, 91, 92
Johnson, Ian, 74
Joint Operations Command Center, 30
joint ventures, 6, 51, 147
journalists, 10, 42, 89, 110-12, 128, 155
Justice Department, U.S., 17, 26, 148

Kagan, Robert, 143
Khrushchev, Nikita, 14
Kleinman, Arthur, 62
Korea. *See* North Korea, South Korea
Korean War, 190
Kowloon, 190
Kristol, William, 143

Land Bureaus, 101
Lausanne Congress, 91, 216n27
law enforcement institutions, 64, 65
Lenin, Vladimir, 43, 106, 160
Leninists, 66, 145, 153, 155, 156
Liaoning Province, 26

liberal democracy, 10, 13, 160, 174, 188, 198
Chinese advocates of, 164
coronavirus in, 137-39
financial crisis impact on, 85, 145
institutions and values of, 184
political and economic reforms leading to, 126
religion in, 105
technology and, 48, 145-47
totalitarian conflicts with, 156, 198
of US and its allies, ix-x, 169, 196
Li Keqiang, 7-27, 126, 173-87
Central Committee address of, 26-27, 177-87
China-US collision course anticipated by, 9, 11
family background of, 10
military backing of, 16-21
political change approach of, 13-14
political leadership experience of, 3
Securities and Exchange crisis response of, 3-4, 7-9, 11, 21-24
speech to nation of, 26-27, 173-77
university degrees of, 10, 208nn8,9
"war on pollution" declared by, 114
Xi denounced and forced to resign by at Politburo meeting, 32-38
Linfen, 101-3
Liu He, 33, 56
Liu Xiaobo, 72, 106, 162-63
Li Wenliang, Dr., 20, 120, 128, 132, 137, 164, 175
Li Yining, 208n9
Li Zehua, 128

lockdowns, coronavirus, 120, 128, 130, 133, 135, 139–40
London, University of, 130
London Stock Exchange, 198–99
looting, 63, 100
Lou Jiwei, 6
Lubman, Stanley, 115
Luckin Coffee, 4
Luther, Martin, 78
Lu Xun, 69–70

Ma, Jack, 155, 169
MacFarquhar, Roderick, 65
"Made in China 2025" program, 145, 147, 155
Mai He, 129
Ma Jian, 63
Mao Zedong, 27, 97, 116, 158, 171, 184, 189–93
    centralization of authority of, 34, 41, 179
    damage inflicted by, 59–61, 185–87
    death of, 61, 73, 159, 188
    re-education programs initiated by, 58–59, 104
market economy, 52, 157, 160, 184, 192, 198
    transition from command economy to, x, 17–18, 44, 85, 156, 158, 179, 188
Marx, Karl, 182
Marxism-Leninism, 43, 160, 165
Marxists, 62
Massachusetts Institute of Technology (MIT), 191
    Energy Initiative, 108
McNamara, Robert, 192

media. *See* news media, social media
Meng Jinghui, 69
militarization, 146, 149, 157, 181
Ministry of Environmental Protection, 111
Ministry of State Security, 137
Ministry of Water Resources, 108
Minsky, Hyman, 53, 211n4
modernization, 159–69, 178, 184, 189, 193
    Charter 08 manfesto on, 162–63, 169
    democracy essential for, 162–63
    Christianity and, 74
    in communist period, 14–15
    political, 160–61, 166, 172, 187
    pragmatic approach to, 161–62
moral crisis, 57–58, 64–54, 70, 72, 81, 181
Munich, 5
Muslims, 73, 180

Nanchang (destroyer), 32
National Air Quality Action Plan, 114
National Center for Medical Intelligence (NCMI), US, 129
National Congresses, ix, 24, 144, 183
National Health Commission (NHC), 128, 131, 132
National Institute of Finance and Development, 53
National Intelligence University, US, 144
National People's Congress (NPC), 35, 42, 53, 150
National Team, 24–25, 28
Navy, Chinese, 31
Navy, US, 30–31, 197

Nazi Germany, 41, 48, 156
netizens, 27, 110, 121, 127, 164
New Citizens Movement, 124
news media, 4, 30, 31, 118, 138–39, 143
  censorship of, 26, 38, 160
New York Stock Exchange, 3, 169
New York Times, 4, 93, 124, 143, 191
Nguyen, Viet Thanh, 119
Nobel Peace Prize, 72, 163
nongovernmental organizations
  (NGOs), 86, 111, 114–15, 117–18
North Korea, 17, 26, 153

Obama, Barack, 4, 8, 10, 143, 146–49
Ohio State University, 129
one-party dictatorship, 159–60, 162,
  166, 184
  American hostility toward, 18–19
  censorship in, 42, 61, 75
  corruption in, 28, 51
  economic policies supporting,
    54, 55
  environmental catastrophe in,
    117–18
  transition to democracy from, ix,
    18–19, 48, 72, 162, 163, 184
  uremia metaphor for, 48

Paracel Islands, 30, 31
paramilitary forces, 64, 103
Parton, Charlie, 109
Pearl River delta region, 108
Pei, Minxin, 65
Peking University, 54, 64, 84, 97, 155,
  176
Pence, Mike, 143, 144, 153
Pentagon, 130
Pentagon Papers, 181

persecution, 59, 73, 86–88, 95–97,
  104, 106
People's Armed Police (PAP), 21,
  30–31, 38, 63, 103
People's army, 63
People's Bank of China (PBoC), 26
People's Daily, 20, 65, 127
People's Liberation Army (PLA), 30,
  184, 189
People's Procuratorate, 95
"Pivot to Asia" strategy, 8, 143, 146
Poland, 21, 79, 198
police, 27–30, 37–38, 42–44, 64, 82.
  See also People's Armed Police
  religious restrictions enforced by,
    81–82, 84, 90–91, 94, 100
Politburo, 57, 130, 131, 177, 189, 195
  military members of, 16, 20, 24, 33
  Standing Committee of, 15, 25, 64
  Xi Jinping resigns at meeting of,
    ix, 34, 169–70, 173–74, 178
political reform, 17–19, 38, 149, 157,
  162
  economic reform without, 12–13,
    18, 36, 42–45, 62, 174, 182, 193
  repression of demands for, 9, 17,
    22, 65–66, 149, 152, 183, 197
pollution, 66, 101, 107–8, 110–15, 117,
  180
Pompeo, Mike, 150
Ponzi schemes, 52
pragmatism, 13
princelings, 9–10, 14
private sector, 17–18, 50–56
  Communist Party authority over,
    52–53, 155
  churches and, 93
  debt and, 52–53

one-party dictatorship undermined by, 55
profitability of, 22, 49, 145
state-owned companies favored
over, 54
property market, 22–23, 140
*Protestant Ethic and the Spirit of
Capitalism, The* (Weber), 76
Protestantism, 29, 73, 80–82, 88,
101
Calvinist, 76–77, 89, 106
campaign against, 94–96
evangelical, 76, 91, 212n27
growth of, 74, 84
Public Company Accounting
Oversight Board (PCAOB), US,
3, 5
public health concerns, 107, 124, 127,
131, 136
Public Security Bureau, Soviet, 43
Pulitzer Prize, 119

Qing dynasty, 226n1
Qinghai Province, 111
quarantines, 121, 126, 127

Red Guards, 196
"red lines," 81, 83
"re-education," 58, 104
Reformation, 78
Reform Era, 62, 68, 83, 89, 160, 174,
182
reforms. *See* economic reforms,
political reforms
religion. *See also specific religions*
freedom of, 62, 77, 85, 173
regulation of, 44, 83, 85–86, 104,
182

suppression of, 72, 85–89, 92–97,
105
Religious Affairs Bureaus, 82, 84, 101
Renmin University, 56, 89
Ren Zhiqiang, 125, 166
Reporters Without Borders, 215n23
Republican Party, US, 7, 142, 144,
146
resistance, 87, 95–96, 198
resources, allocation of, 25, 48, 54, 55,
82, 134, 145
of Communist Party versus
churches, 83, 101–3
environmental, 108–10, 116–17
Reuters, 3, 100
Rhinoceros in Love (Yimei Liao), 68
River Runs Black, The (Economy),
115–16
Rogoff, Kenneth, 53
Roman Empire, 73
Rubio, Marco, 5, 142–43, 149
rule of law, ix, 34, 164–65, 200
absence in China of, 70, 94,
115–17, 163, 168
citizens empowered by, 186
constitution based on, 29, 191
in Hong Kong, 150, 164, 190
popular movement for, 63, 162,
175, 194
Social Credit System and 176
in Taiwan, 152
Russia, 153, 200. *See also* Soviet
Union
Russian Empire, 106
Ryzhkov, Nikolai, 70, 156

sanctions, 47–48, 67, 87, 105, 152
against North Korea, 17, 26

in US economic war with China, 6, 12, 19, 154, 209n16

Sanjiang Church, 94

SARS CoV-2, 130

Scissors, Derek, 134

Securities and Exchange Commission (SEC), US, 3–8, 11, 22–25, 29, 31, 35

security apparatus, 14, 20, 36, 64, 104

Shandong Province, 26

Shanghai, 23, 114

Stock Exchange, 208n11

University of Finance and Economics, 66

Shanxi Province, 101–3

Sha Tau Kok Observation Post, 189

Shouwang Church, 89–92, 95, 97–98

Sichuan Province, 28, 72

earthquake in, 29, 78

Singapore, 35, 44, 192

Sino-British Joint Declaration (1984), 150

Sino Forest, 4

Social Credit System, 9, 13, 46, 47, 87, 176, 185

Social Ethics in a Changing China—Moral Decay or Ethical Awakening? (He Huaihong), 64–65

socialism, 97, 192

Chinese constitution inclusion of, 42

Communist Party abandonment of, 63

Mao's rush to communist collectivization from, 160, 190

in one-party dictatorship, 188

social media, 28–29, 67, 95–96, 110, 113, 121, *See also specific platforms*

during coronavirus outbreak, 120–21, 125–27, 132–34, 141

social stability, 83, 91, 95, 100, 103, 174

social welfare system, 23, 51, 75, 140

Solidarity, 198

Sony, 51

South Africa, 91, 216n27

South China Sea, 16, 30, 35, 146, 149, 157, 181–82

collision of American and Chinese ships in, 31–32

Southern People Weekly, 77

South Korea, 75, 80, 107, 135, 192

Soviet Union, ix, 13, 26, 59, 155, 159, 167

collapse of, ix, 70–71, 156, 198

Communist Party of, 43, 70, 179

totalitarianism of, 41–43, 48, 156

speech, freedom of, 121. *See also* expression, freedom of

Spratly Islands, 150

Sputnik, 155

Stalin, Josef, 42, 43, 64, 70, 87

Stalinism, 59

starvation, 59–60, 160, 189

State Administration for Religious Affairs, 73, 84

state-owned enterprises (SOEs), 49–56

debt of, 49–55

favored over private sector, 54

state property, 63, 116–17, 181

statistics, 53, 110, 111, 167

coronavirus, 130, 133–34

United Kingdom, 136, 151
United Nations (UN), 17, 36
United States (US), ix, 9, 26, 86, 157,
    187, 193, 209n17
    Beijing embassy of, 113
    ChinaAid NGO in, 88, 103
    and Chinese leadership changes,
        36–37
    Chinese students in, 164, 192
    during coronavirus pandemic, 119,
        129, 132, 134, 136–37, 139, 145
    economy of, 16–18, 51, 145–46
    policy changes toward China of,
        141–50
    population of, 116
    potential confrontations between
        China and, 30–33, 35, 45–46,
        169, 174
    religious freedom in, 77
    sanctions imposed by, 19, 205n
    stock trading in, 3–8, 11–12, 21–25,
        29, 31, 35–36, 152–54
    Taiwan strategy of, 150–51
    trade war between China and,
        55–56
United States Strategic Approach to the
    People's Republic of China
    (Pence), 144
universal values, 75, 84, 86, 144, 155,
    156, 162
uremia, 48
USS Jeremiah Denton (destroyer), 31–32
Uyghur Human Rights Policy Act
    (2020), 209n17
Uyghurs (Uighurs), 19, 186

Vietnam, 119, 199
    War in, 191, 192

"Viral Alarm: When Fury Over-
    comes Fear" (Xu Zhangrun),
    122–24

Wang Qishan, 14–15, 21, 33, 35, 183,
    187
    during Cultural Revolution, 15
    family background of, 10, 14
    political change approach of,
        13–14
    marriage of, 14
    vice presidency of, 14, 125, 126,
        173, 186
Wang Yang, 7–16, 21–25, 33, 35–36,
    126
Wang Yi, Pastor, 29, 72, 76–79, 82,
    106
Washington, DC, 25, 146, 149, 191
Washington Post, 191
Washington University School of
    Medicine, 129
Watergate affair, 191–92
Weber, Max, 76
WeChat, 26, 27, 50, 126–27
Weibo, 134
Wei Jingsheng, 196
Wen Jiabao, 53, 57, 109
Wenzhou, 93–95
West China Presbytery, 78
whistle blowers, 111–12, 164
Winnie the Pooh, 10, 208n7
Wolf Warrior 2 (film), 222n38
Working Group of Financial
    Markets, 6
World Bank, 107–9, 191
    China 2030 report, 13, 54, 182
    East Asia and Pacific Department
        of, 192

World Health Organization (WHO), 114, 131, 133, 135
World Trade Organization (WTO), 147
Wuhan, 7, 20, 120–21, 124, 126–51, 164, 175
Health Commission, 131, 134

Xi Jinping, 9, 15, 83, 118, 173, 174, 208n10
anti-corruption campaign of, 56, 57, 66–67, 96, 133, 135
censorship reinforced by, 71, 75, 86
China Dream of, 12, 145, 154
confrontational foreign policy of, 19, 30–33, 35, 36, 45
coronavirus response of, 120, 122–26, 128, 130–31, 140
economic policy of, 4, 7, 10–13, 16–18, 23–24, 29–30, 49–51, 53, 56
professors' denunciations of, 164–66
religion suppressed by, 85–86, 92–93, 96–97, 105
resignation of, ix, 34, 173–74, 178
US awakening to dangers of policies of, 142–56
Winnie the Pooh image associated with, 10, 208n7
Xinjiang, 44, 96, 144, 152, 180

alienation in, 19, 36, 46
campaign against Islam in, 74, 104
Uyghurs in, 6, 186
Xu Danei, 121
Xu Qiliang, General, 16, 19–20, 24, 33
Xu Zhangrun, 119, 122–25, 138, 150, 166
Xu Zhiyong, 124–25

Yang Li, Pastor, 102–3
Yan Lianke, 69
Yan Yunxiang, 62
Yaxue Cao, 133–34
Yeltsin, Boris, 13, 26
Yugoslav Communist Party, 70
Yunnan, 4

Zambia, 199
Zhang Ming, 56
Zhang Qianfan, 124, 166
Zhang Weiying, 54–55, 155
Zhang Youxi, General, 16, 20
Zhao Leji, 33
Zhao Lijian, 137
Zhao Ziyang, 38
Zhejiang campaign, 92–96
Zhongnanhai compound (Beijing), 32, 38
Zhou Enlai, 161, 188, 192, 192, 193, 196, 197
Zhou Yongkang, 14, 64
Zion Church, 82, 97–100